the five-forty-five
to cannes

also by tess uriza holthe

When the Elephants Dance

the five-forty-five to cannes

Tess Uriza Holthe

 Crown Publishers • New York

Copyright © 2007 by Tess Uriza Holthe

Grateful acknowledgment is made to Roto-Rooter Services Company and Roto-Rooter Corporation for permission to reprint an excerpt from the Roto-Rooter jingle. Reprinted by permission.

"Home Coming" originally appeared in *The Louisville Review* in Fall 2005.

Library of Congress Cataloging-in-Publication Data
  Holthe, Tess Uriza.
    The Five-forty-five to Cannes / Tess Uriza Holthe. — 1st ed.
      p. cm.
    1. Railroad travel—Fiction. 2. Cannes (France)—Fiction.
  3. Accidents—Fiction. 4. Loss (Psychology)—Fiction.
  5. Reminiscing—Fiction. I. Title. II. Title: The Five-Forty-Five to Cannes.

PS3608.O4944F58 2007
813'.54—dc22

2006025620

ISBN: 978-0-307-35185-2

Printed in the United States of America

Design by Lauren Dong

10 9 8 7 6 5 4 3 2 1

First Edition

To Salvador Uriza

We be of one blood ye and I.

—RUDYARD KIPLING

acknowledgments

Jason Holthe, scrupulous critic, love, and all-around bully, for always believing.

Judy Holthe for shopping in Cannes and without whom this book would not have been possible. Mary Ann Naples, agent and godsend. My superb editor, Kristin Kiser; Steve Ross; the exceptional Bonnie Thompson; Lindsay Orman; and the fantastic team at Crown Publishers. Debra Goldstein and Elizabeth Little of The Creative Culture.

For moral support, Salvador and Gloria Uriza—thank you, Mom and Dad. Nellie, my angel. Bernadette Crisologo, Sarina, Gino, Roman, Karl and Chelsea Uriza. Anthony Mandap and Paul Sirate. Thanks also to Olav Holthe, antiquarian, father-in-law, and best martini-maker in town. Dee Holthe, my other mom. Bill Wooldridge and Dolores Velasco. Fellow writers Ellie Wood, Katrina Davidson, Jeanne Saito Felton, and Julie Boles.

For their expertise, Heidi Soholt and Ian Proctor for help with the Glaswegian. Wendy Walsh for the Italian. Sholom Morgan and Benjamin Shamir for the Hebrew. I would also like to thank the editors of the *Louisville Review*.

I am grateful to all.

contents

The Five-Forty-Five to Cannes   1

The Necklace   33

The Flame   55

The Pointer   67

Weightless   99

The Bruiser   143

The Three Widows of Signor Alberto Moretti   161

The Ferry Driver of Portofino   191

The Last Bullfight   221

Homecoming   245

the five-forty-five
to cannes

tHe five-foRty-five
to cannes

CHazz JoRGeNseN knew that if he hustled he could catch the five-forty-five to Cannes, France, and make up for lost time. First he needed to make this one to Ventimiglia and in Ventimiglia connect to the five-forty-five. But his shoes and the Italians were not cooperating, everyone moving in slow motion, strolling as if they had time overflowing from their trouser pockets though the conductor had already blown the whistle once from *binario undici,* track eleven.

He checked the large overhead board under *partenza* to make sure he had the right departure train. He did. Voices filled the Milano Central station, speaking in various tongues. Rapid-fire Italian, Austrian, German, French, Spanish.

He dodged travelers rolling their carry-ons on hard leashes. He had nothing but his old gray duffel bag with the black straps, and in his bag nothing further but his dog-eared copy of Chesterton's *The Man Who Was Thursday, Runner's World* magazine, a pair of beach shorts, and a catalog of the new line of stainless steel Jorgensen Faucets his father wanted him to look over for His Thoughts. In case he had any Additional Ideas. Even though the catalog was already printed and thousands of them sent out. It was a ritual they performed, perhaps so that his father could tell himself, when he handed over his empire to Chazz someday, that his son had always had a hand in the family business. They both knew what a crock that was. It was embarrassing really.

Chazz waded through the throng. It made him tense to think of the heavy catalog. In fact—he stopped, unzipped the duffel bag, pulled out the catalog, and dropped it in a round metal trash receptacle. Then, as an afterthought, he took his plastic amber container of lithium pills and dropped that in the can, too. He felt lighter and picked up his pace. His black Louis Vuittons were slipping on the dirty platform. What was he thinking wearing dress shoes instead of sneakers? An Armani suit instead of jeans and a T-shirt?

That was just it. He wasn't thinking, again. No surprise there. Chazz Jorgensen, only son of Terge Jorgensen of *the* Jorgensen faucet empire. Chazz Jorgensen, the fuckup of the family. But still he felt right now like he could do anything. Like he was on the right track. During these times when he was on the upswing, a phoenix rising from the fire, he was golden. Everyone wanted to be around him; he was a savant of charm.

Then there were the other times. The ones that anchored cement weights to his ankles before he could take off and fly. It all depended on whether you looked the dark cloud in the eye and tried to wrestle with it or not. If you zoomed straight through like a car cutting through fog, maybe, just maybe, the clouds wouldn't detect your presence and start to gather.

"All right. All right," he repeated. He was starting to feel panicky. He knew what always came after these moments of euphoria. *Don't think about it. If you start wrestling with it you're screwed. Don't worry.* Maybe he should go back and fish those lithium pills out of the trash. Or get more. *You can always get a prescription in Cannes. Good to cleanse your body now and then.* Though the doctor had told him that it did more damage to keep starting and stopping on his prescriptions. The best thing to do was to adjust the dosage, try different combinations, but not to stop cold turkey . . . *Doc doesn't know everything. Live a little.*

Besides, there was the medicine cabinet in Cannes, stocked full of whatever he needed: Zoloft, Celexa, Elavil, Tofranil, Wellbutrin, Effexor, SSRIs, tricyclics, MAOIs, hocus-pocus allydocous, on and on.

He hit "1" on his cell phone; there was a long pause, and then the connection. His wife's voice, his soon-to-be ex-wife, his separated-and-still-trying-to-be-together wife? Her voice came on from their San Francisco Victorian: "*Bonjour,* this is Claudette Dumont, leave a message please."

This was his second call. The first call he had made yesterday afternoon at four, just around the corner from their house as he sat in their car holding a bouquet of yellow roses, too afraid to pressure her. They had talked briefly. All the while he kept telling himself to go to their front door. That he would be welcome. But he couldn't read her voice. It sounded as if she was happy to hear from him, but he couldn't tell. She never knew he had been so close to home. He found the roses, wilted, later that evening as he hurried to catch his plane.

For an instant their remodeled three-story Victorian came into view. The butternut-and-cream exterior trimmed in rust. The polished maple floors, white magnolia–detailed wainscoting, and cathedral ceilings superimposed on the loud tourist-filled station. The image blocked out the many college students with their thumbs hooked, pulling their backpacks forward. A pyramid of blue duffel bags belonging to a soccer team was arranged in one corner as the coach with a clipboard and whistle hanging from his neck tried to maintain order.

Chazz smiled into the phone and lost the panic from his voice. "Hey, babe, it's me. You'll never guess where I am. I'm in

Milano, headed for where we first met—*Scusi, permesso.*" He bumped shoulders with a man in suspenders, who stopped to throw his hands up. "I know if I just take some time, go back to simpler times . . ." He swallowed. "Listen, I got to catch this train to Ventimiglia but I'll call you back, okay? Wish you were here with me." He was about to hang up. He was almost home free.

There was some fumbling noise as she picked up the phone. "Chazz?" Her voice Amercan now, the lilt of her native French sweet and far away.

He couldn't answer.

"Chazz? I was worried." She hesitated. "We were supposed to meet tonight, remember? To talk. What are you doing in Italy?" A practiced, careful voice.

He swallowed. It was hard, it hurt his throat, but he swallowed. "Listen, I got to catch this train. Hang on, okay?" He waved frantically at the conductor. The man was leaning forward from the train steps to check for any late boarders. He nodded at Chazz. Chazz stepped onto the train and wedged his hip and arm between the glass doors separating the compartments, then pushed. They didn't move easily. He had to wrestle with them a bit. Get his hip shoved further in, and then push. He walked down the smoking aisle, breaking through a screen of smoke hovering like a ghost over rows thirty to thirty-six. The windows in the first car were halfway down, letting in the humid heat. The cheap forest-green curtains rustled from the hot air.

He took a seat by the window. *Uff da.* His joints were sore. Trains moved past on either side of him, arriving and departing. Caked in black dust. It was hot in the train, sticky. Dirty. Sweat trickled down his shirt. His pants were wrinkled from his having slept in a janitor's closet, his dirty-blond hair greasy now. A two-day stubble had taken root on his face like a fungus. He remembered only bits and pieces. That was all he could ask for whenever his mood swung this way.

Once, during winter, he had awakened from one of his lapses after a three-week blur and was dead certain he knew the full meaning of Einstein's theory of relativity and how it related to pi, that they were, in fact, inversions of the other. That and a vague image of having swum at Ocean Beach at three in the morning in his Ralph Lauren wool suit, trying to get away from the Nazis. Hitler on a surfboard. But then the lithium started to work. And the side effects started to diminish. He was clear-minded. Calm. Whatever that meant. At least he was sleeping and eating regularly again.

"Chazz, are you taking your lithium?"

It hurt to hear her voice. It hurt as if she were already gone. This was the week, after a month of no communication. The week to check in as if she were his probation officer. To see if it was truly over between them or if they wanted to continue this life, married but not living together or seeing each other. But he couldn't bear it. If she said, "No, this will not work," his life would end. This way they were still married.

It was all up to him. To shape up. That's what his mother had said, with her sugary sweetness. With her red manicured nails and plump fingers stuffed into her gaudy rings as she squeezed his shoulder. That was what his father had said, seated across from Chazz at his giant oak desk, shuffling papers from his in-box like they were having a business meeting. As if it were that easy. Sure, Mom, Dad, I'll just pull it all together from here on out. Even keel. Even Steven. He laughed.

His mom, what a joke that was. She had had the same types of problems, but she had kept them a secret. Safeguarding her vanity was more important than helping her own child. Even when he was younger and the doctors were misdiagnosing him with hyperactivity and giving him a prescription, which had sent him into a downward spiral of depression, and then later giving him another for his low tides, which had sent him into hyperdrive. When he felt as if he was going insane and she could have helped him the most, through what he called his "straitjacket time," she had said nothing.

Instead she had volunteered things, in the guise of trying to be helpful. "He's always been hyperactive. Even when he was in my stomach. He wouldn't let me sleep at night. Always moving. It's no different now." That was what she had volunteered to the doctors regarding her family history. Not her own depression, nor her desperate giddiness. She hadn't even let on that it ran in her family, that her own father had had it. This seesawing of emotions. Only after Chazz had suffered sufficiently through his teens and his sleepless spells and cries for help had started to disrupt her life, calling her home from a Caribbean getaway, did she have the guts to share her own struggle with the disease. And now she had the gall to tell Chazz that really it was up to him to control his mood swings. To make his life what he wanted. "Look at me," she said. "I've whipped this disease. Use your mind, Chazz. Will it away."

Yes, look at her. Her breath sweetened with alcohol and her clothes sprayed over with a douse of Gardenia perfume that concealed nothing. Her makeup frighteningly perfect. Her fears that never went away. She had not succumbed to the darkness.

Well, could he blame her really? Wasn't it in the end a matter of survival? He knew how precarious it was to stand too close to the edge of a bottomless cliff. Didn't his friends, the few who knew about his problems, the well-meaning ones, the ones who let him appear at their doorsteps at all hours of the night, didn't they at times pull back in horror? A small wince when he met them at the door?

Even his closest friend, Elliot Ambrose, had shut his bedroom door quietly on his sleeping wife and newborn son and ushered Chazz into his drawing room one evening. Elliot had sighed, brought out two crystal tumblers and a bottle of Laphroaig,

and asked, "When's all this going to end, Chazz? I mean, ultimately, where's this obsessive, erratic behavior going to take you?
You got to settle down, man. You've got a wife to think of, for crying out loud."

"You're right, yeah." Chazz had brushed his hand up the back
of his neck. All that time he'd thought Elliot was the one person
aside from Claudette who understood, but in the end, there was
only Claudette. Could he blame them? Who wanted to be close
to infinite pain? Maybe it was contagious.

He understood, about his mother. On certain levels he understood. Maybe she was afraid of being pulled back down into the
abyss with him. Maybe she had fought it off and barely made it
out, clawing her way back up to the light. Diminished from her
waltz with madness. A tattered remnant of her former self but
still alive, if that counted for anything. He was a tentacle, an
extension of the monster below threatening to wrap around her
ankle again and take her back down. Here she was, a safe distance now from the abyss, whereas he was toes to the edge, arms
outstretched, leaning forward, and hypnotized by the impending
fall. Who could blame them? Except for Claudette, he was on
his own.

He could pull his hair out from how much he wanted to
make things right. He'd tried all he could to quiet his demons.
He was trying. He'd told his wife, *"Claudette, I'm trying."* Trying
not to run. Trying to be a better person. Trying not to make an ass
out of himself to all his friends who had it together. There were so
many forms of trying. How was he supposed to know which one
was right for him? He felt guilty, too, because he hadn't told her
the extent of his condition before they were married. He'd been
afraid she would run. But lately he had had it under control. For
almost a month now.

"Sometimes these things quiet with age. As with schizophre-
nia. You never know," Dr. Cameron had said. Healthy living.

The right environment. And one could lead a normal life. The hallucinations, the aggression, the volatility, the manic swings, the depression all could be controlled with the right environment. "If you keep to your meds. If nothing triggers it."

"Triggers it?" Chazz had asked.

"Yes. Big things can trigger an episode. Like losing your job, even good things, like marriage. Graduation." *Like your wife asking for a separation, Doc? Could that trigger it?*

Claudette, she was all he'd ever wanted. Not his father's empire, not the house in Pacific Heights or the one in Tiburon facing the bay, not his Carrera S, his vintage Austin Healey, his BMW 740i. That could all go to fuck for all he cared. He knew that was not where his happiness resided. Happiness was Claudette in the morning, Claudette holding his hand.

He had just gotten nervous, that was all. He had been doing well. He wasn't running anymore. He was going to therapy, taking his meds. He was living right, but this date, this final check-in for the fucking verdict of your life date . . . *How's that for a trigger, Doc?* He had started to fall apart a few days ago.

So it had seemed like a good idea at the time. Go back to where they'd first met, in Cannes, for luck. To remember what it was he was fighting for. She would understand. He was halfway over the Atlantic when he realized it was just another one of those half-baked ideas of his to hide the fact that he was running from things again. Still, he could have hopped on the next plane back, called to tell her he'd be a day late, and made their date. She would have understood. She always did. But he was feeling great again and flying high on the idea of going to Cannes to get back in touch with that feeling. That feeling he had had when they first met.

"Chazz," she said again.

He could hear fear in her voice, and he hated himself for it. Here they were, ironic really, an American in France, a French-woman in America. His tanned hands pulled out a wad of euros. He sorted them by color, then folded them back. His fingernails were dirty. His hands shook. He wiped his hand across his nose. "Okay. I'm on the train."

"Chazz, when you didn't show up today . . ."

He could see her now: petite, fine-boned, medium height. Just short enough so he could put his chin on her brunette head. The concern that would mar the surface of those lavender eyes. Eyes the color of a silvery-blue butterfly's wings. Eyes that could reflect the waters of the Côte d'Azur or a field of lavender in Provence. He would much prefer to see the world and all its beauty reflected in her eyes than through his own muddled vision. Everything was happier, clearer, more promising through hers.

When he was in one of his swings he could see things almost painfully clearly. The pale softness of her lips, the perfect precision of her toenails against her golden skin. A sharp reminder of what he had to lose.

He could envision her now, maybe a bare foot rubbing the back of the calf. The way she dressed, still French-like, with the delicate sweaters and the soft pink dresses with tiny ruffles on the bottom border. He cherished these, the sweet, small details. She would smell of citrus. He could watch her sleep all day. When she woke she always had a smile for him. He just wanted to take care of her. That was all he ever wanted.

"Are you taking care of yourself?" he asked. He caught his reflection in the window. Dirty. Blond brows angry-looking.

"C'est bon." A couple of Frenchwomen giggled, giving him the once-over as they walked down the aisle. Tank tops stretched taut over their lean forms. Loose peasant skirts and sandals. Shopping in Milano for the day, on their way back to France. As the women got closer the one nearest him wrinkled her nose and laughed. He stank, he knew. He hadn't bathed and God knows what he had slept in the previous night. He had assumed it was a puddle of water, but the way he smelled now . . . He watched the woman's face for how badly he stank with an indifferent, almost amused curiosity. She looked back over her shoulders two more times, as if trying to reconcile his smell and filth with his looks.

"*Oui,* I'm taking care," she said. Care. That's what the doctors said was important for bipolarity. A stable household, therapy, meds, and someone to guide the patient when he could not make simple decisions. In this environment, a person with his condition could live a happy, normal life. All he had to do was know his triggers. Things that would send him into a tailspin. For a child it might be divorce or a death. *Or maybe, as in his family, both parents swimming in scotch and involved in a string of conspicuous affairs.*

"My compass is broken," he had told Claudette after they had had their first argument.

"What?"

"I have these compulsions sometimes. Hard to think clearly. It usually happens when I'm really anxious or really happy." And he had been so happy with her. He cared for her obsessively but was careful not to show her too often. *That was another trait, obsession.* He didn't want to suffocate her or frighten her away with too much attention.

On her birthday he had decided to give her a gift. To buy her a new car. He had gone back and forth, back and forth so often, trying to make a decision, that he got physically dizzy. So he had solved the matter by purchasing both a Porsche and a Volvo wagon. And she had insisted he take one back, that was all. She was trying to be frugal even though they had all this damn money. And he remembered now how irrationally offended he had been. Out-of-control offended. So hurt he couldn't talk for days.

But she was good to him, always good to him. She told him she understood. There was her own mother, didn't he remember? Claudette knew how to take care of someone when they couldn't do so themselves. From now on she would be his compass whenever he was lost.

"I have to go, Dettie." He spoke to her gently, the way one would to a child. His pet name for her. Claudette Dumont, the daughter of a fisherman. She was an only child and so she had asked Chazz if he wouldn't mind if she kept her maiden name, Dumont, and not take on his. "Of course," he'd said. He had even suggested that if they had a child they could give it the surname Dumont. It might even be wiser, because Jorgensen was so well known.

There was silence on the other end. He could picture her eyes filling up. Long brown lashes wet at the tips. He closed his own and kissed the corners of hers in his mind. He tried to sound jovial, in control. "I wanted to come here for luck. You know. You were going to tell me. Ah—what the verdict was. Today was—I was so nervous." He chuckled, his throat was tight. He could hear her breathing. He placed a hand on his stomach. "I have to go."

The two men he had shared a joint with the previous night strolled past. Gaunt Italians, brothers. Lean like wolves. His age, possibly. Frick and Frack, he thought to himself. They had promised him some good dope to return the favor, but he had not seen them for an hour and he'd decided it was just a passing promise. They sat down now in the two seats facing his and lifted their chins in greeting. He could use something right now. To calm the nerves. To forget that he was screwing his life.

"Okay," she whispered. She always whispered before she cried.

"I'll call you in a little bit, okay?" he said and clicked "end" before she could answer. He was going down that road, he could feel it. The adrenaline. The premature remorse. He could feel the sinking in his stomach. His aggressive behavior always preceded his downfall, but before that there were the moments of feeling really good. Super. Fantastic. And then slowly it would happen, the aggression would give way to a kind of flailing of his thoughts, his body.

He always pictured it as his brain misfiring, not making connections. Like when his Internet feed was real slow, clogged, and then finally not moving at all. It was hard to think when he was in this state. It was literally painful. His nerves and muscles stretched taut, his skin hypersensitive. Simple things like whether to eat a hamburger or a hot dog could take hours. Things like whether to hop on a plane when he really should be checking in with his wife were muddled.

How had he come to this again? Why was he so cursed while others walked around with perfectly clear minds, their moods always stable? How could you love your wife correctly when you swung high and low like a roller coaster? All he'd wanted was to visit Cannes, infuse himself with the memory of Claudette and himself when they first met until it was a steely resolve, a code to live his life by.

It had seemed a simple enough plan. He would sit at the La Croisette restaurant or the Libera Italiano, eat a filet Robespierre with green peppercorns, toast his wife with a bottle of Valpolicella, and come home a refreshed man. He imagined himself in Cannes now, strolling down Rue La Croisette toward the Quai St. Pierre, making a right at Festival restaurant just to see the tourists all sitting in pink director's chairs with the names of different American actors on their backs, Al Pacino, De Niro. All of this under a pristine blue sky and the never-ending row of healthy palm trees waving in the balmy weather, the Côte d'Azur stretching out into the Mediterranean.

He would gather his thoughts together as he strolled past the bright umbrellas, each boasting the banner of the hotel across the street it represented and the entry price per person. An ambient stream of car engines revving in front of the main drag. The banners furled on the beach: *Plage Gray d'Albion, Plage Royale, Les Plages Riviera, Les Plages Carlton.* Red-and-orange umbrellas, royal blue, orange and white, yellow gold, purple, springing from the sand like beach flowers. The sidewalk above broken only by menus for the beach restaurants below.

He and Claudette had danced one evening on the *plages* across from the Noga Hilton. A salsa band had been playing, and the people spinning and dipping so perfectly had intimidated the two of them into snuggling and laughing, content to be bystanders as they watched the women roll their shoulders and undulate to the music. That had been toward the end of summer, two years ago.

This was the beginning of finding that magic again. He would bring it back to her and they would be happy again. A new beginning, he told himself. Today was the first of July and the annual film festival crowd of actors, cinema people, and paraparazzi of May will have given way to the sale signs in every boutique lining the narrow streets of the Rue d'Antibes. *Les soldes,* the signs would boast.

The tall, flat-faced stone houses with their small terraces above the boutiques would have the shutters thrown open. Rectangular pots draped with purple bougainvillea. Local women would be strolling around in the highest of fashion, so different from their American counterparts with their masculine clothing choices. The Frenchwomen embraced the feminine: the small stitched details, the tiny tank tops and the elegant backless evening dresses that harkened back to Grace Kelly and Audrey Hepburn.

Everything so slender and delicate. Even the cars that lined and backed up the narrow street in front of the La Croisette, choking people with their exhaust, were tiny. The delivery trucks were a quarter of the size of the minivans back home.

Back home, the red dragonflies would be skimming over the lawn in Mission Dolores Park and Claudette would go to see them without him.

He had met Claudette at the La Croisette restaurant. She was working the lunch shift and living in one of the small apartments across from La Croisette, above the sandwich shop Aroma Bagel, with its blue neon sign in cursive. "Look at the light that comes through these big windows," she'd said, hugging herself, as she waited for his reaction.

"Nice," he said. He hadn't had the heart to tell her he was living out of three places in Cannes, the Carlton Hotel, with its tall closet doors and even taller ceilings; the Hilton, with its outside café; and his château that overlooked the Quai St. Pierre, complete with a live-in cook and a refrigerator filled with fresh clams, sea bream, peaches, potatoes, depending on what he felt like that week. Not to mention the yacht parked just outside the Plages du Midi bearing in bold letters *Jorgensen* and *Viking*. No. Not to mention that. That would come later, when he trusted that his possessions would not overwhelm her. Those were simpler times then.

But for all he knew, she wanted to get back together, was going to tell him so tonight, and this played heavily on his mind and made him want to forget this ill-fated decision. But his fucking nerves. No, can't always blame the nerves. *He* was the fuckup, like his father so aptly liked to say.

It was just difficult trying to live up to an angel every morning. She was a mirror that reflected how poorly he managed his own self. But he never hated her for it. Just the opposite. It was just . . . he worried about getting her wings dirty sometimes.

"We gonna jet, man?" the taller of the two Italians asked. His face was long from hunger. Chazz noted distantly that the guy might look completely different if he weren't so gaunt. He hadn't gotten their names, but he assumed they were brothers from the look of them. Both had curly black hair, dark olive skin, high sharp cheekbones, and sleepy eyes. Their skeletons were the hangers that their clothes hung on.

"Let's go," Chazz said.

"We ride to Ventimiglia, yes?" the tall one asked. He seemed to be the spokesman of the pair, the other one the observer.

"Sure," Chazz said, folding the mental picture of Dettie into his breast pocket. He felt his pocket and frowned. "Where's my smokes?" he asked.

"Don't know." The tall one shrugged.

The quiet one just grinned.

"Fuck you, man," Chazz said.

The quiet one took the pack of cigarettes out of his pocket and with a flick of his wrist tossed them to Chazz. Chazz caught them midair and shook his head.

The quiet one finally spoke. "I save for you."

"Right, but you smoked the other half," Chazz said, pulling one out and placing it in his mouth. "It's cool, man. Just as long as I have enough for myself."

When Chazz was little and his parents weren't home to wake him with a smile each morning, his nanny Madame Broussard would take him on outings on Chazz's money. His parents trusted her capability more and more, and so Chazz saw less and less of them. His father would put her in charge of his spending money for the week. "Don't let him spend it all in one place, Hélène," he would say.

"Of course not, Monsieur Jorgensen," she would answer with affronted charm and his father would drive off and Madame Broussard would take Chazz out and spend all his money and then pinch him into not telling his father. "Spoiled little brat," she would say as she bought her Chanel lipsticks and her slices of princess cake with the green marzipan topping. He could remember how the frosting would smear her lipstick.

She would not take Chazz to any of the museums she'd promised his father to, nor the zoo, nor even the library. He would have to tag along as she lived out her fantasy of being rich, of having extra spending money.

And Chazz would say, "Please, Madame Broussard, just give me enough to buy one thing. A candy bar. Or how about a Matchbox car? Please, Madame Broussard."

She would pinch him harder, shove him around, and degrade him in public, calling him a brat and an idiot. "Are you deaf?" she would shout. "Are you dumb?" And then in the evenings as he cried, she would comfort him, then kiss him on the lips like a lover. She was forty years old.

This continued for ten years, until when he was sixteen, jealous of his new driver's license and the Audi 4000 his father had bought him, she pinched him for the last time in the pantry. Chazz returned the favor by punching her lights out. She lost three front teeth. They settled out of court. Madame Broussard went away with a new set of bridgework, a great chunk of Jorgensen stock, and a lump sum of cash, and that was the start of it. His father, frantic about the reputation of his empire, dubbed

Chazz a fuckup. "I give you a new car and this is how you repay me?"

Yet she had given him one thing, Madame Broussard, and Chazz was grateful for it. She had given him the language to speak to Claudette ten years later. He spoke fluent French. He had overheard the lovely brunette, who had kept him coming back to La Croisette every lunch hour, telling a coworker about the grumpy American woman on sidewalk table three.

"Why can't they all go home?" she had said. "They're all so very bad and impatient. Why does it take you so long to bring the check, she asks? How was I to know she wanted the check? I cannot read her mind. Everyone enjoying their cappuccinos after their meals and this woman wants her check! To go where? She is already in the most beautiful place. These Americans. All rush to go somewhere. And then when they're there, they want to leave! *Tout de suite.* So why don't they just go and never come back?"

And he had asked her in French after having ordered in English, "But then how would I ask you out?"

Claudette had covered her mouth with horror and laughed. She gave of herself so freely. It was the same when they were together. How did one react to that? With his mother, a gift from her was credit for future obligations. To chaperone a daughter of a friend. To make a showing at her charity events. With his father, a gift was to buy Chazz off. His good-looking Norwegian-American face on the publicity photos. A small shot in one of the catalogs. *The next generation in the Jorgensen line,* one advertisement had read, with Chazz's signature reproduced in the bottom right-hand corner, below a smiling, strong-looking Chazz.

With his friends, their friendship was bestowed in return for the Jorgensen name, which opened doors to the Cliffs at Telluride, dining at the French Laundry, Jardinière, sold-out concerts,

Erykah Badu at the Fillmore, John Mayer, prized De La Hoya–
Vargas fights in Las Vegas, private jets. It became second nature
to Chazz to expect strings attached to gifts and giving.

How, then, did one react to Claudette Dumont, who loved
unconditionally? No coercion, no twist of words in her giving.
Captivating. Frightening. Paralyzing. If she would only say what
she wanted in exchange for her staying forever.

So, instead, he had been the one to take excursions, a fearful
test of sorts. One day, two, three weeks, to see if she would still be
there when he came home. She always was.

"Hey, American, what you have in Cannes?" the taller one
asked. He jerked a chin up. "A girl, American? American has lady
friend in Cannes? Fancy people in Cannes."

Chazz studied the Italian. He had to be at least twenty-eight;
the quiet one, the observer, twenty-six. He would have been
surprised to know they were twenty and eighteen, respectively.
Hunger did that to you; it ate up your age.

"Business," Chazz said. He didn't want them to muck up
his vision of paradise. Cannes belonged to Claudette and him.
Cannes was tropical weather in July and palm trees and restaurants on the beach. Women on the promenade in their tanned
skin with natural elegance in their walk and a certain sensuality
in the way they regarded you. It was not two gaunt-eyed men on
a dirty train with him.

"You do business like that?" The taller one laughed at Chazz's
clothes. "No, you have girl. Only a woman would take in man in
dirt suit. Our mother was the same. She take anyone in." The
man grinned at this.

A piece of his memory of Claudette unfolded. Dettie in a white
bathing suit lying on the Plages du Midi, her skin gold but not
savagely dark. Full shoulder-length curls—not bobbed like her
hair was now—where he could run his fingers through the ends.

"We go to Cannes, too. To get the good dope," the taller one said.

"Which train?" Chazz asked. "What time?" He'd do some dope, call it an early night. Check out the beach and sort his marriage out.

"The five-forty-five to Cannes. We make transfer in Ventimiglia. *Cinque quattro cinque,*" the taller one added more to himself.

Chazz nodded. It was the train he'd be taking anyway.

Two hours later they were in Ventimiglia. A voice announced the stop over the speaker. He met their eyes and stood. "Let's go."

The two Italians stopped at the exit.

"Well?" Chazz asked.

They consulted in whispers with each other. "We have no currency, man. For the connecting train. No lire—ah—*scusi.* No euros."

Chazz looked off to the side. He should just chuck the whole idea and go with his regular plan. Drugs didn't go well with his meds. "I got you. Come on." Out came the wad of dirty cash to match his dirty fingernails. A mixture of bills totaling three thousand euros, with a couple of U.S. twenties thrown in.

"Thanks, American. You good friend."

"Where's your stash at?" Chazz asked.

"Che?"

"Your dope. Where is it?"

"We get. We get in Cannes."

"All right, then I split," Chazz said.

"Like a banana," the taller one said.

Chazz nodded and the three of them stepped down from the train to wait for the five-forty-five to Cannes.

It was odd standing next to strangers in the light of day after you had laughed the entire night like the best of friends stoned on pot. He had made Claudette feel as if she were the stranger many times, he knew. He had called her from various pay phones and ghettos in the city at three in the morning, the scummier the place the better, with his voice full of remorse and a little fear. "Not sure where I am, hon. Going to be a little late, all right?" He had taken some perverted pleasure in knowing she cared so much to be concerned for him.

Sometimes, though he hated to admit it to himself, sometimes even when things were good in the beginning he hoped that he would come home one evening and she'd be gone. Cold turkey. Just get it over with. It was the fear and the waiting for it to happen. A suspended blade over his neck. When would she leave? It became an obsession that made him prowl the streets in the evening looking for a cure for the pain that was sure to come when she decided to leave. A head start of sorts.

There were times he'd be so terrified of her leaving that he would leave himself, for weeks at a time. He would return only after the fear had left his body. A kind of epileptic seizure of fear. She had asked once when he had been gone for a week, "Are you cheating on me, Chazz?"

"What?" he had asked in astonishment. "Hell no!" That had triggered his going away for two more weeks, because certainly she would leave him now if she thought that.

The five-forty-five arrived, a rusted pale-yellow-and-silver train sprayed with dirt, and the three of them stepped on. The train, like the first, was a cattle car of people, not the luxurious bullet train with air-conditioning or even the clean TGV lines with the reclining sporty red, black, and gray cushioned chairs, the lunch car with hot food. The windows were even grimier than those in the first train and again half opened. He could have taken a first-class luxury train if he'd wanted. But when he was like this he picked things that fit how he was feeling inside.

He watched the houses and the sea through his window. The train stopped in Menton, Beaulieu sur Mer. People strolling down the streets living peaceful lives. He saw a young woman and a little boy walking hand in hand as the father, in a wheel-chair, caught up and adjusted the boy's hat, tucked in his pants, then fell a few feet behind them. The train was moving again. Soon they would be in Cagnes de Mer, Antibes, Juan-les-Pins. They passed by oleander trees in pink, white, lavender; wildflow-ers dotted the countryside and always the sea following him. Cannes not far now, perhaps another forty minutes.

It would be steamy in Cannes. They used to walk hand in hand as Claudette threatened to waltz into every single store. Time was simpler then. *Will you marry me?* He hadn't expected that his greatest wish would be his greatest curse. He couldn't believe his good fortune. Never had believed it. But Cannes would bring his mind-set back to simpler things. He would remember how to live peacefully in the desire just to be next to her. Like when they first met.

The food vendor came, a porter rolling a heavy cart, causing the passengers to gather their packages from the aisles as he apolo-gized, *"Pardon, pardon."*

He was selling burnt black coffee and sodas, small quarter cans of Pringles chips and candy. Chazz's stomach growled and he asked for the salt-and-vinegar chips in a lime-green container.

"Merci." He nodded. He placed a hand on the porter before he could leave. *"Et un Coca-Cola."* The two Italians looked over at him. Screw them; he wasn't going to buy them food, too.

"Oui, monsieur, un Coca." The porter handed Chazz the drink and they exchanged euros. *"D'accord,"* he said, okay, and continued down the aisle announcing his wares.

In St. Laurent du Var a familiar face stepped onto the train. "Monsieur Jorgensen?" It was the waitress from La Croisette, a friend and former coworker of Claudette's.

Chazz could see her reflection hovering over him in the window next to the two brothers and pretended not to hear her. He could see her frowning, her eyes going from his hair, to his clothing, to the two men sitting in front of him.

She tried again, "Chazz? Monsieur Jorgensen?"

The Italian brothers were watching him; he could see that, too, in the window. He felt bad but he did not move his chin from his wrist. The waitress's name was Justine and she took care of Claudette and him whenever they visited. They always tipped her nicely. Over and above the mandatory amount, the *service compris.* If it weren't for the two Italians he would have seen Justine as a good omen. He would have walked with her to La Croisette and started his evening with a bottle of Champagne. She was wearing her uniform of white shirt and black skirt, no doubt on her way to start her evening shift.

He was angered suddenly by the presence of the two men. They were infringing on his plans. He watched Justine hesitate and saw the frustration and sureness in her face that he was who she thought he was. She looked at the other passengers, embarrassed. Chazz saw that the passengers looked back at her with an amused relish. An older woman with a scarf around her head and a white mustache shrugged. A little boy with a chocolate-covered mouth giggled and whispered in his mother's ear about Justine.

Still, he refused to turn to Justine. She looked anxiously one last time from the two men to Chazz, her gaze pausing at his hands below his chin. His dirt-caked hands, which used to touch Claudette's smiling face.

Cannes, the signs said. The three of them stood in silent acquiescence and walked through the smoke-clouded car right in front of a confused-looking Justine, who stood sideways to let them pass. In that moment, walking through the connecting cars, with the sun flowing through the windows, through *fumeur* and *non-fumeur* cars with the red circle and line through a smoking cigarette, he caught a movement from the taller one. A handing off of something to the other.

"What was that?" Chazz asked.

"Is nothing, American. Just a—how you say? Jump start. Something before the real party."

"Just give me enough to coast myself," Chazz said.

"No, is cheap stuff. We get good stuff for our American."

Chazz clenched his teeth. It wasn't that he was some drug addict. He could go months, years without smoking or snorting. But he needed something without the lithium to pop. Something to take the edge off. "Come on, man. Just a bump. Give me just enough for myself."

The two brothers looked at each other, then shrugged and handed him a folded piece of paper; within it there lay a small sliver of transparent paper. "Acid?" he asked.

The taller brother didn't seem to answer. He looked straight ahead, moving his head from side to side as if looking for someone through the crowd lined up to exit the train, and he said in a low voice, "Yes, yes. You take. Hurry. We go now."

Chazz shrugged and placed the paper on his tongue. He looked around. Justine was gone. He would go to see her at La Croisette tomorrow, catch her up on Claudette, and apologize with a rose. He would tell her he had been in a foul mood but he was better now. His hands were shaking again. His stomach growled loudly. Had he eaten the Pringles chips? Had he fallen asleep in between stops and not noticed when he'd woken up that he had been asleep?

The quiet Italian's shirt looked suspiciously crumb-ridden. A slash of pain cut through Chazz's right ear, diagonally downward to his chin. "Ugh." He clenched his eyes shut. One of those weird pains from sitting too long. He rocked his head from side to side to get the kinks out. The two men were staring at him, at his hand that flexed and clenched, flexed and clenched. He felt a moment of fear.

"Okay, American?"

"I'm cool." His brow had broken out into a sweat. A bead trickled down embarrassingly over his eye, and he swiped at it quickly.

"What?"

"Nothin', man." If the guy would just shut up for a fricking moment.

"Is nothing? It's nothing." The Italian frowned and shrugged, turning his back on Chazz.

Nothing. Chazz shook his head. It was so cloudy from no sleep. What day was it? Had he gained or lost a day over the Atlantic? A train arrived on track three as they stepped down onto the platform. *St. Raphael,* the destination board blinked. He remembered St. Raphael.

Outside of St. Raphael there was one winery, in the town of Fréjus. You could reach it in an hour on foot or just hop a taxicab. But if you were with someone you loved, an hour on foot was nothing. Maybe an hour and a half if you counted the time to stop and ask if you were going the right way and the time it took to wipe your hand on your pant legs so you could hold hers and not sully it with sweat. If you don't count inhaling deeply as both of you admired the little colony of sailboats that you could see from the boardwalk. If you don't count the seconds it takes to tickle her ear, to check your reflection in the market windows to make sure you look good for your girl, pet dogs that come out to greet you with tails wagging from under oak trees or the time it takes to tell stories of other dogs you have known to have greeted you in your life.

No, Fréjus is not that far at all from St. Raphael, if you stop at only one boutique and wait outside to smoke contentedly while she goes in to check on the price of the lavender camisole that matches her eyes in the store window and you take the time to note how calm the seas are in your stomach. How content. Otherwise, it is an hour at a good pace or a five-minute hop in a taxi.

The small winery was in Fréjus and Claudette and he found it was a blessing from the sun. Its cool, stone cavelike quarters boasted only five red tanks, where the locals brought in their own jugs to fill by using a hose connected to each of the five vats—five large containers of the four reds, marked *Vin de Table Rouge 12, Vin de Table Rosé 12, Côtes de Provence Rouge 13, Vin de Pays Rosé 13* and the one white, *Côtes de Provence Blanc.* And surrounding the tasting area, shelves of port and grappa and previous wines. But that was just the start of Fréjus, the quaint little *distillerie* of whose name he had forgotten now. He could still remember the wooden sign. Hmm. If he thought carefully he would remember later. If not for this pain in his head. But where was he? Once in Fréjus . . .

First of all, once in Fréjus, you sit your girl down and tell her it is all going to be all right. Even though you know your father has tried to buy her off to make her go away quickly. You don't care about the money anyway. And no, you will not have her sign a prenuptial agreement. That is for losers and business transactions. It was never about the money.

"So, here is the good stuff. La dope." The Italian rolled his fisted hand as if he were throwing dice and said an American version of "Seven come eleven, baby." Only it sounded cheesy. Sneaky. He opened his hand. There was a small plastic bag that fit just inside his palm.

Chazz's eyes were blurry from lack of sleep. He kept focusing on the guy and unfocusing. He stared at the loud one's violet lids. He nodded and lifted the bag from the guy's hand. "Coke?" he heard himself say faintly and he clenched, then licked his teeth from memory. Just one snort. He would take just one. He wiped his hand on his trousers to dry the sweat. He was nervous. This would make him not so nervous. "I thought you were supposed to get it in Cannes."

"Yes. And here we are. In Cannes. While you sleepwalk I got dope." He pointed down at the station floor. "*Il mio amico.* My friend works here."

"Where is he?" Chazz squinted, looking around as people moved by in a blur. Arriving and departing. Everyone leaving. Always leaving. "I wasn't sleepwalking. Where's your guy?"

The Italian shrugged, then laughed. "*Non posso.* I not gonna tell you that. *Un segreto.* Secret."

Chazz shrugged. "I thought you had to leave the station." He followed after the brothers as they walked to a corner. The taller one had cut three lines. "*Salute,*" Chazz said. The two men laughed. He bent down his head, plugged one nostril, and inhaled. The taller one jostled the other. It happened right away. The pain, the dizziness, the stomach convulsing. Chazz could feel his eyes roll up. He tried to reach for people, but he was dirty, with these two other dirty guys laughing beside him, and the people with their good, normal lives pulled away. "Aggh, bad shit. What kind of coke is this?"

The two men were laughing. "Is no coke. Is heroine. Is good American?"

"This is fucked . . ." He staggered up. He was scared.

In Fréjus, if you do go, Chazz Jorgensen, only son of Terge Jorgensen of the Jorgensen Faucets empire, would suggest visiting the corner of Rue Caponne and Rue St. Armande. When you are there and if you are hungry you must visit Fréjus François, a small section off from the main shops. There are hardly any tourists because the town is not in the guidebooks. It is a place to be stumbled upon with your loved one. On a day, perhaps, when you are looking for something else. A winery, perhaps, and you find this jewel instead. Isn't that the way you always find good things?

The restaurant Fréjus François sits in a scrupulously clean alleyway of flat-faced houses in colors of rusted peach, pale blue, champagne, honey, with shutters in varying colors to accent the main scheme. Peach with blue shutters. Beige with green shutters. Sage green with yellow shutters. There is even a corner grocery store across from the restaurant, manned by a sixteen-year-old boy named Carlo and a black-and-white cat sleeping in one of the window openings.

The grocery store, a small beauty store, and Fréjus François are the only stores in the cobblestoned alley. And there François sits with his wide back against the corner of his tiny restaurant with his two small white dogs the size of Jack Russell terriers. The littler dog has a pink porcupine toy he likes to chew as he jealously watches the patrons eat François's delicious fare.

But at first you do not notice François or his little dogs, until you sit down. It may be the girl of your dreams on your arm or the ring in your pocket. But as you sit down and you both order the meal of the day, consisting of filet of white fish, tomatoes halved and steamed in garlic and pepper, included with this a carafe of house red wine and a plate of quiche in Bolognese sauce so that it is moist and flavorful and not at all like its dry American counterpart, you may start to notice François with his walking cane and his beret. Or you may be distracted still by the side of lemon for the fish and real French dressing in a little porcelain bowl for the hard-boiled eggs that also come with the meal.

But after you've stared at the set of five small black chalkboards posted on the outdoor café boasting, *"Tous les Jours: Couscous à Emporter; Omelettes—Natural, Fromage, Champignons, Lardons; Frites ou Salade Compris; Spaghetti-Beurre 30 francs; Bolognaise 45 francs; Carbonara 48 francs; Fruits de Mer 48 francs,"* and after your eyes settle in beneath the blue-and-white umbrellas and the blue paper place settings printed with van Gogh haystacks, you may yet be distracted.

Maybe after you've fingered the purple velvet box in your pocket for the tenth time, you do notice François in a powder-blue polo shirt, plaid navy-and-white trousers, fat feet in beige sandals, and white hairy legs.

You notice François because a young African boy about twelve years old on a skateboard almost careens over one of his terriers, who skitters quickly beneath your seats to resist becoming pancake. You think François will be angry, François will stand up in a storm, yet you are surprised to notice he talks softly to the boy, who looks at the ground, nodding at the gentle reprimand. Then the boy walks over and puts an arm around François's shoulder as François puts an arm around his waist, gently shaking him. The kid grins widely, then takes the terrier for a walk on a leash as François tries to wave the older dog to go along, to no avail.

You notice François next because your soon-to-be fiancée, though she doesn't know it yet, points out, "That man in the corner must be the owner because everyone who passes calls out hello to him. Isn't that sweet?"

You will notice how perfect this street is because the only other business establishments are Emiliene's Beauty Parlor and the fruit store manned by the kid, who is now covering the fruits in blue plastic tarp for the lunch hour, when all the shops close for the three-hour siesta and mealtime. You will grin not unlike the little boy on the skateboard, walking François's dog, because life is slow and easy on this balmy afternoon and the sun falls softly through the arched footbridge connecting the narrow street of houses with the unlit brown lanterns and the clean streets.

The alley is given further shade by the tall apartment houses towering fifty feet high. The sound of an old two-seater plane drones above, and a small moped leans unchained against the opposite house. Every twenty minutes one or two people pass. One or two people open the doors to their houses and step out to smoke a pipe and wave at François. The place has the feeling that everyone is on a perpetual vacation. The postcard black-and-white cat continues to sit in his postcard-looking window, content because he has the secret to life.

When your girl asks, "What are you smiling at?" then shyly sneaks a smile at the charming older couple next to you, you just continue to smile. The slender older man, balding, in shorts and green plaid shirt, smiles unaffectedly back at you. The woman, stylishly dressed, her black hair wrapped in a white-and-gold bandanna and a royal blue Chanel blouse tied at her waist to cover her turquoise dress, does, too. "*C'est bon,*" this is good, the old man indicates, lifting the same red carafe of wine that comes with your order.

The woman's eyes are kind and intelligent and you think, *This will be Dettie and me someday, but I will suggest the Bordeaux.*

You check the chalkboards once again; they boast pasta, desserts, *vins,* and, yes, Bordeaux. You will tell the next kid sitting in your shoes many years from now to take the Bordeaux.

And your eyes will be like the old woman's, full of kindness and intelligence, because from now on you will wake up beside a smile that will never go away, never steal your day money for lipsticks and princess cakes, never tell you you are a fuckup and because, when she is away from your side, you get an ache in the pit of your stomach. And you will think life has never been this good and you will worry and overdo your worry and not sleep. You will worry that heaven will take her back, her little handbags, her sweaters, her smile, her hand around your waist, and tell you it was all a sick joke. But that will come later. The worry. It always comes after the happiness.

"Do you like, American?" The tall one laughed. "The good stuff? Like crap, no?" he asked as his eyes went from Chazz's pockets to his face, Chazz's pockets to his face, so that Chazz felt as if he were being frisked by hands and not eyes. Maybe he was.

They wanted his money. It was obvious now. So obvious. If he weren't such a screwup. If he had taken the time to think. "You dirty—" Chazz tried to swing but he couldn't balance himself and he stumbled and people got out of his way.

"Just leave me enough for a present for my wife. There's a ring I want to buy her."

Frick and Frack frisking him now.

"No." Chazz tried to pull away with a sudden surge of strength. He needed the money for his sorry-I-was-an-ass present to Claudette. He broke away and ran up the stairs and he could hear them chasing after him. Something from Cannes to prove he was in Cannes and not just screwing off in town and pretending to be away. Maybe some of the soft square *calissons* she loved so well. In different flavors, passion fruit, *fraises, framboise,* grape, peach. He wasn't sure if they'd keep but if he brought them home in the bag with the 21 Rue D'Antibes address, she would know he had really gone to France.

He stumbled again, then picked himself up. The trousers of his Armani pants had a gaping hole in the left knee. He ran and ran and they caught up to him once and tumbled but somehow he got up and ran up the next flight of stairs and then he was breathing fresh air. He heard the small insistent *beep beep* of a motorbike and then a car screech and then a thud.

He could see the Cannes sky now skimming past the train windows. But he wasn't on the train any longer, was he? He felt the air as he leaped from car to car. But somehow his legs weren't moving. He was on his back staring at the cloudless sky. Something wet caking his face. People stopping, saying words. But it didn't matter. Because he would be home soon. He could feel himself floating that way. He had made it to Cannes. He had stopped his wandering. Now he was floating home to Dettie.

tHe NeckLace

tHe womaN was tiny, nondescript, and pale next to the crowd of gawkers standing outside the Cannes train station and staring down at the body of the handsome American. "She-ti-chô-yâ," she prayed. May you live! But he was dead, anyone could see that, and yet his right hand still shook in reflex. It seemed to want to rise of its own accord to complete some unfinished business. As if his body were unbelieving of the close call from the small motorbike that had jolted him off balance, giving him a brief interlude of a smile of relief before the impact from the oncoming taxi had taken his life.

The ambulance and the gendarmes had not yet arrived, though their mournful wails could be heard from blocks away. He looked so vulnerable. A thin stream of crimson starting at his temple had begun to pool in the dip just below his right eye and cheekbone. The remnant of a smile was still on his lips. The face was still perfect but on the back side, where the pavement had started to steam, a darker red poured like a halo. On the back side, she knew, the bones would be soft and broken in many places. She touched her necklace as she stepped closer. *Mon Dieu,* his eyes were still open, reflecting the cloudless Cannes sky.

She touched her necklace again and said a quick prayer for this boy who died away from home. Away from his mother. She noticed a group staring too long at her necklace and she pulled her collar close to hide it. It was the Hebrew word *chai,* the Jewish symbol for life. You couldn't be too careful these days. Though she was French herself, she was also Jewish, and the French were not favoring Israel right now, she believed. They favored the Arabs. It was not always wise to flaunt the necklace.

She had a son about this young man's age, Laurent, but they were not talking for eight months now and the thought of it was an acid that burned a hole into her heart. Daily. Daily she thought of nothing but this. That she and her son, once so close, so interdependent, were now behaving like sworn enemies. Well, possibly not that bad, was it? She voiced a chuckle at her catastrophizing. At times, she could not tell if she was exaggerating or if really this matter of the two of them not talking was not *très sérieux* and needed to be addressed immediately.

A woman standing over the body met Anaïs's eyes, and in that one look communicated her hate. The woman said in a loud whisper to her friend, but meant for Anaïs to hear, of course, "Did you see? The Jewish woman? She was laughing at the dead American. How morbid. How sick."

Anaïs wanted to say, No, no. You've mistaken my meaning. I was not laughing at the boy. I was laughing at my own foolish self. But the two women had tsk-tsked and walked off after saying one last *pauvre enfant* over the dead man's body.

If she were still talking to Laurent she would call him instantly the moment she arrived home. To check that he had not been hit by a car. That he was eating well. That that woman was feeding him. Anaïs tensed at the thought. All because of that girlfriend of his they were not talking. She was his new wife now but Anaïs could not bring herself to say the word because then the woman would become her daughter-in-law. The girl was

Catholic, from Brazil, and she was like the plague, like malaria, like a madness that had fevered her son's body and transformed her well-behaved boy into a changeling. Truly there was no other word for it.

But Anaïs knew. She knew some of the thinking behind Laurent's impulsive move to marry his new wife. He had lost a girl once. His first love. They were engaged to be married. Anaïs wonders if he is truly over her. Anaïs is hardly over her. Such a well-behaved girl. What was her name again? It is on the tip of her tongue. Starting with a *K* or *C* was it? Katarine? Ah, it slips the mind for the moment. She snaps her fingers as the name eludes her. Laurent had thought that simply because they were engaged his future was paved in gold. That K was as good as married to him. Anaïs was fond of that girl but for some reason she cannot call her name to mind. Certainly it has been five years; still, one would think she could recall more than the first letter of her name. But in the end the young woman had showed Laurent, by giving him back his engagement ring, that it was just a promise.

"Nothing is set in stone," Anaïs had told him. "You must let go, Laurent."

"Never, Maman. She will come back to me. You will see." But the girl never returned.

Laurent blames her, Anaïs knows. Because Anaïs had advised him to wait the one more year to marry until he graduated so he could fully focus on school and then fully focus on his new wife. "Better she has a change of heart now than when you are married, Laurent." Anaïs had rubbed her palm over his back the way she used to do when he was a child. He had pulled away and scowled at her then.

"Leave it to you to find something good from her leaving!"

"That is not what I mean. I meant only to comfort you." Ah, but that was so long ago. "He cannot still hold that against me.

Can he?" She shakes her head. "Talking to the wind again." She clucked her tongue. So here they were with the rush wedding of a girl he had known less than a year. And this time Anaïs had held her tongue.

The ambulance was here now and the gendarmes were parting the crowd.

"*Pardon, pardon,*" they repeated, brushing past her.

Anaïs looked down at the young man once again. She felt somehow his goodness. *Ridiculous,* her husband would have declared if he were still alive. But it was true. Anaïs had a good *sense* of people. "A practical word; no mysticism attached," she would insist. "*Ho-shem yeesh-mor.*" She whispered the Hebrew words. "May God watch you."

A pair of gaunt-cheeked men were watching Anaïs Barr. She met their eyes over the body of the young American. The tall one possessed eyes glazed over like in death. The other one, the shorter one, was more contemplative, as if he had one foot in each world, heading for the one in which his taller brother looked out from, devoid of emotion. A dark world; Anaïs shuddered. The taller man was staring at her necklace. Not for its symbol, no; she got the feeling it was not for its symbol but for its worth.

Her necklace, a triangle of eighteen-karat gold with a garnet hanging suspended at the top of the triangle, framed the *chai.* The symbol for *chai* was like the Greek symbol pi with a smaller inverted L to the left. The taller man whispered something to the brother, but the shorter one shook his head. "*No,*" he said in Italian. "*Un regular.*" A regular. "*E comunque.*" And besides. "She reminds me of Mamma."

And the realization surrounded her, threatening to steal her breath. They had killed this young man. For whatever reason, intended or unintended, they were responsible. She knew it in her bones. For the wicked there were words as well: "*Laich lo-o-zo-zail,*" may you go to hell. And then like the two young men the feeling was gone. "Silly. Silly." She shook her head. "I am losing my faculties. Too dramatic, as Laurent would say."

But what had started her thinking of Laurent? Ah yes. The young American for whom the stretcher was being pulled out. Two ambulance drivers approached as the police took notes. No amount of scribbling, Anaïs knew, could make this young man rise again.

"He was running up the steps," a young girl said, pointing to the train station. "I could not see where he was running to. Maybe he was late for an appointment." The police nodded and scribbled this down.

"Was he with anyone?" the head officer, balding and with glasses, asked.

The girl looked at her friend, a young man. *"Non."* The man frowned. "I did not see anyone running beside him."

"And then?" the policeman asked.

"And then he was hurrying, hurrying"—the girl made the motion of running in place—"and this motor scooter was coming from the other direction and almost hit him." She gestured in the direction that the motorbike had come from. "He was shouting something. Something." Again she looked to her friend for help.

"What was it?" the policeman asked.

"He was shouting, 'Sing' or 'The ring,'" the young man said, shrugging. Again the police scribbled.

"But he avoided the motor scooter and I was so relieved." The girl placed a hand on her chest. "And then ooh, boom, the light changed and this taxi was turning and, ah—" The woman shut her eyes and shuddered. Her friend placed an arm around her, and she turned her face into him.

The ambulance drivers brushed past the crowd and surveyed

the American for what seemed like an hour. Then, after conferring with the police, they took hold of him on each end. One grasped his ankles, revealing expensive socks and new black shoes, and the other placed hands behind the shoulders of the young man's well-tailored suit. They counted to three, *"Un, deux, trois,"* lifting him as a collective gasp went through the crowd. Just a glimpse was enough; the entire back side of his white collar shone black and crimson as it was pulled away from the darker pool on the ground, which had matted his golden hair red. Anaïs imagined someone placing a finger in that cold pool and writing from right to left on the foreheads of his two murderers the words for the wicked: "You shall die in this life and in the next."

She waited, waited, holding on to her collar, which was no longer protecting her necklace, in the way that the old and forgetful wait, filling in situations and making assumptions. She waited to see if the police needed her testimony for something she had not witnessed. Maybe they needed to hear her comments, how she was purchasing something for her cold at the *pharmacie.* How after that she had wandered into her favorite *boulangerie* and inspected a loaf of bread, saying, *"Bonjour,"* to the baker, and was about to ask him if he could sell her a smaller baguette since she would dine alone.

He knew her from the days when she and Laurent would visit Cannes for a month, and the baker, Monsieur Girard, still sold her the longer baguettes for two of them from habit. She had been in the midst of telling him this when she heard the awful screeching and then the suspended breaths in the store as all waited for the giant crash of breaking glass. There was a crash, but the sound that followed was that of an awful thudding and rolling, not a breaking of glass.

She craned her head again to the police, who glanced over and above her. Did they have enough information? Probably everyone had repeated different pieces of the puzzle. But had anyone told them about the two men? How the murderers had stood around like simple onlookers? Anaïs shook. There was nothing she could tell them. An accusation based on instinct. His murderers would not find their judgment at this moment. The police would not deduce the truth, no. But the murderers could not escape their ultimate fate. It awaited them in hell, and they could not escape it.

But what, where was she? She gathered her things. "Getting forgetful now," she tsk-tsked. "It is this way when you have no one to practice your thoughts on," she murmured, oblivious to the people who looked and frowned when they saw they were not being addressed by her mumblings and, for that matter, that the woman was not addressing anyone visible.

Anaïs let the bread bag hang from her elbow, the loaf sticking out prominently without wrapping. Again Monsieur Girard had given her enough for two to dine. The rest would go to waste as she was too lazy to feed it to the pigeons. She had paid for the loaf hurriedly when she'd heard the screams directly after the accident. She held her sweater close to her. Though it was hot outside, a chill had settled inside her. What had she been discussing again?

Oh yes, the infidel, her son's girlfriend, fiancée, wife, witch. What did it matter what she addressed the woman in her own mind? But she knew it mattered. This was not the way to honor one's son. To say awful things in her mind. It was just that she was so alone. But it had not always been this way. Long ago, she had had a life, a large family like the people bustling beside her, with laughter and children in tow, but time was a thief.

"Now what to do?" This accident and standing around like another gawker had stolen her dinnertime. Now she was too tired to take the train home to Aix and then cook. She would need to go to a restaurant here in Cannes. But they filled up so quickly, and there were a few she would rather avoid. She tried

Le Petit Cassoulet, on the main promenade beside Festival. She stood looking into the window at diners, shifting her weight from left to right, as two groups of people lined up in front of her. A girl of six or so, dressed stylishly in a rose sequined cap, a peasant blouse that showed her skinny midriff, and a matching peasant skirt, tugged at her mother's dress. "Maman, Maman. I want to order my own plate this time, Maman. I do not want to share with Mathilde."

"Shh." The green-eyed woman gave Anaïs an apologetic look and bent down to her daughter. "You are bothering the *madame.*"

"But I will not share with Mathilde tonight. I do not like the food she eats."

A younger, curly-haired girl of about three glanced over her mother's shoulder, dressed exactly like her complaining sister except in beige with her beaded cap clutched in her hand, sucking her thumb as her mother rocked her. "Shh, Louise, *s'il vous plaît.* You are making my head hurt."

Anaïs smiled self-consciously and looked in through the glass windows at the customers seated at matching tables of rose-and-white tablecloths. It took a moment before she realized she was staring through the glass at a couple seated directly in front of her. They smiled awkwardly and said something to each other. Anaïs started, jumping back. So embarrassing.

How long had she been staring at the young lovers? Had the others seen the look of longing she felt as she glanced around at the groups of families? She knew the headwaiter walking hurriedly around with his pink dress shirt stained in the armpits with widening circles of sweat. She tried to lift up a hand to him; perhaps he had room for one in a quiet corner. But he was busy and gave her only a brief passing smile. Her face warmed.

"I won't eat here," she murmured. "Too crowded," she announced. And the mother of the two girls glanced curiously over her shoulder to see whom Anaïs was speaking to.

"*Pardon.*" Anaïs excused herself, already craning her neck to see what other restaurants were available along the promenade. As she walked she held her baguette close to her. The smell reminded her of when she was younger.

When she was younger she had uncles and aunts and brothers and parents and, later, a husband. She still lived in the same house in Aix-en-Provence with the canopy of chestnut trees lining the promenade. Her family had owned two buildings on the street up from the train station, before the train's path turned onto Rue Mirabeau and the main thoroughfare leading to Rue Joffre and the Cézanne walk, where the artist had been inspired by the countryside but which was so crowded with tourists now.

Aix belonged to the students as well. Now it was a university town. *Jeunes* with cell phones and backpacks, tight jeans, cigarettes, sunglasses, and loud greetings in cafés to their classmates, jarred tables and toppled chairs. The louder the better, it seemed. A virtual performance that could be seen all day and was usually preceded by a loud motorbike. But it hadn't always been so.

Her family had owned a *boucherie,* Boucherie Barr it was called. She could still picture the substantial barnlike door of turquoise, with its arched paneling, and the window where the name was again stenciled in gold lettering. Her uncles prepared rabbit, chicken, knuckle of ham, *jambonneau,* sausages *andouilles,* and salami in addition to *pâtés* and *rillettes.* Next door they owned the adjoining Boulangerie-Pâtisserie Barr, selling everything from breads to gaily packaged jellies with orange and red lids that boasted *gelée de citrons, myrtilles, gelée d'orange, mûres,* and shiny *tartes aux fruits* made from their collective gardens behind their butcher shop.

Anaïs's mouth watered from the memory of the tarts. Her Aunt Lilette would cut the peaches in half. "Not the usual tiny slivers but halves, you see? In that way my creations are different and *très délicieux,*" Aunt Lilette would say. And the peach tart would look like a small island of miniature peach-colored hills. Aunt Henriette was the master of the breads. Her breads were works of art, with their fancy twists and top crusts pinched with her masterful hands into the shape of roses and leaves.

In the mornings the bakery would fill with the smells of the warm, baking breads. The scent of the almonds that had gone into the powdered cakes would reach to every corner of the store. The cherries, apricots, and peaches of the cooling tarts would be impossible to ignore. As her aunts stopped to rest, Anaïs and her cousins would sneak in through the adjoining butcher shop, placing fingers in front of their lips at the assistant butchers, who would chuckle and pretend not to see them as they entered the back way to the connecting bakery.

Once inside the *boulangerie-pâtisserie,* the smells would be doubly intoxicating and they had to steel themselves in order to get the job done and not stand mesmerized before a blackberry tart until their aunts returned and grabbed them by the ears. It had been known to happen.

Anaïs and her cousins, usually Marie Claire and Guy, would stuff their pockets and shirts with whatever they could come away with, then run like mad until they were safely down the Cezanne walk, several blocks away. As they walked through the foresty area where the artist had once taken his inspiration, Anaïs, Guy, and Marie Claire would gain their own inspiration from the various tarts. They would giggle as Anaïs and Marie peeled open their shirts, each revealing a wheel of tart plastered to their bellies, and as they peeled them away they would laugh at their fingers and stomachs sticky with cherry glaze or dark berry tart.

Guy was the worst thief. Always in his fear he would grab a simple baguette. Delicious but still! Unworthy. His sister Marie

Claire would lament, *You are not good enough to be a thief. What shall we do with a loaf of bread?* What indeed? After they were through with the tarts they would swab their sticky bellies and fingers with the bread and eat some more.

They stayed away from the preserves that Grand-mère Ruthie prepared. They were both fascinating and strange. Green pickled tomatoes in clear liquid that had hibernated in closets for six months, looked salty, and could not possibly satisfy three mouths of sweet teeth. The word *kosher* had not meant much to them then. And as children the adults had never pressured them. They believed more in the soul and thoughts being kosher than food, which is why it had been such a surprise later when her own son, Laurent, had become, at the early age of eight, infatuated with kosher food. He would eat nothing else.

"My good little Hebrew boy." She chuckled now at the memory. The very same one who would beg for *calissons des fruits,* then drive the candy confectioner mad as he scrutinized the contents of each package for permissible ingredients. He loved the *poires, abricots, cerises,* and *citrons.* "Did you bake these candies yourself?"

And if the confectioner made the mistake of conceit and admitted to having made them, Laurent would follow with the inevitable "Was it made with any pork products?" and other such questions.

"What are you talking about?" the attendant would say, exasperated. "These are sweets. Why should there be pork products?" But still Laurent would continue on.

And no one had taught him this. Their own *boucherie* was not kosher. Anaïs sighed. Such a good boy. How she wished now she had had more children. Maybe if Laurent had had a brother, the boy would be encouraging him to speak to their mother. But she had only Laurent. And everyone else was gone now. Guy, Marie Claire. All moved away. One to Canada. One to America.

The Boucherie Barr and the connecting *boulangerie-pâtisserie* all liquidated.

The shops were now a lingerie shop and a soap shop. At least they had kept the original facades. And the front street still had the arched trees touching from either side of the street to form a natural pear-colored canopy of shade. But it was not the same.

Once Aix had been their kingdom. The Barr family. And Anaïs had been like a princess. Her Uncles Abey and Saul were the brains behind the butcher shop. Their forearm muscles strong and etched with numbers. "You must not show those off so much," Aunt Lilette would chide. "Vandals may appear."

But she knew as well as everyone that neither brother would ever hide the painful legacy of his past. "You tend to your breads, Lilette. Leave the meats to Saul and Abey, eh?" Uncle Abraham would gently joke. And Aunt Lilette would finger her necklace, the one Anaïs now wore. But they were all gone now. From death, disease, time.

She had only Laurent. And now Laurent was changed. All because of that woman. Anaïs had been so thrilled to meet the girl. Whoever her Laurent loved she would and must love, too. She would embrace her immediately and give honor to her son by loving this girl. But it had not been that easy. From the start, from the first look the girl had stated her claim on Laurent. With one look!

She had a mother, her shuttered look said. She didn't need two. She had a family—brothers, sisters, and a father—her squared shoulders and upright posture declared as she summed up Anaïs's worth. And Anaïs had stood timidly, obediently, with a welcome present in her hands, her shoulders slumped, unprepared for the assault.

"Your wedding, I will help you to prepare," Anaïs had said. She had done the traditional thing and called the girl's mother to first tell them how pleased she was at her son's engagement to their daughter and possibly arrange for a meeting. She would be more than happy to pay for their flight to France to discuss preliminary wedding plans. To get to know them better.

She pictured her large house bustling with new soon-to-be family members. She had left the message on their machine and then waited patiently in close vicinity to her phone that day and all through the next, biding her time by writing invitation cards to the party she would throw for them. Leaving the place for the date blank, to be filled in when they returned her call. She had even bought the correct amount of stamps to send to Italy, Spain, to call back old friends, remaining family.

Dear Gabrielle and Jonathan, Dearest Guy, Dearest Marie Claire . . .

Our Laurent has recently become engaged to a beautiful young woman. In honor of their union I cordially invite you to a luncheon . . .

All day she had written cards on stationery she had taken hours to select. *Dear Abraham, Dear Judith, Dearest Rebecca* . . .

But the girl's family had not returned the call.

"They don't speak French or English, Maman," Laurent had explained. "Only Serena does."

The girl was beautiful, of course. She had expected nothing less from Laurent.

"Thank you, Mrs. Barr, but my mother and sisters have already promised to attend to me. Perhaps you could help with the food for the after-party?"

And instead of being embarrassed, Laurent had grinned. He had grinned! "She has it all taken care of, Maman," he said.

"But surely there is something I can do? When you perform the breaking of the glass at the end of the wedding," Anaïs had begun.

But the girl had frowned and looked to Laurent. A line had creased between her brows. And again Laurent had beamed. "We've decided to just do all Catholic, Maman. No longer the joint Jewish-Catholic celebration like you and I discussed."

"Ah." Anaïs had nodded stupidly. What kind of response was that? "Ah . . ." Why hadn't she spoken up, protested? Maybe Laurent had not yet been deeply imbedded with this woman's wiles but now, now certainly it was obvious. What was Anaïs to do with the date she was to give to the rabbi for the ceremony? After that long conversation she had had about his need to be flexible and not so stringent in welcoming the girl, who was a Catholic. What to do with the tentative reservation she had made for the synagogue? How could someone whom Laurent loved look at her that way? How could Laurent fall for such a person?

But it was clear at the end of the day who Laurent would choose. He no longer needed Anaïs; he had his girl. And Anaïs? She had evenings like this where she walked and walked, looking not so much for a restaurant but company. She had a family to whom she rented out the bottom floor of the big house she owned, not for need of money—she had plenty of that, ever since the shops were sold. She rented the house out to a family just for the comfort of the noise, of voices.

But again she had erred, because the family was a contained unit. They, too, did not need her. Many times she has regretted not renting out to one student or a woman like herself who might seek company in the evenings. How nice it would have been to have someone to share idle time with. Instead of filling the void, their closeness emphasized her loneliness.

It was only during the long, quiet winter months that she intruded on them. Standing by the rooms below, hovering a fraction longer than appropriate, on the pretense of checking in. She didn't want to intrude. "The pipes—how are they serving you? I can check them myself," she would say hopefully, the laughter of the boarders' children putting a momentary spring in her step as she craned her head to the side to see what they were giggling about.

"Oh no, Madame Barr, the pipes serve us fine. Thank you."

"And the furnace?" Anaïs would ask, trying not to let her gaze wander into the sun-filled room.

"It heats our floor perfectly, Madame Barr."

There would be an awkward moment when Anaïs would be peering in through the doorway into the family room with no more questions left, and the boarders' children would be playing cards quietly or drawing. This was the same room she once shared with Laurent. The children would be reading a book as they sat comfortably with blankets tucked in around them. The woman boarder would look to her husband for help.

"And you, Madame Barr? How are you faring? Can I help you with anything?" he would ask kindly.

The question would jolt her back to reality and she would thank him and hurry out, never quite having stepped in. "No, no thank you. I did not mean to intrude."

"You are not intruding."

"I have things to attend to. Yes, there are things. I meant only to check. I did not mean to intrude."

And the man and woman would look at each other and clasp hands and smile at her as she walked upstairs to her quiet quarters. She had once heard snatches of the woman boarder saying in muffled tones to a friend, "Yes, alone. Poor thing. Son no longer visits. Married now." The family did not seem to care either way. They did not send their children up to say hello or bring her flowers, as Laurent used to do. To them she was just the landlady. She had no one to care for.

But this was not winter; this was July, and the hot weather kept the family outdoors and Anaïs, seeking company, also propelled herself outdoors. She bumped shoulder to shoulder with someone. *"Pardon, madame,"* a young man said, doffing his hat but still walking ahead, catching up with friends as they hurried across the beach to the ice-cream stands that dotted the walkway. The crowd was becoming too thick now. She checked her watch: *sept heures,* seven o'clock now, and Friday evening at that. She shook her head. There would be few restaurants that were not already full. Her stomach rumbled. If she didn't eat soon she would become faint.

She had made this day trip to Cannes, and for what? To see a poor American lying on his back while his life leaked out onto the tar-blackened streets. Just one day. That was what she was reduced to now. Long ago, she and Laurent would go every year to Cannes for the full month of July, without fail. When he was at the university in New York he still came back for Cannes in the summer and to Aix for the holy month and for her birthday. But he had not come now for eight months, and habit had drawn Anaïs here, if only for the day.

She had not bought half the clothes she had last year. Last year the two of them had walked arm in arm on the promenade above the beach. After purchasing a bag's worth of *chocolats, marrons,* and *fruits confits* at Bruno's and dipping their hands into the crinkly gold-ribboned container every few steps, they had talked of introducing Anais to Laurent's new love.

Today she had bought only practical things: underwear, a *huile d'olives* that she liked to cook with, and the anis-flavored Homeodent toothpaste she favored. And, of course, the hemorrhoid potion she was always embarrassed to ask for. Ordinary things that she could have bought in Aix.

She circled the Rue des États-Unis back around to Rue d'Antibes until she came around to La Croisette again and passed La Malmaison. People were gathered in front of the building—a grand opening of some sorts. Anais could not concentrate as the Rue des États-Unis threatened to come around again. She stopped walking. Her bones filled with exasperation. All the restaurants were full except the one she dreaded the most, La Maison du Gaston. Her son's favorite restaurant. To be reminded of him on such a day when she felt such loneliness. But where else was she to go?

She swallowed, rubbed her arms, and stepped one foot across the threshold. She buttoned her shirt, but not before the waitress saw. So Anaïs dropped her hand and lifted her chin. She waited another ten minutes. The waitress had seen her necklace, Anaïs was sure of it, and now things would be different. The waitress placed the menu before the table Anaïs was contemplating. *"Bonsoir, Madame."* The woman bid her good evening, but there was a falseness in her voice, Anaïs was certain.

When she asked for a carafe of water she was given a bottle of Perrier.

"I asked for a carafe of water," Anaïs said.

"Ah, pardon, Madame. It is on me. *Voilà."* The waitress produced a carafe.

"But I do not want this also charged on my bill," Anaïs protested. "It is already opened."

"Yes, of course. It is free. My fault."

"Well then, I would like the *fruits de mer* tonight." Her mouth watered as she looked around her at the other tables that had ordered the same mixed grill of prawns, sea bass, salmon, and vegetables. On one plate the butter glided over a hill of zucchini.

"Ah, sorry, Madame, we are all out. *Finis.* Something else?" the waitress asked, with her pen ready to take the order.

"Well," Anaïs sighed heavily. "Perhaps I shall just have the lamb, though I do not want this."

"Um, *une minute,* ah?" the waitress asked.

"Where are you going?" Anaïs asked as the woman hurried away.

The waitress returned. "I have asked the chef, Madame, and

he apologizes. He does have some special oysters and mussels, brought in only an hour ago. They were to go in tonight's bouillabaisse, but he will make them for you any way you like, as an apology, though he suggest *au beurre blanc*. Also, he has, if you like, lobster—it is not on the menu, but he can prepare lobster *cardinal* with the meat chopped and mixed with truffles and sprinkled with a little bit of butter and cheese, yes? Or however you like. It is no problem. I can run across the street to purchase fresh lobster. Whatever you like. He realizes it is early for us to be out of the *fruits de mer*, but we had such a crowd this evening."

"However I like? How should I know? Isn't he the chef?" Anaïs gathered her black patent leather handbag, dulled with fingerprints. "If I were the chef I would not be here but at home, cooking my own meal!" She pried open the snaps and then snapped them shut. She sighed heavily and looked around. There was an abundance of the dish on each table. "If the chef had not been so generous there would have been enough to go around."

"Yes, Madame." The woman's smile was undaunted.

A test of will, Anaïs thought. She is trying to see which of us is the stronger. Smiling when she is not really smiling inside.

"Well." Anaïs's face took on a pinched look; she had forgotten that she loved fried lobster, or that she usually scanned menus for mussels *au beurre blanc*. They were making things difficult for her. She was certain there was more of the special in the back room and that they were keeping the dish from her. Everyone had the dish on their tables. "What is that?" she asked, pointing to a plate of *fruits de mer* just being served beside her.

The waitress smiled patiently and opened her hands before her. "Again, Madame, we apologize. That is the special, but they arrived fifteen, twenty minutes before you. Won't you try something else?"

"Well," Anaïs sighed. "I suppose I will have to. I shall have the oysters and mussels *au beurre blanc*. How much is it? He had better not charge me too much."

"No, no. Same as—" The waitress turned, picked up a different menu. "See? The other evening we had the same thing, for fifteen euros. Same price tonight."

"Not the same mussels from the other evening, I hope," Anaïs said.

"No, madame," the waitress said.

"*D'accord.*" Anaïs crossed her arms and shrugged.

"*C'est bon,*" the waitress said, writing the order down and setting the handwritten duplicate below the glass ashtray on Anaïs's table before disappearing to place her order and greet other customers.

Anaïs crossed her arms. They were conspiring against her, she knew. Because of her necklace. She ignored the tall blonde seated two tables away wearing the same *chai* necklace and happily eating the special of the evening with her husband. She had experienced such poor service ever since Laurent had stopped speaking to her. People were being difficult with her because of the necklace and what it represented.

When Laurent accompanied her, these things seldom happened, because he was big and strong of spirit and very articulate and outspoken. Not an old woman like she was. He had once picked up an entire table and thrown it across the street to another café when they had been refused service.

She finished her meal, denying to herself how exceptional the flavor was. Light, with just enough wine so as not to detract from the oysters. She was so busy pining for the *fruits de mer* that she was certain people were being served even after they had told her they were all out. Every fish platter looked like the special. She finished the meal off with half a carafe of white wine, gulping it down as if it were rubbing alcohol, when in fact it was superb. She stood too soon, quite dizzy from the meal and having battled her own thoughts. She was convinced that the waitress smiled just to annoy her. And at the waitresses's *"Au revoir, madame,"* Anaïs did not respond.

Outside, the weather was warm but she was cold. She walked toward the train station in the dark. Her mind was filled with annoyance at the smokers. Smokers in the restaurant, at the street corners, in the train station now. So concerned was she with the smokers that she did not notice one of the men from earlier in the day until it was too late. He was so swift. He ran in front of her so fast, disturbing the air in front of her and sucking her forward in the same way that a train does in passing.

"The murderer from this morning," she gasped and placed a hand to her throat as he jumped onto a departing train at the very last minute. It was then that she noticed her neck was bare, and she screamed. She hurried up the steps, unable to articulate to the security guards or the group of policemen headed below for another bomb threat. Her hands were shaking as she rushed to a phone and deposited the necessary amount of coins.

"Hello?" the woman answered. It was the infidel.

"May I speak to my son, please," she asked.

"Hello, Madame Barr—"

"My son, please."

There was the sound of a hand covering the phone, then her son's voice. "Maman?"

"I was at the train station in Cannes. I do not mean to bother you. Were you having dinner?"

"It is all right, Maman. Tell me, what is it? Your voice is shaking."

"I did not shop for clothes today. They were all too small for me anyhow. And the restaurants, they were all so full. But how are you, Laurent? We have not talked."

"Yes, eight months." So he was counting, too! "Is everything all right, Maman?"

"Ha? Yes. Of course. It's just that I was on my way home, you see. After eating dinner at that horrid restaurant. They would not serve me because of the necklace."

"Which restaurant?"

"That Gaston's." But that did not matter now. Laurent had counted the months!

"Really? But that is one of the best restaurants. We have never had a problem there before."

"But I did. Today I did. Every day. But I just wanted to hear your voice, I suppose. There was a young man today. He was killed."

"Are you calling from a phone booth?"

"Yes. You see, that is why I was calling you. I was at the train station and my necklace. The murderer stole my necklace!"

"The mur—? Stay there, Maman. I shall come get you."

"No. Do not bother. I am fine, really. I was just frightened. You see."

"Stay, Maman. I will come. Will you wait?"

"Yes. I will wait. It is no bother?"

"No. None at all. Will you walk back to a safer area? Ask a policeman to escort you. I will pick you up at the lobby of the Carlton, is that okay?"

"Yes. Where we used to have tea."

"Yes, there. I will come to take you home. Will you wait?"

"Yes."

tHe fLame

serena barr chooses that precise moment to escape, as husband and mother-in-law proceed downstairs to breakfast at the Ritz-Carlton. There are so few windows of opportunities in a day; one must take them when one can. Her headaches were threatening, she told them. "The two of you go on without me. Perhaps I can join you for lunch. Besides, I am sure you have much to discuss." She can barely stand to be in the same room with Laurent's mother; the woman is so draining. So quietly demanding, with her sloped, defeated shoulders and her endless heavy sighs of self-pity. Serena wonders what the woman was like in her youth. When she was physically stronger. She hates to refer to her as Laurent's mother because then she will become her mother-in-law. Serena had been perfectly happy to have son and mother not talking.

In fact, it had taken a lie to have Laurent pick up the woman five nights ago. The woman woke them in the dead of night, and they drove down from Paris. Paris! Imagine pretending to have had her purse stolen. How pathetic. How juvenile. Why doesn't she simply relinquish her claim to Laurent? Serena is certain that Madame Barr's memory lapses are ploys to win Laurent back.

She puts on her sunglasses and hurries across the lobby, a bird in flight. A quick glance in the direction of the dining area confirms that mother and son are seated at a corner table, deep in conversation. Above them, several very large pictures of famous actors and actresses. One in particular catches her eye. The flavor of the year.

Why the fascination with cinema? She understands, the film festival, but still it seems a silly gesture. Why not portraits of the movie stars instead of these petrified photographs, why not art? It cheapens the hotel. Ah, the air outside is lovely. To be free of them both. When Laurent is with that woman his entire being is focused on her. Like a footman to a queen. Serena is unused to being second best. When she is with Laurent and that woman she loses her place. Back home in Brazil she is the one treated like royalty. She takes her white Hermès scarf and wraps it over the top of her head and around her neck. It floats behind her like a flag of surrender.

A lift of the wrist and the slim silver watch shimmers in the sun. The face and sleekness of the watch are pleasing to her. There is time. Her pace slows. How Laurent held his tongue when he saw the watch she purchased. *He skimps on me, but would he have done so with his old flame?*

Did she bring the invitation? In goes the wrist with the silver watch, disappearing into the depths of her fashionable patent leather bag. What does one wear to an open-house viewing? An eighteenth-century château. She isn't even sure if it is *their* house. Though she had heard Laurent whispering over the headlines in the local paper. "Do you think it is Claudette's husband? Claudette's Chazz?"

"The man who was hit by the taxi?" Madame Barr asked. "Could it be?"

"It gives no mention of his wife except that she is formerly of Cannes and that the deceased, Jorgensen, is the son of a millionaire."

"One cannot be sure. You must not try to contact her, Laurent. Leave well enough alone."

Even now Serena's body cringes. How she hates that name. Claudette. Laurent's old flame. And not even an old flame but a torch he carries in his sleep whenever the woman's name escapes his lips. And what's worse, his mother had been the one to warn him not to call her. There must have been a look in Laurent's eyes. There must have been. Oh, why had she not been sitting in the same room? So that she could have witnessed the exchange. Could have witnessed the kind of look that crossed his face. Was it a look of pity, sadness, or regret? But ah, if she had been present, the two of them would not have been discussing his old flame. They enjoy excluding her.

But it wasn't the paper that had started her on this mission. It must have been fate. Shortly thereafter she phoned her friend Camille, a real estate agent, and Camille mentioned a château that was on the market. "Too large for Laurent and you, I know, but if you wish to see it, I can get you an invitation to the open house."

"No, probably out of our league. What is wrong with it? Why does the owner wish to sell?"

"Well, I'm not supposed to disclose this but, you see, the owner was American. He died unexpectedly in Cannes last week and the widow wishes to sell the property. I have seen it; only ten rooms but they are substantial. It is amazing."

"Repeat that again?" Serena asked. *Was it possible?*

"It is amazing."

"No, not that part."

—ᴍ—

There, there it is; her hand closes around the envelope with the impeccable stationery announcing, in black type, an open house. By Invitation Only.

France Premiere Real Estate proudly presents a magnificent eighteenth-century château above Cannes with an unobstructed view of the sea and the mountains. Superb property boasts 2,000 square meters of living space plus 800 square meters of independent apartments on four hectares of grounds with incomparable trees. Pool house, automatic sprinkler system, greenhouse, outdoor lights, automatic portal. Very complete, with quality materials. Protected site with direct access to the sea; beautiful monumental stairway in courtyard. Garage for five cars and outbuildings. Fully equipped kitchen, dining room, and two salons. Guardian's house of approximately 80 square meters. French gardens.

Region: Above Cannes
Price: 10,050,000 euros
Address: 9854A Rue St. Pierre
Viewing from 9 A.M. to 2 P.M. By invitation only.

Was this wrong, what she was doing? This self-imposed secret errand. Not an errand, a mission! She pauses for a moment in the crisp morning light. The air from the sea is invigorating, intoxicating. Cannes has always had this effect on her but not on Laurent. He prefers Paris. Cannes is too sultry. He likes the shade. Give him Aix, where he grew up, where all his memories are shaded from the glare. *Where his memories of that girl still linger behind every tree-lined street. She used to climb these trees, you see, when we were children. She was such a good climber. Are you sure you want to know this, Serena? It's such an old affair.*

Of course she wanted to know. She wants to know everything. No, that's not true. At first she didn't care in the least, not until he started talking in his sleep. But is this wrong, what she is doing? Is she a schoolgirl searching for old pictures? Of course it is wrong. Will that stop her? Of course not. She wants to see, once and for all. Laurent swears he has no more pictures of the girl. But Serena is certain Madame Barr has plenty. Probably squirreled away in those old moth-smelling boxes of hers in the closet.

She must look out for herself. She has a valid curiosity. A burning curiosity—and nothing will satisfy her until she sees for herself. How can she fight what she cannot see? What if the girl were to search for Laurent even now? She needs to be prepared.

The real estate woman, Madame Guerlain, is smartly dressed in lavender, with a matching jacket of the same length with slits for pockets, as if she herself could take up residence in the large house. Auburn hair knotted in a French twist above her head and rose-colored lipstick. She greets Serena in the entryway, where a large turquoise pot housing a tall palm is situated and, on the hallway secretary, a silver bucket of long-stemmed yellow roses.

The agent's eyes reach over the invitation to take inventory of Serena's attire.

Serena instantly feels inappropriately dressed. She is not quite sure what the dress should be, but she feels certain that what *she* is wearing is below standard.

She knows I'm only here to look. She can tell.

"How did you hear about us, 'demoiselle, may I ask?"

"A friend of mine. We—I am searching for a house."

The woman's lips turn upward in a wry smile. "This is more than just a house, as you will see. Please, *entrez*. There are others viewing the property. If you have any questions, I will be here. The garden was designed by Le Nôtre. There is a house for the guardian. If you wish a recommendation, I have the names of several reliable keepers."

"Wonderful," Serena says. "May I?" she asks, because the woman still blocks the entryway.

"Of course. Please do not touch any of the furnishings." Her smile is pleasant, but Serena feels as if the woman is mocking her. Witch. For all she knows, Serena could buy ten such homes. It can't be the way she is dressed. She is wearing her Hermès scarf. Her Ralph Lauren white suit. It is only when she steps into the foyer that she sees what the other three couples are wearing. A man in Levi's, leather loafers, and a pink polo shirt and a woman in a beige peasant-style dress with short sleeves and a beautiful tan.

The man of the next couple is in trousers and a silk shirt, the woman in sandals—sandals!—and a tank top and blue peasant skirt. She herself looks too severe. The people move by her, inclining their heads the way one would at a museum. It isn't what they are wearing so much as their bearing.

Compose yourself. It's not as if you're some lowlife. Your husband is a respected engineer. You yourself an upcoming Brazilian artist. Remember that as you look at them. Probably they are just looky-loos themselves. Besides, that is not what you are here for. Right. You are here to see. To sniff for clues.

She takes a deep breath and for the first time brings her attention to the house itself, the texture and quality of the room she is in. To gaze at the impeccable taste is a sip of fine wine. Her eyes land on an oil on canvas spanning the length of the cobalt-blue leather sofa below it. Could it be? An original Modigliani? She unhinges her sunglasses from her eyes and steps forward, one hand on her chest, the other reaching out toward the painting. Bright colors of ripe green, tomato red, copper, indigo blue.

"Amedeo Modigliani, do you know of him?" Madame Guerlain asks. "He is Italian."

"Only from the galleries, the museums."

"Please, I must ask that you do not touch the furnishings."

"Yes. Excuse me." She snatches back her hand, which is just inches from the canvas.

Madame Guerlain inclines her head, leaving Serena to study the portrait more carefully. She wants to jump with joy at the beauty of the work. The color. Nothing makes her happier than a beautifully conceived work of art. She is like a child again.

The portrait of a couple reclining on the sofa, a silver-haired Scandinavian-looking man in a suit and a woman, a redhead, seated beside him. "It is exquisite. I've never seen this one."

"It's a private collection, of course. The owners' grandparents. It's not for sale. None of the furnishings are."

"The owners' name?" Serena asks.

"They asked to be kept anonymous."

"Yes, of course," Serena answers.

The house is a wealth of easy elegance. Nothing is spared. Everything of the highest quality. How had Laurent described his Claudette? The woman who was too lazy to teach, who preferred to work in a restaurant? *She was such a good climber.* Serena can see where the owners expanded the windows for a larger view of the sea. A mahogany-paneled library. And throughout her wanderings, the paintings follow her. Everything done with such love. Such care. The château is a sanctuary. A delight.

She walks into the master bedroom unexpectedly and there is a portrait. A black-and-white photo of a woman. Not at all like the stiff photographs in the Ritz-Carlton. There is movement here. The portrait is of a woman with long, wavy, shoulder-length hair, the light dancing around her. The woman is looking over her shoulder with a wide smile, as if she was walking away and the photographer called to her lovingly. Serena's breath catches. The woman's smile is open, seductive. The dress she wears, gossamer in texture, has spaghetti straps; one has fallen over the shoulder. Her thick bangs are draped over one eye. Her eyes are light-colored—blue, gray?

Serena searches for a name. The house so full and yet everything tucked away neatly. Everything smelling fresh and citrus-scented. Fresh-cut flowers in almost every room. Old farm-looking buckets filled with roses on top of Italian marble. The fireplace in this room massive, yet light touches of the whimsical. Everything in balance with everything else. The house speaks of harmony.

She tiptoes to the hallway in time to see a couple retreating down the hall, where a stained glass window beckons, then hurries back into the room. She steps quickly to the cedar closets and pulls the doors open. There are clothes still hanging. The woman is petite. The dresses like the ones she has seen in fashion magazines. One in particular catches her eye. Frivolous cream satin with large yellow roses and yet beautiful. The other dresses are understated. Small sweaters on matching wooden hangers.

And to the right, men's clothing. Suits. Tuxedos. An entire wardrobe. This was their summer home?

She envies this woman in the portrait. She imagines her barefoot, running through the long corridors of this house. This woman who may or may not be Claudette. This woman who has everything, even Laurent's love, after all these years.

Serena has the urge to gather a pair of scissors and cut the dress in half. Not all the dresses, just this one that speaks of sunshine and gifts given in adoration and not a care in the world.

"Can I help you, Mademoiselle?" The real estate woman is standing in the bedroom.

How long has she been standing there? "I'm sorry. I wanted

to see how large the closets were. I had no idea. I was mesmerized by the clothing. Such beautiful dresses the owner has. How old is she?"

"I'm sorry. I should have mentioned. The house is still fully furnished. The madame has not yet requested the clothing to be shipped to her."

"She will not do it herself?" Serena asks. The moment she speaks the words she wishes to fly after them. They are like wayward children laughing over their shoulders at her.

"Of course not. When one has this much money, one does not pack things for oneself. She sends others to do so."

Serena feels put in her place. She nods, points in the direction of the portrait. "Lovely picture." The smile on the real estate agent is thin. For a moment Serena expects she will be evicted. *Don't be silly. For accidentally looking into a closet? No. For thinking such things. For wanting to tear the dress to pieces. Oh. For that.* She feels almost hysterical from the pressure. The real estate woman follows her out of the room.

The phone rings, and Serena is saved. Granted a reprieve. But it is a cell phone, so she is not as free as she thinks.

"Ah, Madame Jorgensen. *Oui.* It is proceeding nicely. The house has many visitors. Do not worry, Madame. Leave it to me. I shall take care of it."

Serena's ears are straining. *A name. Just give me a name. And I will leave this place.* The agent has seen her hovering and lowers her voice, giving Serena her back.

Serena wanders into a study. How envious she feels. This woman of this house lives like a princess. The man from the newspaper is smiling at her. He catches her off guard. His small portrait on a woman's desk. Something about the room says it belongs to the woman. The Cleopatra-styled white reading chair. And, of course, the picture of the man in a crystal frame. She feels churlish suddenly. Her mother would be ashamed of her. *Have you forgotten the reason this house is being sold? A man died. A young man.* Serena studies the picture. If this is *Claudette's Chazz,* as Laurent had called him, in the picture, then this would be the man Claudette eventually left Laurent for. The man is unmistakably handsome. Striking. Nothing at all like her bookish Laurent.

The woman lived like a princess. And here is the real estate agent barking like a circus dog for her. Calling the woman *Madame* as if she were her superior.

"*Oui,* Claudette. We will speak again. Thank you," Madame Guerlain says, smiling into the phone. And with a click of efficiency the agent hangs up.

Serena is frozen. The princess in the portrait is indeed Laurent's Claudette.

"Mademoiselle. I do not wish to ask you again. Do not touch things. I must ask you to leave."

Serena looks to her hands in embarrassment. She is holding the small portrait of Chazz Jorgensen in her hands. "But I—"

"I do not think this house is for you, eh?" the real estate woman asks.

Serena feels humiliated, her cheeks burning as the woman escorts her toward the door. "But I have not seen the upstairs. My husband and I may want to make an offer."

"Thank you, Mademoiselle. Please have your agent contact us with your bid."

"Yes, of course." Serena smiles. "I will do that." She finds the door shut in her face. When it is an open house. She feels a headache coming. This one will put her out for the rest of the evening. This Claudette is adored by all. The real estate agent. The house that showcases her presence. How can Serena compete with a princess? A woman loved by two men. Missed by a jilted mother-in-law. *"When Claudette left, Maman was devastated."*

Oh, to be ignorant again. To have the woman be only a name

to which she could attach warts and a pinched face. How will she ever sleep now? She has opened Pandora's box. She knows what the competition looks like; only her essence could fill such a house, and Serena cannot compete. Cannot. Serena points herself in the direction of the hotel. Her feet are leaden. Her head throbbing, throbbing.

Why fight it? Why not simply surrender to the ugly brutality of it? So that the pain blocks out every worry, every insecurity? Let this be your world.

"Yes," she whispers. *I must go gracefully. Succumb.* She assumes the air of a martyr and suddenly notices that she has gone down the wrong block. She meant to take the next one over, not this narrow alleyway.

A young girl with a mincing voice asks, "Madame, do you wish to purchase a puppy?"

Serena must reach down the lengthy corridor of her mind, from where she has retreated from the pain, to answer. "What is it?"

"A puppy, Madame. Would you like to purchase one? Maman will not let me keep her."

"A puppy, you say?" Serena crouches, pleased at being referred to as *Madame* and not *Mademoiselle*. Through the white glaze of her pain she reaches out for the puppy. She is near the train station when it happens. She had thought to avoid the shopping crowd and go the circuitous route. There is a whirl of activity around her. Young boys kicking a soccer ball. Men and women emerging from the train station. She feels her bag being lifted, and for a moment she thinks it is the wind. She stumbles back and lands on her backside. Not bruised, just shaken.

"Madame, are you all right?" the young girl asks, looking afraid. Still coddling the squirming puppy.

"My purse. My watch!" she screams. On this day she has been stripped of her possessions.

—∿∿—

They are seated in the hotel suite. Room service has just left a cart of silver-covered plates and tea. Madame Barr crouches beside a dazed Serena.

"I wanted to avoid the crowds. I suppose I was in a daze."

"Why in a daze? Were you hurt?" Laurent asks with concern.

"No. I don't know. I—my head was hurting again, you see. I thought to take a walk, that perhaps the air would do me good. I stopped to talk to a child. An adorable girl. And then there was pushing. Shoving."

"Shh, child. Let me take care of your hand." Her mother-in-law reaches out, and Serena is surprised to find that the woman's hands are warm. Not at all cold and deathlike, as she expected. She has a warm cloth and is gently ministering to the cut and bruises.

"My watch," Serena protests.

"We'll shop for one today. A new one to replace the old. Just like Maman's necklace." Laurent is so full of energy he makes her ears ring.

"Laurent, let me take care of her," her mother-in-law says gently. Serena lies back as Laurent brings the cushions around her and lets his mother attend to Serena.

the pointer

GIANCARLO VILLORESI was a watcher of people. He watched
people arrive and depart Ventimiglia station with great interest.
He knew every passenger who had boarded the train in this car
and in the next. He knew their nationality, the number of people
in their group, and, if he was listening correctly, he knew their
destination and how much time he had to plan the theft.

He knew the tricks, too. He knew what a wealthy business-
man trying to dress below his class looked like in peasant clothes.
The clean cut of his hair. He knew because over the years he had
studied and knew what type of mannerisms to anticipate. How
some businessmen were used to first-class service, liked to be
first in line for the best seats, checked their watches repeatedly,
tapped a foot in impatience, how they carried in their face abhor-
rence of rowdy children. Sometimes the clothes could not hide
the person.

He knew what a decoy purse looked like when it swung too
lightly from a woman's shoulder and that there would be the
real purse closer to her body, possibly beneath her blouse. He had
once come across two tourists trying to be clever by placing all of

their credit cards, cash, and traveler's checks on their infant child. Every so often the child's face would fill with irritation and it would pull at the wallet strapped around its neck. That was too easy. Sometimes they tried to outsmart him, leaving notes in a fake wallet that said, "Ha, ha, fuck you." And he had laughed, appreciating the joke while he counted the take from their real wallet, which he had also pocketed.

He also knew to look for tells, easy things, like the man at this moment constantly touching his right pocket every five minutes. Lucky for him, GianCarlo had already dismissed him. He was one of those who could be easy to pick and yet if fate intervened to alert the man, he would also make the loudest stink. Have the least cash.

At sixteen, GianCarlo was a connoisseur of this life-and-death game. He used none of the coarse, blatant strategies, like accosting a stranger and handing them your baby while you took their wallet. Nor did he ride motorbikes to swoop down and pluck handbags from unsuspecting tourists. There was no style in that. Vulgar. That was for the rival gangs, who had no class. Anyhow, he was no longer an ordinary pickpocket, though he had been an expert at it. He was too good for that. He was the star of his group, the pointer. He scouted out the targets and set them up for his brothers. He no longer got his hands dirty. Perfect targets were his business. He made sure the transaction had the easiest possible circumstances with the highest possibility of success. That left less room for accidents. His plans were always carried out with precision.

If GianCarlo had been present during that last transaction, the American would never have lost his life. He felt somehow responsible. It had started out wrong from the beginning. His brothers should never have been on the French train lines. Ventimiglia was as far as they went. They never stepped down from the train past that. But his eldest brother had gotten greedy.

Worse than greedy—desperate—and you cannot lose your head over these things. You must wait, wait for the correct opportunity, no matter if you had to starve for a few days. You had to wait. Also, they had picked the wrong target. The American was too wealthy. The *polizia* and the government always got involved with those cases. The *polizia* had no time for average citizens. But going after the American, a disaster! GianCarlo would have known this immediately. And now the *polizia* were coming down hard. The train lines, already under heavy watch for bomb threats, would be under enormous scrutiny after the death of the American. The American had been well known, and neither his father nor his widow would let the matter rest. It was in all of the papers.

Three young tourists, Chinese girls, chatted happily in the seats across the aisle from him. He watched their reflection in his window. They felt safe beside him, he knew, because the moment they had entered the car the smallest of the three, attempting to lift her suitcase onto the top rack, had almost dropped it, a heavy, steel-colored Samsonite, on top of an old woman's head.

GianCarlo couldn't have hoped for a better opportunity. He'd jumped from his chair immediately and saved the suitcase from falling. Afterward he had helped the other two load their suitcases onto the top rack. Now he was their friend, not a threat, and they ignored his presence.

The three women spoke almost no English, and that, too, was an unexpected blessing. The harder it would be for them to explain to the *polizia* once they were robbed. Every now and then they glanced his way and blushed. He had his father's good Italian looks. This he knew as well, for it helped to distract his targets. His brothers, Marino and Angelo, took after their mother, Vilma Potvan, and her French-Romanian side.

His mother would wake from her grave if she could see Gian-Carlo and his brothers now. He knew exactly what she would say: "We have been persecuted for centuries by the *gadje* and now you hurt our people further. You do things to further confirm their contempt of us."

Gadje was a Romany word. It was the opposite of *roma,* the Romany word for "man." His mother's people. But they were not always known by such a name. Even now, within his group, they were known as Gypsies. The *gadje* had been misunderstanding them for ages. For one thing, they assumed all Romany came from Romania. But that was not so. Though there was a high population of them in Romania, not all Romanians were Romany. It was a common mistake. His kind was allowed no home. They could live in an area for hundreds of years and they would still be considered outsiders, be told to return to India, to Egypt, to Transylvania, to "wherever it is you people come from."

For many years, though the old people insisted otherwise, the *gadje* had thought his people, his mother's people, descended from Egyptians. The word became shortened through the ages to *Gypsy,* but they came from everywhere, as his grandmother used to say.

His maternal grandmother, Olga Potvan, used to rub her heavily veined hands in glee when she explained, "We are descended from the Middle East, from India, from Persia, plucked to Transylvania and sold as slaves long ago to the Impaler and his cousin. We have since traveled to Poland, Portugal, Brazil, France, Scotland, America. They cannot put one name to us. We are always moving. We come from everywhere. We are everywhere."

They *were* everywhere, his mother's people, everywhere and yet they kept to their own. His mother had been the one to break the cycle in her family when she married their father, a non-Gypsy, a *gadjo.*

GianCarlo knows what he would say to his mother if she

were here now. He would say, We do not steal because of our nationality; we steal for the same reason other poor people steal, because we are hungry. Because people take one look at us and refuse to give us jobs. He would rather die than go into the city to seek work and see the disapproval reflected in their faces merely for his being who he is. No skills. Lazy. Once before, he had tried to explain that his eldest brother was an artist. That his middle brother played the guitar. "They stink," the woman had said from the back room.

That last comment had repulsed GianCarlo, for his brothers and he took great care in bathing. It was something their mother had been strict about, so afraid was she of disease. So instilled in her ways of worrying about contamination from outside forces. And yet the woman had complained that they stunk. She'd seen their tattered clothes and added that last part for effect. It was such a blatant lie. Perhaps even the woman did not realize she had done it.

"Can any of you read?" the next woman had asked. No, Gian-Carlo had answered, bowing his head. Except for a few words. No. *But I can speak Italian, English, French, German, Spanish. I learned myself, from listening and asking. And Romany*—but he would not tell her that.

Perhaps that is why his people travel on and on. Not because they wish to be nomads but because they are not welcomed anywhere. No, his mother would not have approved of GianCarlo and his brothers making peace with her family after her death, and yet they'd done it anyway. During the annual May trek to Les Saintes-Maries de la Mer in France, for the ritual cleansing of the black wooden statute of Saint Sarah in the Mediterranean. Where his Grand-mère Olga took his face in her veined hands and told him, "I knew you would return. I shall make an offering to Saint Sarah, for returning you." She pointed a crooked, shaking finger at him. "Ah, but the old ways are dying." And in

Les Saintes-Maries as they danced and drank, people locked their doors at night.

They were two stops away from the designated destination. He checked the three girls in the window. They were still talking with one another. They knew their destination, that they were on the correct train, that the sun was out, and so they felt safe. This was the best situation for GianCarlo and his brothers because the women would not expect this. He knew that the first girl, the one he had helped, carried the bulk of their money in her bright pink backpack and not the handbag she kept close to her body. She had a map inside, which they took out from time to time, a cell phone, and money. He knew this because the other two would nudge her whenever they needed to purchase something and she would glance around before deeming it safe to go digging inside her bag to pay the food vendor.

GianCarlo stretched and stood. He went to the sleeping cars, where there were private rooms and the seats unfolded into beds at night. He stepped into the compartment and sat down like a stranger. He kept his eyes down the hallway to ensure that there were no train personnel watching. When his oldest brother, Angelo, glanced over and lifted his chin, GianCarlo looked away.

He still wasn't sure they should be out in public this way until Angelo's moon-shaped scar healed, but Angelo had convinced him otherwise. He could hear Angelo suck his breath in with annoyance. He thought GianCarlo overly cautious.

"Well?" Angelo asked.

GianCarlo looked straight ahead and said, "*Tre cinesi*. Car five. Pink backpack. Seats twelve to fifteen. You will see my empty shopping bag across from them."

"Good. We go," Angelo said to Marino.

Marino looked over at GianCarlo. "We see you tonight?"

"Not tonight. I have dinner at Uncle Paolo's, remember?"

"I shall accompany you to their home," Marino said. "Wait for me. We shouldn't be long."

GianCarlo bowed his head. "I can take care of myself," he said, feigning annoyance. He knew that Marino worried about his being alone. That sometimes the *gadje* could be taunting, cruel, brutal to their kind. Also, when a Rom was alone, he was looked upon as a leper, as *marimé*, possibly unclean by other Roms. Being alone during work was different. But, in truth, GianCarlo hated to see his brother turned away from their uncle's home, so he refused the company. "Besides, then you would have to walk home alone."

"Me, it does not matter, but you—it is not good for you to be seen alone. It will be hard to find a match for you. The others will think something is wrong with you. That you are unclean. How then will you find a wife?" practical Marino asked.

"What would I do with a wife?" GianCarlo asked. "The two of you have no wives."

"It is too late for us," Marino said. A match was usually made at the age of ten by Romany parents, and the couple would marry two or three years later. They were all three considered old bachelors at sixteen, eighteen, and twenty. GianCarlo knew that Marino was obsessed with the idea of continuing their lineage. Perhaps because their parents were gone.

"I have visited their home alone many times. I promise I shall be careful." GianCarlo stood, then hesitated before leaving their compartment.

"What is it?" Angelo said.

"Don't hurt them," GianCarlo said. "The three Chinese. Do not hurt them."

"Why would we hurt them?" Angelo asked.

"I don't know." GianCarlo gritted his teeth. "Why was the American hurt?"

"It was an accident," Angelo snarled, but GianCarlo was already walking down the aisle.

At the next stop, GianCarlo gathered his backpack and descended from the train. He watched from the platform as his brothers walked from one car to the next until they were in the same one as the three tourists. They walked past the three women and sat at the end of the compartment. He watched until the train and their figures blurred away.

He took the next train going in the opposite direction.

There was a local newspaper on the seat beside him. He picked it up. In it there was the picture of the running of the bulls, something he was very interested in. The paper had been left behind, but GianCarlo could not read. He recognized only a few words. *American,* maybe; possibly the other word was *girl.* But he couldn't be sure. He tried again: maybe another word was *ru-ru-nning.* He took the paper and flung it across the aisle. A woman glanced his way but found nothing of interest. He propped his feet onto the seat and lit a cigarette. People looked down the aisles at him, some glared. A woman fanned the air in annoyance. The car, as the sign indicated, was *Vietato fumare.*

Three American boys his age boarded the train. *Stop observing.* He had to remind himself sometimes that he was not on duty. The Americans were wearing label T-shirts from America. GianCarlo could neither read nor understand their meaning. The boys wore baggy trousers and billed hats. The redheaded one picked up the newspaper.

"Dude, you hear? Another girl got gored in Pamplona. Shit. I think we ought to do that before Verona."

"I want to see the Arena," the fair-haired one said. "I think we can get tickets for *Carmen.*"

"Screw Verona, man," the third said. He looked Japanese.

"Screw that Romeo and Juliet crap." He was laughing, giving his friend a hard time.

A Japanese speaking English. GianCarlo couldn't get over it. No different, probably, than a Senegalese speaking Italian. Right? Or the native Chinese speaking French. Still, it caught him off guard now and then.

His ears were straining to hear more of the running of the bulls, but the Americans were standing up. "No, he's right. We got to stick to the program, man, otherwise we'll be all over hell and creation," the redhead said.

GianCarlo stood, too. He followed them all the way to the Hotel San Luca, just outside of Corso Porta Nuova and L'Arena. He peered down the alley as they disappeared into the fancy hotel with the automatic glass doors; then he continued walking toward the arena and under the twin stone arches of the Piazza Bra. It was only four-thirty. His uncle wouldn't be home until six, for his dinner break. He walked through the piazza and watched as the area began to fill with the opera crowd. Women in high heels, shawls, and fancy dresses struck poses and measured themselves against one another. Men in tuxedos, in suits. A woman with beautiful wide hips, a backless dress, her ripe breasts jiggling, walked hand in hand with her date. GianCarlo shook his head. He couldn't help but grin. He watched as men turned full circles to watch her pass.

Two *poliziotti* in uniform on regal horses watched the crowd from in front of the Arena. The show tonight was *Aida,* and the cafés were already filling up. Latecomers without tickets were standing in long lines. GianCarlo leaned against a lamppost and watched the slow gait of the waiter at Café Giulietta. While the younger waiters were breezing past the diners, delivering their food, he was almost stumbling with his two plates of paella, an Italian twist on the Spanish dish of mussels in yellow saffron rice.

GianCarlo knew the dish well. His mouth moistened at the smell of the Italian sausage. It is what he would like to order someday. Someday he would like to order that very dish and sit in the corner seat before attending the opera—*Aida,* like they were showing tonight. Preferably he would like to do this with a beautiful girl on his arm. An older woman, twenty-one. He would sit in the corner where the old man served and tell him he was in no rush. At the end of the meal he would tip the man greatly. A man like that had nobility. A man like that should be the owner of the restaurant.

GianCarlo based this thinking on the man's ability to stay composed as the tourists yelled for him to hurry up. And the times he had witnessed customers complaining about a mix-up in their order that the waiter had taken—the man would nod and lose none of his dignity. He wouldn't grovel. He wouldn't mewl and whine. He simply nodded and went back to fix the order. Sometimes it brought angry tears to GianCarlo's eyes.

He spent the rest of his time going in and out of shops. He liked to browse in the corner bookstore and look at the picture books. Someday he would like to learn to read. He didn't linger long at the bookstore because the shopkeepers had seen him a few times and he knew, though he didn't steal from the shops, that they had a sense about him. The *gadje* store owners would cast glances over and over, and GianCarlo would know it was time to leave.

"When I was younger," his Grand-mère Olga had told him, "my brother and I went to town without our father's say-so. At ten and twelve we thought we were grown and knew our own minds. But we didn't know the minds of others. Bald-headed *gadjes* followed us down an alley. They would not let us pass. They beat us until I lost my front teeth. And the *polizia,* do you know what they said? They called us tramps. They told us to stay in our camps and keep to ourselves. They didn't want our trouble in their towns. But we were only there for the sweets."

GianCarlo stayed an hour longer at the piazza. He pointed out ten people to himself who would be such easy pickings. But he was not working. And it was difficult to cover too many areas. You had to decide on either the piazza or the train lines. Not both. Because you had to know the *polizia* in that area, and every little detail. If one wanted to do a job right, one had to specialize, or there would be slipups. Like the one his brother Angelo had made with the dead American. He had chased the man into another territory when he knew specifically they had agreed to do only the Italian lines and not the French. *Stupido.*

He left the piazza half an hour early and decided to meet his uncle at the train station. He was staring at the arrival board to see if Paolo would be late or not when a hand clamped over his shoulder.

"Gianni."

GianCarlo jumped. His Uncle Paolo laughed. He had his oil-stained backpack slung over his shoulder and his train conductor's uniform still on.

"What are you doing staring at the train tracks?" Paolo asked. His uncle was handsome. He looked exactly like GianCarlo's father had when he was alive. GianCarlo could have passed for his son. He knew sometimes, when his Uncle Paolo looked at him, that Paolo was remembering his older brother. "You are ready to eat? Manuela is making *spaghetti con pesce* tonight."

GianCarlo nodded.

"Did they make their usual snatch?" Paolo asked gravely. Again GianCarlo nodded. His uncle was the conductor for the five-thirty Ventimiglia line, the one just before the five-forty-five connection to Cannes. He didn't approve of what they did for a living, and he had not yet asked if Angelo and Marino were responsible for the American's death, but he knew there was no controlling them.

He'd once told GianCarlo that he believed GianCarlo was the only one worth saving. He tried to encourage GianCarlo to become interested in becoming a conductor. He knew people in the offices who would hire GianCarlo on his say-so as long as he passed the easy tests. But the tests GianCarlo had to take, and the forms he needed to fill out, required reading the questions asked of him. Therein lay the problem.

"Who did they target today?" Paolo asked.

GianCarlo was aware of the kindness of tone in the line of questioning. That his uncle never said *you,* as if GianCarlo were not involved in the snatch. As if it were not he who specifically pointed out the right targets. His uncle was never one to pretend that things were different. There was no accusation. Only heated arguments once or twice between his brothers and uncle. Specifically with Angelo and Paolo, where it had come to blows and the two had rolled on the ground.

Paolo had the upper hand because he was well fed and much bigger. He stood at six foot two, with broad shoulders. But Gian-Carlo was afraid in those instances for his uncle and he watched Angelo for a long time afterward. Because he knew his brother Angelo. He knew Angelo was not above evening the odds while Paolo and his wife slept. But he also knew something more painful. He knew that before his parents had died, Angelo had not been this way.

"Was it tourists?" Paolo asked. "The *polizia* are watching closely. And now with the rival French gangs roaming the lines—"

GianCarlo was uncomfortable. He didn't wish to speak ill of his brothers. And also, he liked to pretend when he visited his uncle that he himself was just an ordinary boy. He could see his uncle would not let the matter drop, so he told him, forgetting that he was talking to his uncle and not to his brothers, "Three *cinesi* tourists. A group of girls. They did not speak an ounce of English or Italian. Highly hysterical in temperament. You should have seen the animated way in which they spoke." He could not help but grin when he remembered how happy the girls were. But then he saw his uncle's lips press into a thin line, and Gian-Carlo stuttered. He blushed and studied the train tracks once again.

His uncle's frown faded. "Come. Let's go home and eat."

Another kindness. The word *home*. To remind GianCarlo that Manuela and Paolo welcomed him if he wished to move in. They had a spare bedroom. Small as a broom closet but open to him if he wished. But not for his brothers.

The feeling was mutual. Angelo and Marino called Paolo things like the "goody-goody with a job" and "whore's husband." It was out of the question anyway. Such a move would widen the disparity between his brothers and himself even more, and things were already strained between him and Angelo. He knew instinctively, the way dogs do, that you do not turn your back on your own pack.

They walked the last set of steps up from the train station. It was July and the sun was still strong at six-thirty, causing Paolo to blink. He did not notice the women who stopped to stare at his handsome figure. Instead, Paolo put a hand casually on Gian-Carlo's shoulder and kept it there as they walked. GianCarlo loved these times with his uncle. He was proud of Paolo's conductor's uniform. His uncle had a job. All perfectly legal. Walking next to his uncle like this almost always reminded him of his mother when she was alive and how he did not need to be sly and cunning to survive. He could be sixteen again and sometimes, though he was careful never to ask, his uncle would suggest they kick the soccer ball around after dinner as Manuela watched and cheered GianCarlo on against her husband.

His stomach rumbled as they walked. He knew his uncle heard it, but they silently agreed not to speak of it. He was looking forward to this meal. GianCarlo was always careful to turn down a few dinner invitations so as not to wear out his welcome.

"You must watch out, GianCarlo." Manuela let her fingers linger through his hair as she placed a plate of spaghetti in front of him. "The French gang, I hear they are possessive of their territory."

"We stay to our lines. We never go past Ventimiglia."

There was an uncomfortable silence.

Except for that one time. When I wasn't there. The words lodged in his throat.

Manuela glanced at Paolo with concern. GianCarlo did not miss the exchange. That was his job. This was what he did all day. Observe. But he did not let on that he had seen this. He loved his aunt for her concern. She was a strong one. And beautiful, too. He knew that even though Angelo and Marino joked about whether she was truly blond between her legs as well, that was only jealousy talking. *"No true italiana has green-blue eyes and blond hair."* Manuela was a beautiful woman. Probably descended from the German lines that had settled and mixed long ago in Verona, but still *italiana.*

"That incident with the American should never have happened. That poor man. And his wife! She was a native Frenchwoman, did you know? It was horrible. They played it over and over again on the television. Her sobbing to the cameras. Oh." Manuela placed a hand on her chest. "I thought if that were to happen to me. If someone took Paolo that way. Or you!" Her hands shook.

Paolo reached across and put his hand over hers. GianCarlo liked to witness these exchanges. It gave him hope.

"How did it happen, GianCarlo?" Manuela asked. "Was it Angelo?"

"Manuela," Paolo said softly, chidingly.

GianCarlo shrugged, embarrassed. "Angelo said the American owed them money. That the American told them to follow him to Cannes."

"Owed him money? For what?" Manuela asked.

GianCarlo could not answer. He wanted to know the same thing.

"It is late. Are you certain you will not stay?" Manuela asked.

"No, *grazie,* Manuela." GianCarlo kissed her on the cheek as Paolo stood with his arm around her.

"Tomorrow you will come back? What shall I prepare for you?" Manuela asked hopefully.

"Thank you, Aunt, but not tomorrow. I have other obligations," GianCarlo said, studying his shoes. He could not stand to look at her when he left. Always she looked as if she would cry.

"Stay alert. We are just around the corner. If you need us for any reason. At any hour," his uncle said.

"I know," GianCarlo said.

"On Friday then? Dinner on Friday?" Manuela asked. Paolo squeezed her shoulder lovingly.

"Maybe." GianCarlo smiled.

Manuela reached out and pinched his cheek softly. "You are harder to court than your Uncle Paolo here."

Paolo wrapped his arm around her neck and she giggled, trying to wiggle out of his embrace. They waved from their lighted doorway. GianCarlo thought, *I shall remember this on my way home.* It helped. Mr. and Mrs. Sweetlife, Angelo called them.

—ⱮⱮ—

Around the corner the neighborhood became seedier. Gian-Carlo's house was farther than Paolo would have liked it to be. He had to walk several blocks before he got to the house he shared with his brothers. The streets, as he turned onto Viale Monte Nero, were unwashed in front of the storefronts. They were sticky from the afternoon heat and smelled of cooked piss. The familiar group of Senegalese men in African garb were selling knockoff handbags on blankets and other trinkets, shouting "Hello, Madame. Madame, you like?"

A woman tourist stuck out like a whore at a garden party. Obviously, she had not noticed the change in streets as she'd gone from shop to shop. It was still light out. Fading but light. Soon she would be in trouble if she did not go back to the safe part of town. One of the sellers cast furtive glances left and right as the woman picked up an imitation Louis Vuitton purse and tried it on her shoulder. "How much you want for?" he asked. "I give to you for eighty-five euros."

GianCarlo jerked his chin up to the man. They knew each other.

"How about seventy?" The woman was still bargaining when a low whistle from their group got the other sellers packing quickly, threading arms through bags and pounding down the cobblestoned pavement. The man, unable to agree on a price with her, grabbed the bag from her and took off with his friends.

"What?" she asked in confusion.

GianCarlo shook his head as a *poliziotto,* the big cop who was wise to their ways, came strolling around the corner with his hand on his baton. GianCarlo watched for a moment to see if his friend would get away.

"*Signora.*" The *polizia* walked quietly up to her and pointed her toward a safer direction.

—∿∿—

On the corner in front of their apartment, GianCarlo saw little six-year-old Pietro sitting cross-legged with his plastic soda cup filled with coins. He was playing with the strap of his sandals. He was unnaturally dark from sitting in the sun all day. Tiny even for a boy of six. And his eyes were very old and much too calm for a child.

"*Ciao, Pietro.* How much did you make today? Did you do good?" GianCarlo asked.

"*Così-così.*" Pietro held out his hand palm down and tilted it from side to side to indicate so-so. "*Non c'è male.*" Not bad. He held up his coins for GianCarlo to see. "Eighty cents in euros."

"And on you?" GianCarlo grinned.

Pietro patted his pocket and lowered his voice. "*Due euro cinquanta.*" Two and fifty euros.

GianCarlo nodded. "Did you watch my house for thieves today?"

"Of course. No one went in or out. Except your brothers. They returned twice."

GianCarlo pulled out one euro and a pack of gum he had lifted and handed both to Pietro.

"*Grazie, Gianni.*" His face lit up. "When I am rich I will hire three guard dogs to watch your house."

"Maybe by that time neither of us will need to watch this house, eh? Maybe we will live in another house?"

"*Sì.*" Pietro nodded eagerly. "Someday, maybe we have a house big enough for my grandfather to live with us." GianCarlo liked that the boy still believed in such things.

"See you in the morning." GianCarlo yawned. "*Buona notte,*" he said, bidding the boy good night.

In the evenings they let him sleep on their doorstep. Gian-Carlo sometimes brought him out an extra blanket when it got too cold. Angelo refused to let the boy in the house. "We cannot take every beggar in."

"Ah, here comes the prince now," Marino joked when GianCarlo stepped inside.

Angelo nodded. He no longer smiled at GianCarlo when they greeted each other at the end of the day. In fact, he no longer smiled at all.

"How much did you give Pietro?" Angelo demanded.

"Is nothing. A few coins and some gum."

"The money is ours to split. Just because you are a prince with Wednesday dinners with the Sweetlife family doesn't mean you can give our money away like you are rich. I will take that money out of your share."

"Angelo," Marino laughed. "Go easy with him. *Che c'è di male?* He was just being kind."

"Kindness doesn't feed our bellies," Angelo spit out. That's the harm in it. "How much did you give him?"

"One euro. What's my share? Take it all for yourself if you like," GianCarlo said, turning his back on Angelo's bullying and placing his backpack on the ground.

"No, no," Marino protested. "Come on. Let us start over again."

"Fuck him," GianCarlo said.

"What's that? What's that?" Angelo walked up, and Gian-Carlo turned to meet him. They stood nose to nose. They were the same height now, and GianCarlo was well fed.

"Here, then here." Marino, ever the joker, tried to relieve the tension with his antics by extending a butter knife to each of them. "Go ahead, kill each other."

GianCarlo was so angry his eyes watered.

"What's this?" Angelo frowned, taking the blunt knife and

flinging it over GianCarlo's head to the wall behind him. "I can't fight a baby."

Marino's smile faded. He turned his back on them and looked out the window. There had been a time when Angelo was the charming one. When he used to draw incredible sketches of people. But you could hardly tell now with his eyes so dark, his new half-moon of a scar pulsing purple and ugly beneath his right eye.

The way he looked now, GianCarlo could imagine him really frightening the American before he threw himself out in front of the car. Perhaps he had been trying to wave for help. Gian-Carlo wasn't sure what had happened that evening. Marino and Angelo were hiding something, and their stories did not match. He'd never thought Angelo possible of hurting someone. He just could not see it—his brother who used to sing his mother to sleep as Marino played the guitar in the next room. But he saw it now.

"Is this how you talked to the American before he threw himself against a car to get away from you?" GianCarlo asked.

In a flash and a curse they were rolling on the ground, his brother breathing with cigarette lungs through his gnashing teeth. The same mouth he used to sing with before their mother passed.

Marino was trying to pry them apart. "Enough."

"Go ahead, kill me. Like you did the American," GianCarlo said, no longer fighting.

Angelo backed away, doused by the words.

GianCarlo got up and scrambled for his backpack and out of the house, down the steps, down the street with little Pietro calling after him, "Gianni! We play cards tonight?"

It had rained overnight and GianCarlo was soaked. He paid one euro and fifty-two cents at the Verona station *bagno* for a shower and the use of the bathroom. How Angelo would have sneered at this. "Go wash in the river or the fountain," he could almost hear him say. "Spoiled prince. Little prince."

He walked until his clothes dried in the heat, and then he paid to tour the Castelvecchio, gazing at the old oil paintings. His favorite was the one of the Roman with a platter of coins. The figures were gigantic. Titan-like. And the point of view was from the bottom looking up, which gave the figures an even bigger image. It was hung at least twelve feet off the ground, so the point of view would be emphasized. He could not read the description below the art, but he knew the title was *Eliodoro si fa consegnare da Onias il tesoro del tempio* by Giambattista Tiepolo, because his mother had once asked the docent to read it to them.

Once, long ago, his brother Angelo had pointed the painting out to him. GianCarlo must have been about ten years old, Angelo fourteen. This was when their mother used to take them to see the different *musei*. She was so different, their mother. She wasn't what people expected a Romany to be. She was clean but poor. She was learning to read and trying to instill this in her young children, but it was difficult when all of them had to work.

She taught Angelo how to draw. She told him that someday his paintings would hang in such a *museo*. She gave Marino her charm and GianCarlo her kindness. Their father worked long hours in the factory and had no time to teach them what little he knew. But GianCarlo remembered her dignity and her kindness the most.

Vilma Potvan, the beautiful Roma. How she kept her chin up with the natural grace of a dancer, even in the face of snide remarks from local *gadjes*. How she had certain herbal cures for ailments and how a neighbor had once brought his infant to her for an uncurable stomach malady and she had cured it, not by magic but by close attention and a few herbs. She knew how to dance flamenco just by being part of the Potvan clan. Her brother had struck it rich, but he never came back for her or her parents, as he had promised. It was said he had a stable of Arabian horses and a big house on Santorini and that he had changed his name. She did not blame her brother. She wanted this same thing for her three sons. To break free of the cycle of poverty, become educated, and grow roots, but to return and help others. How she would have shuddered to see what had happened to them after first her husband's and then her own death. Six years can wreak tremendous havoc on the lives of three boys unwilling to give up their home. To follow her dream. When perhaps they should have been with her family. With the Potvan clan, forever moving like the wind, like the drifting sand. Like her own ashes.

He checked the tower clock in the courtyard of the castle: seven-thirty A.M. He had been daydreaming too long of her again. He could catch the seven-forty-five and still have plenty of time to meet up with his brothers. He picked up his pace, cut through the Piazza Bra, and headed toward the train station. He was passing the Hotel San Luca when the automatic glass doors opened and the three American boys from the previous day stepped out.

They were talking about the bullfights again. "The running of the bulls only goes from July seventh through the fourteenth, man. If we don't go soon we'll miss it."

"I'm still up for it," the dark-haired one said.

"When?" the redhead asked.

"Today. Now. The whole day. About six hours from here to France. Connect from there to Spain."

They looked at one another for a moment, laughed, and then said, "Let's do it."

GianCarlo followed behind them all the way to the train station. They talked about the "fucking term papers" they would have to do come fall. Screw finals. Girls. Girls. Mom and Dad. More girls. The Italian girls versus the French girls. GianCarlo was so engrossed in their talk he found himself getting on the train with them. *I shall follow them for an hour just to hear the rest of their story of the bulls. I wish to go someday, too, and I wish to hear of their preparations.*

An hour later, as they changed trains, GianCarlo conceded an hour more. *Their talk entertains me.* Six and a half hours later he was in France, where the Americans noticed him getting off and waiting for the connecting train to Spain.

"Hey," the Japanese-American said. "Hey, man. You going to see the bulls, too?"

"Yeah," GianCarlo said, mimicking the way they had been using the word for the entire day.

"You local?" he asked as his friends also became interested.

When GianCarlo frowned he said, *"Tu italiano?"* with a bad accent.

Yes, he told them and gave them his name: *"Sì, mi chiamo GianCarlo."* Then he smiled and said, "But I speak English. Some words I do not understand so well."

"Good," the kid said with relief. "I'm Paul."

"Thomas," said the redhead.

"Tony," said the fair-haired one.

Thomas ripped open a bag of chips and extended it to Gian-Carlo. "You ever see a bullfight?"

"No. First time. Like you," GianCarlo said.

"Hey, Tone, give him a soda," Paul said. A backpack was opened and a drink handed over.

Soon they were all sharing stories of what they expected from a bullfight. Of the two American girls who'd been gored and trampled the other day during the first running of the bulls. They were going to spend the night in a hostel in Spain—did Gian-Carlo want to join them? He said yes, he would like that very much. They reached Pamplona at ten in the evening, found their respective beds, and went to sleep.

———〰〰〰———

They were awakened at five A.M. by Paul's wristwatch, which had fluorescent numbers.

"Hey," Paul said to the dark. "We better get started. The running of the bulls starts at seven."

The others grumbled. GianCarlo was instantly awake. He had not had so much fun in many years, and he was excited. He eased out of bed slowly, mimicking their sluggish movements, stretched his arms out over the top of his head, pretending to yawn, and smiled broadly into the dark.

The excitement in the air matched that of a grand festival. Everywhere they looked were posters advertising Pamplona's annual *Fiestas de San Fermín, and the running of the bulls.* Other posters advertised the recent bullfights at the Plaza de Toros and the current ones. They were all thanking Paul for their first-rate positions along the fence of Calle Santo Domingo, which swerved past City Hall to Calle Estafeta and eventually to the bullring. By six-thirty the crowd was starting to press in behind them for the running of the bulls.

"So they come out over there, see." Paul pointed down to the corral. Obviously the aficionado within the group. "Six bulls take off at a run and they have these oxen mixed in called *cabestros,* trained to herd the bulls down toward the coliseum. The trick is to run alongside or just ahead of the bull. If you fall, they say you want to drop and stay put and the bulls will instinctively jump over you." The four of them shared a look of disbelief and laughed at the suggestion.

"What are those rolled-up newspapers they're all holding?" Tony asked, standing on the low wooden fence.

"Well, if the bull gets a bead on you, you're supposed to smack it on the nose to startle it and then run like hell."

"Yeah, right," Thomas said with a low whistle.

"I'm gonna do it," Paul said, hopping into the fenced enclosure.

"Can you just jump in there?" Thomas asked. "Don't you need to sign up or something?"

"Nope." Paul grinned.

They watched in silence as he walked toward the other people in the enclosure. GianCarlo wondered sharply if this would be the last time he would see Paul. Perhaps he would be the first to fall and the next to be written about in the papers. *Third American gored in running of the bulls,* his Aunt Manuela would read to him. It saddened him greatly, for he liked Paul the most and had planned to try to stay in touch by writing even though he did not know how to write.

He would live vicariously through these new friends, through their talk of college and final exams and other adventures such as this. He imagined asking Manuela to help pen the letters he would write to his new friends. It was irrational, this sadness that overtook him, almost as if Paul were already dead.

The rocket shot announcing the opening of the gate rent the air, and the bulls came pounding out of the gate. The crowd screamed, clapped, shouting directions to the people inside the enclosure. The people inside pressed their bodies against the walls as the bulls pressed dangerously close. Others ran just a few feet ahead of the bulls, grinning stupidly.

GianCarlo soon found that it was not Paul he was cheering but the bulls. The poor creatures, as they slipped on the cobblestones, were without dignity. It stabbed at his heart. All the talk he had heard for many years of *the glory of Spain, the proud tradition* vanished quickly before his eyes. His eyes and mind were glued on the bulls. The massive creatures slipping on the pavement as people laughed and shouted. His anger confused him. A Spaniard fell and was gored quickly, his stomach and blood trampled and trailing on the cobblestones, and that in itself seemed a sport as onlookers pointed and talked and smoked, and then it was all over and they were talking about the bullfight and getting tickets.

"Did you guys see me?" Paul came back with an addicted look in his eyes. "I had to climb over that man and then *he* got it! Shit, wait till I tell my brothers."

They bought the cheapest tickets available—the ones directly in the sun, labeled *gradas de sol,* which GianCarlo explained meant high up and directly in the sun all day. There were more expensive ones, for sun and shade or all-day shade, but they had their own "shades," they said, and so "no problem."

"I got an extra pair of shades. Cheapos, but they'll work. I'll lend 'em to you, man," Paul said.

"Let's get something to eat," Tony said.

GianCarlo nodded and rubbed his stomach. "I think maybe I wait." He furrowed his brow with a helpless smile.

Paul grinned. "GC's grossed out. Should we wait?"

"No. No wait." GianCarlo shook his head. "Is no problem. What I mean to say is, you eat. I drink some wine. Maybe later I eat. Is no problem. We go."

At the café his friends looked over the menu and boasted of the big meals they would order. GianCarlo had only two euros left in his pocket and he didn't want to be a charity case. He excused himself and went to the bathroom. They said they would wait for him before they ordered. In the bathroom he stood in front of the urinal with his zipper down and waited, scoping each person who came in. A man bragged about a restaurant called La Mesa a block down the street and around the corner that was better than this one. GianCarlo pretended he was just finishing up. Finally, when a well-dressed, slightly drunk man staggered in, Gian-Carlo began to use the urinal. When the man went to wipe his hands, GianCarlo did the same.

There were no napkins, but a damp towel hung from a ring. When the man finished washing, GianCarlo finished wiping his hands and turned to hand the towel to him. *"Grazie."* The man coughed.

The towel fell, and they both bent to pick it up, bumping shoulders and GianCarlo's head. *"Scusi,"* they laughed. Gian-Carlo left the man combing his mustache in front of the mirror.

In the hallway he checked that the man's wallet had money. It did.

"What do you think, GC?" Paul said. "Two bottles of wine? What sounds good to you?"

"I just remember." GianCarlo held one finger up.

"You like real Spanish food?"

"Yeah, man," they chimed in.

"I know of a place better than here. Authentic. Is called La Mesa."

"Why didn't you say? Is it far?" Paul asked.

"No. Just around the corner."

The recommendation did not disappoint him. The restaurant was nicely done, and his friends seemed very happy. At La Mesa, GianCarlo ordered three glasses of expensive wine. Two Riojas and one Cigales. For courage, he told himself. He wanted badly to accompany his friends, but he was not so sure he wanted to watch anymore. *Don't be a sissy,* he told himself.

When it came time to pay, they all pulled out their wallets.

"Geez, GC," Paul laughed. "Is that your grandfather's wallet?"

GianCarlo then saw that they all had the American wallet

with the scratchy material that held together like magic. Velcro, Paul told him. GianCarlo laughed. "Is old. I grow used to it." GianCarlo studied his new wallet.

"But it's as big as a hamburger, man," Thomas laughed. "What you got in there?"

"In here? Let me see." GianCarlo licked his finger, first paying his portion; then he pulled out a photo of a pretty young girl. "My sister Alma."

"Dude, she's hot," Paul said. "When you going to introduce us?"

"Next time. All of you come to visit."

"And that? Must be your mother—she looks like you."

"You think so?" GianCarlo grinned, though his mother was ten times this woman. "Yes. You see that scar? Is faint. Just above her lip? I caused her to fall one day when I was a baby, and boom. She hit her lip on the floor. From then on she would always say to me, 'Ah, Gianni. You always cause me great pain and great joy. That is why you are my favorite of all.' Our father. My brothers." GianCarlo laughed inside at how similar to these people he did look. Dark-haired. Wide-browed. Instant family.

He finished the last bottle of wine when the others could not. The wine helped to confuse him back into normalcy, and soon he was standing in the coliseum next to his new friends with the sun cutting directly into his eyes and the crowd cheering the first fight. He overheard two Spaniards talking.

"This man. They bill him above Córdoba; how is it possible? He is a fraud."

"Yes, there is no grace in him. Possibly he knows the commissioner's daughter and that is how he could be billed this way. Did you see his name on the posters?"

"Yes. A shame."

GianCarlo watched with a sinking stomach as the matador

strode out on his horse with his picadors, their capes furled around their arms. The picadors started first. Taunting the bull and cutting the poor animal with their blades. Tiring the animal.

"None of the bulls are tried. You understand?" a Spaniard was explaining to a young boy. The young boy nodded. His mouth clamped around a straw, making loud gargling noises. GianCarlo and his group listened. When the Spaniard saw they were listening, he spoke in English. "Once a bull learns about the trick of the cape and that there is an actual man behind the taunting," the Spaniard said, opening his palms, "he goes next time for the man, avoiding the cape completely."

Is it not enough, GianCarlo thought, *to bring an innocent animal into the ring untried? That they also have the advantage of an animal forced to fight outside of his territory? Must they tire him first before the brave matador steps in?* Long ago the rags-to-riches story of many matadors had appealed to GianCarlo. It was something he could aspire to. Granted, he was not Spanish, but if an American could become a matador, like John Fulton, why not an *italiano?*

But standing here, relating more to the plight of the helpless bull forced to fight for the entertainment of others, he felt a sickening in his stomach. The wine rolled up in his belly in a great wave. He watched with disgust as the matador called to the bull.

With a flamboyant flourish, the matador took over. The crowd was mixed in their welcome. Obviously, they, too, felt him undeserving. But it was not the fool with the cape GianCarlo was worried about. It was the poor creature. When the bull came charging toward the man, a hush fell through the crowd. The bull was magnificent, brandishing on his haunches the symbol of the ranch where he had been sired. A trident within a circle. His muscles possessed great dignity, and the way in which he carried his horns was breathtaking.

And his eyes. Even at this distance GianCarlo could see a certain look come over the bull. A look of life or death; he recognized it instantly as what he felt when he boarded the trains each day. That he would rather be somewhere else. That he would rather not steal. His brothers, not he, held his future in their hands. He had heard long ago that bulls in a field were not naturally given to fighting. That they felt safe in their herd. And that ranchers could usually walk through and even pet them on the flanks. It was only when they were taken out of their natural habitat that their killer instinct for survival manifested in such a brutal way.

His friends were clapping, cheering on the matador Gelmirez, as the Spaniards nudged and talked in low voices about the Americans who did not know a bad matador when they saw one. GianCarlo wished to shut his eyes and run from this scene, but he stayed on and watched as the matador spun and twirled. It was only by the grace of God that the matador fell and his leg was hit at such an angle that he could no longer fight, and so the bullfight was discontinued. The crowd jeered him loudly. The matador cursed back. Finally he broke away from the escorts who were helping him walk out, and in a show of defiance he limped to the center of the arena, took off his coat, and with a sneer of disgust looked at the crowd and wiped the dust from his coat to signify that he wished not even to have their dust on his person. This outraged the crowd to such an extent that they wanted blood for the next fight.

GianCarlo was in a drunken haze by the time the second bull came out of the pen. He bought some cheap beer, which he drank from a plastic container. His ears numbed to the announcement of the next matador. All he could see was the bull silently charging at a gallop out of the pen, before the hush of the crowd. This bull was even bigger than the first. The hump on his back like a menacing mountain.

Soon the bull was stumbling, bleeding from the cuts aimed at his back. But he had to fight. The horror of it. He could not even leave if he wished. Brought here to die. The shouts of *Olé! Olé!* crescendoing as the matador strutted like a multicolored cock in his red, black, and gold as he aimed his last thrust with a flourish.

GianCarlo forced himself to watch. The bull took the metal into his body and swaggered from side to side before his front legs buckled. The people were throwing flowers down to honor the matador, the coward who had done this hateful deed.

The poor creature. Brought against his will . . . were the only thoughts GianCarlo could form. And in his anger he looked at his new friends cheering and jumping. How horrific they looked to him. He cursed them and the crowd, the stupid women fawning over the butcher, throwing kisses at him. The sun was in Gian-Carlo's eyes now. It was hot. The waves in his stomach rolled again. Now it was cold inside his body. *Molto freddo.* Very cold.

He wanted revenge for the bull. Brought here against its will. He wanted revenge for himself. Forced to live a certain way against his will. And he did the only thing he could do. He picked their pockets, all of them. His new friends, the Spaniards hovering near him, clapping his back. He took their currency, dangerously dropping the wallets without care. The blood thrumming in his ear, bile swirling in his stomach at the insanity. At the bloodlust of the crowd.

He became like a fool, weeping uncontrollably, and he kept telling himself, *You have lost your mind. Stop this. Against his will. Against his will.* His mind repeated. He staggered out of the sunlight as his friends roared with the crowd for the next matador, the next bull. He jostled the Spaniards away, "Move, move, *scusate,*" he shouted in Italian and made it to the wall and vomited.

A couple of Spaniards nearby clapped him drunkenly on the shoulder. "The *italiano* has not the stomach for our sport. Do not worry, young one. We will corrupt you yet. You will never get this out of your blood. Once you see a bullfight, it cannot be undone. You will come back again and again. You cannot purge it from your system. Then you will realize"—the man speaking handed him a flask and wiped his wet lips—"you are in love with the chase. In love with the kill."

GianCarlo grabbed the flask with a snarl and drank and drank. The change spilling out of his pockets without a care. He shoved the flask at the man's belly and lurched away.

"You drink like a Spaniard, young one," the man called after him. "We will convert you yet. Come back and visit us again, eh?"

GianCarlo did not count the money on the train ride home, but he knew. He knew he had more than enough to leave his brothers and start new and fresh with help from his Uncle Paolo, who would never betray him. He arrived in Verona the next evening and stopped at the Café Giulietta, where the old waiter worked. The noble one.

When the old man approached his table, GianCarlo ordered a big meal. The yellow saffron rice and paella. As the man walked away, GianCarlo noted how slow he was. How much slower than he'd thought. The corner table he had so admired before was at the very outside perimeter of the shade. But he was unused to fine dining and did not realize he could ask for the tarp above to be brought farther out in order to shade him. He sat waiting with his head in his hands and his stomach feeling much worse than it had yesterday.

Hurry up, old man. My head is pounding. GianCarlo's brow had broken out in a sweat. He pushed away the people trying to sell programs for the evening show of *Aida*. The meal took forty-five minutes to arrive because of the crowd. And in that space of time GianCarlo was convinced the man was making him wait because of the way he looked. Because he knew GianCarlo to be Romany.

Finally the old man appeared with his meal and gave Gian-Carlo a smile and an apology. GianCarlo cursed him. The man blinked back in shock and again tried to apologize. The other customers were staring at GianCarlo as if he were dirt. *They think I am dirt? I shall act like dirt then,* he thought and turned the table and his beautiful meal onto the ground and ran around the corner. His mind was a riot of confusion. *Why did I do that? Why?* Then an answer came to him. *The money is stained with badness from the bullrings. Picked from the pockets of those who love to watch animals die.*

In his confusion he turned around and edged back to the café. It had begun to rain. He would apologize profusely and give it all to the old man. But when he returned, the man was gone and one of the younger waiters recognized him. "You bastard. Come fight a man your own age. I'll give you a thrashing if you come any closer."

GianCarlo backed away, his explanations falling from his lips into silence. He went to throw the money into the trash but found he could not. He walked in the hot rain and then he ran and ran. He did not hide his tears. People in their fine opera garb and umbrellas stared at him in passing.

weightless

SHE FIRST noticed the flowers in Arashiyama near the Togetsu-kyo Bridge, but the ones she remembered later were the weeping blossoms near the old samurai district in the city of Kakunodate and the long, straight canopy of them leading to Aoyama cemetery.

As the plane drifts over the Atlantic, Sophie's mind reaches back to Kyoto and that February two years ago. It was an early *hanami,* cherry-blossom viewing time, and hundreds of families were picnicking under the umbrella of trees. The *sakura,* cherry blossoms, were blazing bouquets of pink and white just outside the soft-screened studio.

Her first assignment, her father had bragged to his old Caltech colleagues. She was nervous at first, the tips of her fingers almost numb from gripping her mother's Hasselblad, taking picture after picture of the master archer, his forearms flexed, bow steady, teaching kyudo to the Imperial Guard.

After the photo shoot she bowed to the master archer, taking his cue and retreating and bowing, retreating and bowing until the door latch dug into her back. As her boss, Mr. Sherman, went to say their good-byes, Sophie snuck out onto the balcony and took her last picture of the beautiful trees for her mother. Leaning precariously over the wooden railing, she grinned in disbelief at the snow starting to fall. She held out her hand as the flurries melted in her palm.

"*Mujo.*" The archery instructor walked up behind her, his feet making no sound on the bamboo floor. His voice like cedar, fragrant and warm. She whirled around with delight at his stealth. He pointed to an exquisite tree of pale pink blossoms and said again, "*Mujo,* a reminder of the impermanence of life. Lovely yet fleeting."

She had clung to this memory a month later at her family's funeral. Sophie alone sitting bent over, arms crossed at her belly. Staring in a daze at the three caskets, in the space between her mother's and sister's pinewood boxes. If she didn't focus on either one, the images blurred. Orphaned at twenty by a drunk driver and a broken stoplight. She felt her world spin out from underneath her. No anchor. Weightless.

She studies the magazine on her lap. She knows the photographer, Leila Jansen, an older rival. Jansen is nowhere near the photographer Sophie's mother had been. Her schedules booked a year in advance. Her mother had had that extra genius, an eye for a photo's soul. She'd taught Sophie everything she knew.

Still, Jansen's picture is very good. An overhead shot of two lyrical dancers at a festival, wearing garlands and dressed as muses. It's not the angle or the subject, it's that Jansen has caught the movement, the anticipation on everyone's face as if something big is about to happen. Each dancer is holding around her waist a silk ornamented triangle large enough to be a Hula Hoop. The points of the triangles converge even as the muscles on their stockinged quadriceps strain to explode in the opposite direction.

Two triangles meet at a point; smooth out their corners and

you have created infinity. That would have been the observation of her father, the astronomer. He spoke to Sophie and her sister, Angeline, as peers when they were children, engendering an excitement in them of new and different ways to view the world. Though astronomers could be highly competitive, he explained, a collaborative community based on trust and honor was encouraged by the entire scientific association.

He'd given them an observation log to note their impressions, reminding them of the ethical protocol to be as honest and concise about dates, coordinates, and discoveries in the cosmos. Like coordinates, perhaps, to a new star. Once, Sophie had seen a woman step out of her father's Volvo. She had written down, but not shared, the woman's address, the exact location. She had covered his tracks.

"Think outside the old box, girls." He'd tapped the side of his temple. His soft temple; he had worn his sideburns for so long they were just coming back into style again. His temple, where his head had made contact on impact with metal and glass.

Sophie studies the triangles again. Infinity, she thinks. The opposite of one cell dividing. Frozen at the moment of separation.

Sophie likes to ponder these things as she looks through the camera lens. The temperature of the desert at night. Comet showers hundreds of years old still circulating, leaving an imprint every seventy-five years in the heart of the sky. Like the one that happened just after the accident. At midnight, bundled in a fleece knit cap and gloves, she whistled for her cattle dog, Blue, hopped into her station wagon, and drove away from the light poles to Humboldt County. Together they lay on top of her father's station wagon hood as if it were a heated bed and watched the comet shower for three hours straight. *Did you know, girls? Chinese astronomers in the* Book of Silk *recorded twenty-nine forms of comets.*

Shooting stars heralded their return to an empty house. She'd turned to Blue then on the way home, his mouth open in that wide, wolfish smile, his tongue lolling out from happiness, and she'd thought how he was the only one who'd known them, too. Her parents, her sister. She'd called him over to the middle of the seat and kissed the top of his salt-and-pepper blue head.

He'd smelled so sweet from sleeping on her mother's flower beds; she'd lifted his paw and inhaled the musty earth. "Where have you been?" she asked as his pink tongue swept over her forehead. Memories of the beach and their last summer together lingered in his paws. A road map of her family's journeys in his feet. The next day she gave Blue away. Next, she sold the house.

Sophie is certain she saw a pre–comet shower. One comet with a tail at least a hundred feet long crossed the sky at dusk a month in advance of the shower. "It's possible," Mr. Sherman, her boss, said during their lunch break as he read the *Chronicle*. Imagine. A rogue star breaking from the group. Sophie prefers to view the world through a different lens these days, more comfortable being invisible. Someday she would like to study astronomy, maybe work at the Harvard-Smithsonian Center for Astrophysics. Her father once took her there on one of their sightseeing goal-oriented trips. She longs to scan the heavens, as he once did, but for now photography pays the rent and this is her first solo assignment.

"Don't screw this up," Mr. Sherman warned. "You're good, Sophie, but you're clumsy. This Chef Girabaldi and his restaurant is the real deal. Don't embarrass me, kid."

"I won't, Mr. Sherman."

"You sure you're up to this? You haven't had a break since—"

"I'm sure."

After two years as his freelance assistant, she still calls him Mr. Sherman. A month ago they hired a receptionist, and she's already calling him David. Sophie suspects it has something to do with the new receptionist's legs.

The job isn't without its perks. She would never have been able to see the Amazon if it hadn't been for Mr. Sherman. It's just that she always ended up doing the dirty work. Like wading into a pond thigh-deep in order to photograph *Veronica amazonica,* the gigantic water lilies over three feet in diameter. Sophie's pictures came out beautifully, and Mr. Sherman took all the credit. "Photography by David Sherman," the spread had read.

People don't realize what goes into these shoots. When she wasn't taking pictures she was assisting, holding the unwieldy aluminum light refractor like an SOS sign overhead, one foot propped against a mossy tree, the other teetering on a wet, jagged rock as strange spiders stepped velvet limbs onto her ankles and giant ferns gouged at her eyes.

As she waded into the scummy, warm pond, Mr. Sherman barked orders from dry ground. "Farther, Sophie. Move in farther. Light's changing. Quick."

Sophie never mentioned the jagged pebbles and crushed glass she'd plucked from the tender undersides of her feet with tin tweezers later that evening. No one knew about the leeches that had stuck to her calves; they cared only about the brilliant jade water lilies with the magenta underbellies glossed over neatly in a magazine spread.

Milano Central is bustling, kids with cell phones and backpacks. She picks up a local paper, catching a glimpse on the front page of Chazz Jorgensen dying in Cannes yesterday. She blinks, not quite reconciling the two pictures in the paper. One of the body being taken away on a stretcher, the other a candid shot she took two years ago of the handsome young man at the annual Telluride Film Festival. He was uncomfortable in front of the cameras.

"Could we take these in a private room?" he'd asked, contradictory to his father's hiring them for candid publicity shots. She'd done her best to place him in poses that looked candid.

As the snow fell gently outside the floor-to-ceiling windows of the Peaks Hotel, with the local singer Tommy Elskes playing his guitar in the lobby, Chazz Jorgensen had gripped a tall, frosted glass of beer, still wearing his wraparound Revos. Not until his wife joined him a day later did he seem to loosen up and actually fit into his own skin. Sophie sighs, folds the paper into her bag, and catches the first train to Rapallo. *Mujo. The impermanence of things.*

She boards the second car from the front to get away from the crowd, but the minute she sits down she is immediately alert. So preoccupied was she with the article on Chazz Jorgensen that she didn't notice the two men until she was seated. One is sitting four rows away facing her. Dark, tall, gaunt, with a fresh moon-shaped cut below his right eye. The other is to her right. The one a few rows to her right glances her way, then gives the other a familiar look that set the hairs on her arm upright. They know each other. *Not a good sign, Soph. Stupid. Stupid,* she repeats in her head. She can hear her father's words: *"Keep your eyes open. Stay alert."*

She holds her bag close to her, very aware of their movements. Inside her duffel bag is her amateur blue Baytronix AstroQuest 6. It is all she has left of her father, but she'd swing the telescope and tripod like a bat if she had to. The train pulls away from the station and she prays for someone seeking a less crowded car to join hers, but no one approaches. The man facing her stands abruptly and moves somewhere behind her. The one to her right gets up and sits a few seats in front of her. The effect is dazzling, dizzying. They do this two more times, switching seats, moving closer, tightening the circle around her like a noose. Her heart is moving at a serious hum. *Shit.*

She takes a deep breath, and before they can move again, she gets up and walks toward the head car. As she separates the glass doors adjoining the two compartments she hears them stand up behind her. She hurries to the front, passing by a couple chatting heatedly in Italian, their heads nodding in agreement, past a woman sitting with a wriggling toddler, and finally settles in with her back against the conductor's booth. The doors part.

She's lifted one shaking fist to bang on the conductor's door when her two pursuers gaze at a man seated across the aisle from her and stop short. Sophie follows their gaze. The man is tall, at least six foot two; she can tell just from how high his knees come up seated. He is facing the same direction as she is, reading the local newspaper. His oil-stained gray backpack has a thermos sticking out of it, a freckled banana, a book, and a lunch box. She notes belatedly that he has conductor's clothes on.

When she looks back up, the two men are gone. Should she mention them to the train conductor? He must feel her watching him, for he looks up from his paper and turns around.

"*Buon giorno, Signorina. Che cosa desidera?*" Then, in English: "Are you lost?"

"Who's driving the train?" she blurts, unsteady on her feet.

He smiles, an amused frown on his forehead. "Is not my shift yet. *Il mio amico*—my friend Luigi drives. In an hour is my turn." He looks at his watch, smiles at her, and shrugs.

She nods, feeling safe and a little silly. She takes a seat, letting the sun warm her face until she feels drunk from its heat, and asks in a thick voice, "*Andiamo a Portofino?*"

"*Sì.*" He nods. "We stop in Rapallo, and from there you take ferry to Portofino, *sì?* I will let you know when we arrive."

— ⚍ —

A jade field of fire-red poppies surrounds the road to the villa. The scent of wild thyme, lavender, and a hint of rosemary hangs in the sea air. To her left, high cliffs drop to reveal a stunning view of the sea. In a grove of plane trees, a towering yellow house covered in ivy with a red tiled roof comes into sight. It is immense, and she cannot see the top of it until she stands at the doorway and tilts her head back, because the rest is hidden in the heavens.

The servant tells her that the *signore* and *signora* are in town shopping, and she is shown to her room. The room has stone floors and a large red Persian-style carpet at the center, beneath the bed. The windows are thrown open to let the air and the sound from the sea rush in. She sits on the bed, gauging its firmness, then eases herself flat on her back, letting the warmth of the sun blanket her.

A knock, after which a small plate of *pasta alla Norma* breezes in on a tray. Purple-red wine in a small glass tumbler. Deceptively simple-looking. Delicious. Spicy eggplant in a red cream sauce and penne fill her belly. She lifts the glass, studies the alcohol, and spills it out her bedroom window. It looks like blood trickling down the side of the villa.

In the late afternoon, when she wakes, the scent of freshly baked lobster hovers thick and salty in the air. After weeks of canned tuna on white bread, the aroma is an explosion to her senses. She grabs her camera and hurries downstairs. Armande, the chef, Mr. Real-Deal himself, is happy to see her.

"Ah, *Signorina,* welcome to my kitchen. Did the sea sing you to sleep? Hypnotic, no? We dine on the terrace, but first we wait for the spaghetti. This is my brother, Luciano. He has just returned to us from long stay in your America. He stay away two years." Armande holds up two meaty fingers and shrugs, shoulders high up to his ears. "I tell him you are here to take *fotografie.*"

"*Buona sera, Signorina.*" The man smiles and inclines his head in greeting, his tanned hand on a coffee mug.

"Sophie Olafsen," she says, extending her hand. The man looks blankly at her outstretched hand, then stands quickly in understanding and extends his. He is younger than Armande, slender. Sophie guesses maybe twenty-five.

"You see?" Armande grins, placing a hand on his thin head of hair. "*Mio fratello,* he take all my hair! But is nothing. I take all the good looks." Armande turns to give Sophie a profile of his large hooked nose, then points to Luciano. "And he is *brutto,* eh? Ugly?" He claps a hand on his brother's shoulder and musses the black curly hair. "So I must pity him."

A frown flits across Luciano's brow at the word *pity.* "Sit. Sit." Luciano extends his hand to the wooden table. "May I bring you coffee, *Signorina? Aqua, vino?*"

Armande grins, stirring the pot. "My wife. She grows bored with me. She likes for my brother to come to visit. You see? I am a very boring man. All I do is cook."

"I forgot to ask her name," Sophie says, "when she looked in on me."

"She did not give you her name?" Armande waves a hand. "Pah. Bad girl. Her name is Nicola." Armande's good humor is infectious.

For a moment Sophie thinks of her father at their old double kitchen sink, the afternoon sunlight faint and fading through the window, stirring a big pot of his famous prizewinning chili before their soccer games. And afterward, their mother tense about his scraping the white split sink when he washed out his big Cal-phalon pots, Angeline and Sophie trying hard to skate over it all. They were never the same after his affair. They were like that split sink, occupying the same space but separated.

Nicola waltzes into the room, her smile bouncing from Armande to Luciano. Sophie barely recognizes her from the plain-faced woman who greeted her earlier. Nicola is a woman transformed. She has let her thick hair down. She looks more youthful, with the cherry lipstick sparking from her face. Her slender body is complimented by a fitted red-and-white dress and high heels. Her tan limbs bare. Perhaps she is closer to thirty than forty.

Luciano greets her with a kiss to the cheek. "Nicola," he says.

Nicola smiles delightedly and hugs him. She meets Sophie's eyes over his shoulder. "Ah, *principessa*. You rest well?" She flashes a grin of white teeth. Before Sophie can answer, she announces, "Is special night tonight. My brother-in-law. He come once a month to visit. Handsome, no?" She pinches his cheek and turns to Sophie. "How old are you, *bella*?"

"Me?" she squeaks. "Twenty-two."

"Luciano is *ventotto*. You understand?" Nicola walks over to her husband and beams from Luciano to Sophie. Sophie doesn't dare look at Luciano.

A seven-foot-long table made from a slab of three-inch-thick stone awaits them outside on the terrace. Faded pink place settings and silverware adorn the stone table. Armande arrives with two platters of spaghetti with anchovies, tomatoes, capers, and black and green olives to accompany the baked lobster. Posing with a grave face, he lets Sophie take two pictures before he commences the meal with *"Buon appetito."*

A beautiful Valpolicella from a carafe is served to accompany the meal, and Sophie does not mention that she has sworn off drinking forever. Mr. Sherman's voice comes to haunt her. *"Don't embarrass me, kid."* Sophie grips the glass and swallows a big gulp so that a tear rips down the corner of her eye.

The talk and laughter that ensue under the stars is startling to Sophie after two years of hibernating. *Has it really been years?* She hadn't known her eyes were starved for the sight of a family laughing together. She watches them greedily between gulps of wine. At the end of the meal Sophie instinctively swabs the remaining olive oil and tomato sauce from her plate with a chunk of bread.

"Brava," Luciano says.

"She eats like one of us," Armande says. "You have excellent taste." Armande kisses his fingers.

"She eats like a pig," Nicola whispers in motherly astonishment. "Brava!" Then, pouring another glass of wine, she folds her arms and lights a cigarette, studying Sophie. "I know," Nicola announces, red fingernails gesturing wildly in the air. "The *principessa* should try our grappa! We make here in my home."

"Nicola. Is too strong for her," Luciano says in Italian.

"You like, *principessa*? Or maybe you too young to drink?" Nicola smiles sweetly. "Shall we get you more coffee instead?"

The three of them wait for her response, and Sophie, from the wine bubbling inside her, says, "Sure. I'll try some."

"Sure." Nicola lifts one shoulder and gives Armande a look. "She wants to try."

The clear grappa arrives in tiny glasses, and Sophie looks at the three of them as they take up their glasses. *"Salute,"* she says and downs it all as Luciano opens his mouth to protest.

Sophie's eyes nearly cross, and Luciano and Armande erupt in laughter. She tries a small giggle. A tiny bubble of laughter.

"Bravo." Luciano pats her back. "Slowly. Next time slowly."

Nicola pours another. "Here. Try again. This time slowly."

Sophie looks at the glass and takes a deep breath, but before she can reach for it Luciano takes the glass, looks at his sister-in-law with a trace of annoyance, and downs the contents. His back is to the house, and Sophie can see the interior walls painted in different shades of green. The entire house complements his eyes. She is almost incoherent. "The walls," she says before her companions burst into laughter.

In the space of an evening she has stepped into a new family like trying on a new coat. It is foreign but not unpleasant. She leans toward them like a houseplant starved for natural light. She is standing near the corner window, preparing for bed, when she hears Nicola accost her brother-in-law Luciano on the dirt path below. "Luciano," she says.

"Nicola." There is a hesitation.

Mind your business, her mother would have said. *What are they saying?* her sister would have asked, giggling, and jostled her for the window.

She minds her own business, retreats from the window, and sets up her telescope, but the voices flow up to her like a tide, crisp then faint.

"You will return tomorrow?"

"Maybe," he says.

"But your brother. You must," she insists.

Sophie focuses on the sky instead. Where is the Milky Way? For a moment there is a frantic pounding in her chest. It's got to be there. There it is. She sees the gauzy band of ghostly light and can breathe again. Sophie pictures her family there. The three of them in a new house in the center of the Milky Way. A home similar to the one they left behind, with a dog and a neighborhood, a church and a library.

She keeps a journal. Not so much a journal but a place where she writes letters to her sister. Letters she will never send. *Dear Angeline, I wish you could see this house.*

The next morning Sophie receives a note. The man who is to write the article to accompany Sophie's photographs has been held up. He sends a note of apology and says he hopes to appear at the villa within the next few days, adding, "I shall look forward to viewing your work." He signs the note "Alexander Colter." Sophie understands this. Articles come to life whenever the photographer and writer collaborate. Still, she wrinkles her nose at his choice of words, and pictures him stuffy and eccentric, an old man in a three-piece tweed suit. They always are.

She adjusts her camera and takes a couple of shots of Armande standing in the morning light before the rust-colored walls. His copper pots and melon-colored plates will contrast nicely with the rosemary and the earthy black of the truffles. *He was preparing breakfast when I took this one,* she will tell this faceless, prim Alexander.

"Is good news?" Armande asks as she sits down for coffee on the wooden kitchen bench.

She tries another one of her wooden smiles. "It's from the magazine writer. He's going to be a few days late." She takes a shot of Armande in profile. His egg-shaped body and hooked nose are a delight. Full of curves against the sharp angles of the window frame and the flat field of red poppies just outside. "You know, if you need anything at the market, I can run errands for you. I'm going there anyway. If you need garlic, tomatoes—" When he only smiles she asks, "Do you think I can borrow your car to pick him up at the dock when he arrives? I'd like to make myself useful." She sits at the wooden table and sips her espresso from a white, almost thimble-sized cup.

"*Bella,* my car, house, kitchen, everything. Is open to you, eh?" He opens wide his arms. His apron protrudes at the belly, and the butcher knife he is holding showers the room with the basil he has been chopping. "For now, why not go for swim below?" he asks.

"Yes," she says. "That sounds wonderful." She blushes, embarrassed at having allowed herself to feel so at home. She must remember not to get in their way. She takes the towel the servant brings her and goes for a swim.

The sea is as cool as her father's Bombay Sapphire martinis. He would let Angeline and Sophie, bundled in blankets, sip from the triangular glass as he adjusted their family telescope on their deck. They complained that the drink tasted like rubbing alcohol. Their mother used to bring him his usual one glass a night. But after their reunion, the strain had started to show. He had started to have two, maybe three glasses, pouring it straight himself as their mother stared blankly at the stars.

"Did you know," their father asked, "that sailors once navigated the oceans by looking up to the heavens for answers, in the alignment of the stars?"

Floating this way, the water lifting the weight of her, Sophie feels everything. The memories flood her at once. Her sister's laughter, their trips to Kehoe Beach, Blue barking at the seagulls in that light-footed lope of his. Paw prints in the sand stretching after their father as he ran zigzag. Their mother those last few days, a canopy of shadows across her lovely face. Hers was a closed coffin. Gasping, Sophie breaks free from the water, dabs her face with the towel, knowing the heat will dry her bathing suit, and hurries to wait for the ferry.

The tablecloth vendors are under the trees. Women in pleated skirts and linen blouses, their sleeves puckered at the shoulders. Simple shoes for standing all day. Sophie lingers a moment to finger a butter-yellow table runner with white lacing. The vendors inspect her as she inspects their wares.

"*Bella, speciale,*" the woman says to her, taking the cloth down delicately and cradling it like a lover. "Original, this design."

Sophie shakes her head. "Thank you. I'll think about it."

"*Sì, sì.*" The woman shrugs and throws the cloth off to one side. "It may not be here tomorrow, but you will think about it."

Sophie walks alongside their tables, fingertips skating over the satin and lace designs. She cannot resist; she takes picture after picture while the vendors elbow one another, no doubt pointing out the silly tourist.

At the end of the row of folding chairs, beneath a giant palm tree, sit three women, one stiff and gray-haired, wearing her pale blue sweater like a cape, buttoned only at the top over a crisp short-sleeved blouse. The middle one is voluptuous, with her oversized hourglass figure and her copper-red hair pinned back. The youngest is of Senegalese descent, wearing a matronly dress of midnight blue with fine white lace trim. Their clothing is of the highest quality. The handbags that drape from their elbows are designer-made. The jewelry they wear is much different from the other vendors'.

The gray-haired one asks, "You are visiting, *Signorina?*"

"Yes." Sophie turns and gestures upward, in the direction of the villa. "I'm photographing signor Girabaldi."

"*Which* signor Girabaldi?" she asks, her blue gaze like ice.

For a moment Sophie thinks, *There are two signori Girabaldis?* Then she realizes, of course, Luciano. The women watch her keenly. "The chef," she manages to say.

"And the younger, you have seen him? Handsome, no?"

Sophie's feet shuffle a little. "Yes." The three widows giggle, and Sophie reddens.

"Ah, to be invited to dinner now," the African one says before Sophie can answer. She sees Sophie's awkwardness and says, "We are not laughing at you, dearest. Simply the situation, you see. A lovely girl such as yourself. In that big, dusty house."

"Oh," Sophie says. She thinks surely they are wrong. Armande's house is so well kept. But perhaps that isn't what they mean at all. "Well, here's my ferry."

"You go to Rapallo?" the gray-haired one asks. "Visit the Museo del Merletto if you have time. We have our own designs there. We open our own museum soon."

"What name shall I look for?"

"Moretti. Look for the three Moretti widows."

"Oh yes. Of course," Sophie says, thinking them senile.

She feels lost in Rapallo. She sees polo shirts for her father; a silver paperweight in the shape of a fortune cookie and a pen set for her mother; a yellow bikini, sandals, and short, frilled skirts for her sister; even a leather collar for Blue, but has no desire to purchase anything for herself.

She eats alone at a café, not wanting to overstay her welcome at Armande's. She opens her journal to a fresh page and writes to her sister. *Angeline, do you think it's wrong to have laughed with this family?* She doesn't ask how her parents are faring in heaven. She doesn't write to them. She doesn't like to face that she may be angry with them. The thought is silly. As if they abandoned her on purpose, took Angeline on purpose.

Because that evening of the accident, Angeline wanted to laze around on the sofa, watch *Friends* while Sophie studied, but their father had wanted a buffer, someone to blunt the quietness from the stranger who had become his wife. And when Sophie had refused to drive, he had teased Angeline in that slightly desperate voice: "Come on, shortstop, you can carry the pizza home. Your mom can always use an extra slave." Then, to Sophie: "Soph, you sure? Don't wanna drive? Last chance." He had jingled the keys like bait.

Sophie was short with him, tired of the strained silence, and the role of mediator and chauffeur. "I can't always drive!"

So they had left, a tense, bantering group of three, the sweet scent of martinis lingering in the empty glasses trailing behind like old confetti. The last time.

The sun is soft like Christmas tinsel on the water's surface. Sophie stretches her legs along the Lungomare V. Veneto, blinking at the blinding pockets of shining light from the Gulf of Tigullio.

That Christmas after the accident, Sophie decided to take the ornaments down like their mother used to do, wrapping them delicately in red tissue paper, working her way up to the angel at the top of the tree. Sophie began the ritual reverently. Taking down the tree used to be as much fun as decorating. Their father would put on the stereo while she and Angeline danced and joked, working up an appetite for their traditional take-home order of Zachary's Chicago-style pizza. She smiled, remembering their epic battles over whether to order pepperoni or the delicious Greek, smothered with tomatoes on top. But the memory had been too dear, too soon, and in the midst of taking down one ball it had fallen and shattered on the floor.

Staring down the ladder at her mistake, she'd felt a surge of anger, then a fury so fierce it frightened her, and she had started to cry. She'd never felt anything like it. The pain threatened to swallow her. So she'd decided right then and there to detach, to simply let go of them. She stood stiffly, walked into the garage, and dragged the garbage can into the house, trailing oil and debris, like skid marks over the maple floors and white carpeting, then she dumped the tree in angel first.

She decides to visit the museum the gray-haired woman mentioned. The way to the Museo del Merletto detours from the main road and winds up through the Parco Casale, a small forest of trees, a tennis court, and then a miniature driveway and a large house.

The ticket man or the security guard—she isn't sure which, perhaps both, because of his blue uniform—nods at her. She and a boy of twelve kicking a soccer ball are the only customers. The boy appears impatient; he has a notebook. It is the weekend. Extra homework, she supposes. The ball gets away from him, and she fights the urge to tip her foot and swing it up to her knee. She picks it up instead and waits for him to come to her. *"Scusa, Signorina, che ora è?"*

She tells him it is ten to three. He sighs and kicks the ball dejectedly.

The ticket guard appears stonefaced at first. He is balding in the center, the hair on his temples bushy and unruly. He smiles at her. "Is a upstairs and a downstairs," he says, taking the money from the impatient boy, who excuses himself around Sophie and places fifty-two cents on the table and hurries forward. The guard then holds out his arm to show her the way to the first set of lace designs.

The lace panel on the first floor is a sight. Over eight feet long in a rectangular glass case that dominates the center of the room. A court scene. She marvels at how old it is. Downstairs, she searches for the designs of the three women. "Moretti," the gray-haired one had said. There is an emerald organza evening dress that takes her breath away, but she wouldn't fit in it. The dress is so tiny, precious, flirty. She would be too big-boned. It is made for a fine-boned woman, like Nicola.

She turns to the other drawers, and the ones she has just shut slide open. One, two, three. She goes back and shuts them. Now the drawers to her right slide open. She has the sudden feeling that the headless mannequin wearing the emerald gown will step down and dance. The room chills and she decides it is time to return to the sunshine. The security guard waves good-bye with a bewildered smile as she hurries out.

—⚏—

She hears her name on the ferry and turns to see Luciano. His skin is dark from fishing all day and his green eyes glitter beneath black lashes. He smells sun- and sea-kissed.

"I finish work. You return to the villa?" he asks, leaning easily against the railings.

"Yes." She tries to find a posture that doesn't make her look as if she is struggling. Finally she gives up and stands with feet spread hip distance and her handbag dangling from her clasped hands. A decidedly schoolgirl pose, she knows, but it feels very comfortable. She is aware, right now, that she is a young woman standing next to a young man. She liked it better when she was invisible behind a camera lens. Disembodied. Detached. Safe.

"I shall come with you," he says, pulling off his T-shirt to replace it with a fresh one from his duffel bag. Sophie averts her eyes but cannot avoid the sprinkle of hair cutting down the middle of his taut stomach.

"Did you catch any fish today?" She feels silly the moment the words take flight. He is, after all, a fisherman.

"Yes." He smiles.

They laugh at the awkwardness of it. On the way back she feels a warmth spreading inside her.

In the evening, they gather for dinner, and Nicola, like a doting mother hen, pushes Sophie toward Luciano. After watching her adjust her camera lenses he wipes his hands on a napkin and asks, "May I see?"

"Of course." She hands him the camera, praying he does not drop her mother's Hasselblad. She has nothing to worry about. His hands are sure. He is not clumsy at all. She is flattered by his attention, but at the same time she feels a shifting around her. Like figures in a child's dollhouse. Now the husband and wife stand together, now her figure is placed next to that of the younger brother. There is a waiting in the air that unnerves her.

She tells him to bring the camera to his eyes as she adjusts the lenses from behind him. *"Ah, sì."* He nods.

Nicola sits, inspecting her nails. *"Scusi,* I must help my husband." She stands abruptly, spilling a carafe of wine onto Luciano's lap.

"Ah." Luciano jumps up, and the look he gives Nicola is wild before he catches Sophie watching.

As Luciano and Armande smoke near the edge of the large terrace, Nicola brings out a brush and shows it to Sophie. She wishes to arrange Sophie's hair. "Is okay?"

Sophie smiles, stunned, and turns her back obediently as Nicola parts her hair and begins to brush, then plait. Sophie closes her eyes and savors the soft drum of Nicola's fingers on her scalp. Their mother used to do this. The three of them on the porch in the afternoon sun.

But after the reunion, their talks were no longer filled with girlish amusement. She'd get behind Sophie and tell them about the other woman. "I saw her in town today." The woman had been an associate of their father's. In town, her mother and the woman circled each other like repelling magnets. Sophie never saw them in the same place at the same time, until they seemed like one person to her. Sophie could not look at one without thinking of the other.

Sophie would nod and braid Angeline's hair as their mother relived the entire affair, over and again, how she'd found out through a friend. How it had started the week she was gone for that assignment shooting fossils in the Gobi Desert. It was as if they communicated only through the memory of the other woman.

"Mom, stop it," Sophie pleaded one afternoon. "Why did you agree to stay, if you're only going to torture him for it? He's willing to try. Why can't you? You were gone all the time on those assignments. *National Geographic, Vogue, Travel & Leisure.*" She tried to keep the accusation from her voice, but the best she could do was refrain from adding, "What did you expect?"

"Is that what he told you? That I was gone all the time?"

"You *were* gone. We *all* missed you."

"He was gone, too," she said softly. Barely a whisper.

And Sophie had sat straight up, full of indignation and fury. "What're you talking about, Mom? He was right here!"

"You're so young, Sophie." Their mother had trailed her fingers one last time through Sophie's hair, while Angeline sat stiffly in front of Sophie. "Two people can be in the same room and still be gone." Their mother stood quietly, walked into the house, and shut them out.

Nicola tells Sophie about the villa. "Ah, but you should have seen before Armande fix. Was so crazy! I choose the furniture. The paints. Everything."

"And I pay everything," Armande shouts to them from where he and Luciano are smoking.

"Ah, but you can buy anything you wish," Nicola says.

"Yes, this life costs me." Armande's smile sobers.

There is a creaking space in between their words.

"I met three women today; they said they knew you," Sophie blurts. "They were sitting with the tablecloth women, only I don't think they work there."

"Moretti's three widows." Armande winks.

"Ah." Nicola bends over Sophie's shoulder and frowns in

warning. "Those women are horrible. Filled with gossip," she says. "Tell me. What did they say? Ah, do not tell me."

"*Sì,* but if you wish to *know* something. To find someone. The widows know. They see all," Armande laughs. "But is depend. Only if they like you. Otherwise..." He pretends to zip his mouth. "*Niente,* eh?"

"Such foolishness," Nicola says, holding Sophie's hair in two braids as if she will wrap a ribbon around each or pull them apart. She lets go and waltzes toward the edge of the terrace to the two men, leaving Sophie's hair to unravel. Nicola reaches out to tickle Armande at the waist. Her actions appear unsure. Armande chuckles and pulls away. They are like two figurines, one fallen and scraping against the other. As if any moment one will shatter from the weight.

Before Luciano leaves, Nicola accosts him, and again a silent struggle ensues beneath Sophie's window. She listens to their heated whispers below.

"It must be different."

"But all I ask—"

Sophie does not hear the rest of it. A struggling sound. A wrenching curse followed by a loud, stinging slap. Hurried footsteps. "Luciano," she hisses. "Wait!"

There is the sound of shoes straining over pebbles, followed by Nicola's wrenched sobs. The sound makes Sophie frantic. She busies herself with adjusting her telescope. But in the end she cannot resist. She dares a look out the window in time to see Luciano storming down the stone steps. At first she thinks it is a sash flapping near his waist. But it is his shirt, ripped from pocket to waistband.

The moon is full as Luciano ties his little boat to the dock. He can see the path to his cottage clearly. But even in the dark he knows the grounds as if they were mapped on his heart. His family's property. He goes inside and studies himself in the mirror. He stares at the pocket she has torn. He reaches to the middle of his back and pulls off the shirt and drops it into the garbage can.

A cooler empty except for water and floating ice. On second glance he sees a can of beer immersed just below the surface. He reaches in, pulls the can free, and walks back out into the night to sit on his rock. *My rock.* From here he can see the house. The bedroom where Nicola lays her body down each evening. Armande owns everything now, the house, the property, the woman.

Luciano has nothing. Not even his new shirt, which she has ripped. He is a blank sheet of paper swept up in the wind. He is only wealthy by association.

He once thought he wanted to live without her impetuousness. He went to America. He found work in San Francisco on Silver Avenue, in the garage of a house. A sweater factory. The owner was an Italian, but the man never invited Luciano to dinner with his family. The neighbors kept to themselves.

There was no sea to gaze at from his one-room apartment, only black-tarred pavement and cement sidewalks, an empty elementary school yard. He was a fisherman out of water, swimming on asphalt, breathing sweater dust through his pores.

Once when he was thinking about her, he stretched his hand too far into the machinery and the sewing needles stitched red fabric into his palm. He still has a scar from that time. She is etched into his skin forever. He returned, amused, humbled by his trip, only to find that in her anger she had married his brother. His brother, whom he loved more than himself.

"You must tell me, Luciano. I tried to reach you, to ask permission, but you never wrote once," Armande pleaded.

"Permission? Brother, she is your wife now. I have had many

women since. It is I who must ask for permission." He laughed, chuckled, hoping the pain would not show. His teeth clenched so hard he felt they would burst apart.

"Ask anything. I shall give it to you," Armande declared in relief.

"The old cottage on Father's property."

"That is all?" Armande asked. As the eldest son, he had inherited their father's property without lifting a finger. Without venturing out of his circle into another country to try to make something of himself.

"That is all." All that he owns. The cottage and a scar on his hand she dealt from half a world away.

When she heard that he had returned, she went to the cottage in a fury and ripped all of his clothing. He arrived home from fishing and found her a whirlwind of anger. He saw that her anger was wretched, bigger, deeper than his, and she consumed him with flying fists and teeth marks.

And in the morning how she had sat next to him, the sweet, smiling sister-in-law. "More coffee, Luciano?" While under his shirt his body ached from her fists and teeth marks, the cuts muted by iodine and sealed with salt from the sea.

The prodigal son, the three widows called him when he returned. They meant it as a joke. A sign of affection. As if his father had ever given him money. Money was never wasted in their household. It was spent on wise things, like Armande's studies to become a chef. Armande was the favorite. Luciano was an afterthought.

So Luciano looked for a mentor elsewhere. He found him in Aix. A French fisherman, Monsieur Dumont, was an acquaintance of their father's and a supplier for his small restaurant.

Their father was a self-taught cook with a successful *ris-torante*. He looked down on Monsieur Dumont. "How can a man be only a fisherman? Not strive for more? The man has nothing to show for himself except a drunken wife. If he were smart he would marry off that daughter of his. She is his only asset. Yet she has the manners of a goat. Her long hair always in tangles. Yes, marry her to a rich man who will pay off all their bills. Do you know, son, that Monsieur Dumont is just a step away from jail? That if he misses one day of fishing, his bills will catch up with him? They will take away all that he owns, his house, that brat of a daughter of his."

His father's only advice, though he has plenty of advice for Armande: "Make something of yourself. Don't waste your life as a fisherman." So Luciano gravitated toward the French fisherman.

How funny one's path in life can be. How strange. But he is feeling sorry for himself again, he knows. And yet what is he to do? Returned only five months and all of his plans turned to dust. The wife he was to marry. The life he was to lead. And Nicola, he is breaking her resolve he knows. Unintentionally. By ignoring her. Should he stay? Should he leave again? Each day she pushes the young photographer his way, and yet the closer he steps to the girl, the angrier Nicola becomes. Each day she dances closer and closer to him.

She is married to his brother now. He must remind himself whenever she stands close to him. How familiar her scent. Like wild honeysuckle one catches on a breeze and then it is gone. *She is married to Armande now.*

In the morning, Sophie goes to the ferry and waits for the writer with two café espressos in her hands, but he never shows. De-layed again. She shrugs a little in disappointment. She had hoped to be distracted for a day, play guide for the prim Mr. Col-ter, maybe go for a swim, explore the city. Instead she wanders aimlessly.

It is the evening of the Rapallo festival. They wait excitedly for the ferry ride into Rapallo. Armande is in great spirits. He has prepared a snack of ripe green melon slices and tiny kumquats filled with shredded prosciutto. He unveils this treasure on the ferryboat with a sweep of the plastic shrink-wrap.

"Armande thinks of everything, no? So we do not go hungry before the festivities. Signorina, you bring your camera tonight?"

"Yes," Sophie says, feeling very coltish in heels and a soft coral dress that ties at the waist. The tropical air plays at the fringes of the dress and feels like liquid against her bare legs. "Let's take a picture before the ferry docks. The three of you," she suggests.

Nicola, dressed in a rose gown with matching shawl, stands between her two men.

"Good," Sophie says, trying to focus on the three of them and not on Luciano, who refuses to smile. Just as her finger presses down on the button, Nicola, with a slight movement, takes Lu-ciano's hand. The flash goes off and Luciano pulls away with a scowl. Sophie drops the camera slightly and looks over to see if she has seen correctly. Nicola acts as if nothing has happened; she threads her arm through Armande's. Yet Sophie has witnessed it all.

By the time they reach the festival it is in full swing. The music can be heard all along the pier. Set outdoors in the center of the plaza with the Banco di Chiavari signs in green on one end and the various shops now closed for the evening on the other, the festival has transformed the cobblestoned plaza. Tables of Ar-mande's food are laid out, and a live band takes a break from playing Italian love songs to do a rendition of "Bad to the Bone." The younger crowd runs to the center to gyrate and laugh.

The locals have already formed long lines behind Armande's tables. Folding chairs border the dance floor, and older couples show off, the men twirling their partners to the music. A table with a banner boasting the name of the local cafés—La Cucina, La Toscana, Andiamo, Café Bella Mia, and Armande's famous Cucina Girabaldi—stands with barrels of olives, cheese, and wine laid out.

Sophie disappears into her work, taking pictures all evening. Her long hair is braided down her back. She uses an entire roll on the food, another two on the dancing, Armande spinning one of the locals around on the dance floor. She feels important and knows the pictures will come out beautifully. The three widows fan themselves and incline their heads in greeting. *"Signore Moretti,"* Armande says, bowing. When Nicola sees them she lifts her chin and walks the other way.

Couples part and come together on the dance floor. Sophie takes picture after picture, and in between the swaying skirts she catches a glimpse of Luciano through her camera lens. Luciano drinking a glass of wine and watching Nicola on the arms of a young man. When an eager woman tries to pull him onto the dance floor, he shakes his head no politely. The woman is undaunted; she tries to place her arm around Luciano.

Sophie laughs, forgetting that she has lowered her camera and is staring at him outright. She is no longer invisible. But it is too late; Luciano is staring back at her, his lips pressed together in a smile. Her face reddens. She looks away. When she looks up he is walking toward her.

"You wish to dance, Sophie?" His breath smells sweetly of wine, and she finds herself wondering what it would be like to taste the fragrance from his lips.

He is grinning. "You do not wish to dance?"

A couple nearby are watching. "Dance, dance," the man says, gently pushing Sophie forward.

Dancing so close to him she can barely breathe. She stares straight over his shoulder but watches him from the corner of her eye. Sophie feels as if she is floating and falling at the same time. Her shroud of grief lifts, unfurls.

After their dance Luciano leaves to fetch her a drink. Sophie stands to the side beside the folding chairs. "*Signorina,* have you decided yet? Which Girabaldi do you prefer?" the gray-haired widow asks.

That night Sophie wakes to find Nicola watching her from the foot of her bed. She lies still; Nicola approaches on bare feet, then gasps when she realizes Sophie is staring right at her. Without a word Nicola flees from the room.

Luciano arrives with flowers for Sophie. "Where are your pictures?" he asks, pretending to hold a camera and pressing his index finger up and down. His green eyes stray for a moment to Nicola, seated at the end of the table, but he does not give her the normal kiss on the cheek.

The three of them are on the porch in the afternoon sun. "May I see? The pictures?" he asks.

"Like that?" Nicola asks, snapping her fingers in the air so that Luciano's eyes jerk instantly to her. "She take pictures yesterday. Suddenly they appear like magic?" she laughs.

She intends a teasing quality to her voice, Sophie thinks. But it comes out jagged, scrapes the stone table.

A day goes by, and the writer has been delayed again when Sophie meets Luciano in the empty hallway the next morning. Their hands linger. He invites her to spend the day together. They go to Cinque Terre. At the Riomaggiore station, beneath the faded yellow booth, under a clock and a sign that says *Privato,* she tells him about her family.

"I had a sister. I was very close to her."

"What was her name?" he asks.

"Angeline."

"And the other driver? What became of him?"

Sophie pauses. "There was no other driver. My father was the drunk. He hit a light pole."

She imagines a great compassion in his questions, and her heart swells. A shy kiss. By Tuesday evening they are in bed together. His kisses are slow and painstaking along her neck. She arches her back and feels herself thawing inside.

"He licked my skin," she would have told her younger sister. "His breath warm just above my stomach. I closed my eyes." But she has no one to tell. So she simply remembers how the curtains unfurled and snapped in the sea breeze.

She thinks for a moment of Nicola. Unsure of her relationship to Luciano, yet Nicola is married. And Sophie—is she the other woman? Though she has a great affection for Nicola, she feels a power in the possibility somehow. No longer the victim.

She spends the next two days with him, but on Thursday Luciano does not show, nor the next day. She spends her day walking back and forth into town, as if retracing their steps from their last evening together, trying to recapture the scent of promise that permeated the night. Luciano is busy, she tells herself.

The writer arrives the next evening, full of apologies. "Alex Colter," he says, taking in her whole face with his eyes and extending a hand. He is young. Her age. But it is too late. She doesn't truly see him.

"I went to pick you up. I waited," Sophie says, her eyes still dreamy with Luciano.

"I'm real sorry. I got held up doing the story in Pamplona."

"You missed the festival," she says.

"Really sorry," he says as she watches him unpacking his notebooks, his hands in motion.

She likes the worn leather saddlebag strapped across his chest, the rounded flap that holds his belongings, filled with stories, filled with life. She imagines bulls and gaily dressed women, a bottle of scotch, a leather flask of whiskey. The leather of the flask would be burgundy-colored.

She would have liked to have taken those pictures of Pamplona for him.

He is fishing for a pencil now. "The running of the bulls. I would have been here the day of the Rapallo festival but another American got gored. Had to stay over to do the story." She notices from a distance that Alex is a towhead, with intelligent eyes. He has a swimmer's body and wears khaki cargo shorts, Tevas, and a dark green short-sleeved shirt.

"So," Alex says, "is there a story here?"

They follow the coastline, staying a good distance from the cliffs but close enough to see the ocean. Alex has brought his tape recorder. He asks question after question. "What was the temperature like the night of the festival? Was the night clear or cloudy? Did anything unusual happen?"

"It was a gorgeous night. Very warm. Nothing unusual. People really enjoyed themselves, as you'll see in the pictures."

"I saw the pictures you did for the *Planet*. Great shot. The one with the green water lilies. I was supposed to do that story but got assigned to something else. The colors were so vivid. I suppose you had to get into the pond to take the pictures from that angle."

"Mmm." Sophie nods, her mind drifting. She is lovesick from Luciano's three-day absence. But it isn't as if they have made any promises.

"Were there any leeches in the pond?" Alex asks.

It is dark on the way back to the mansion, and they are drenched from the humidity. Alex suggests a swim on the private beach below. "Come on. It will be nice. They've all gone to sleep by now."

The invitation intrigues her. It's not such a bad idea. She has been wiping the perspiration from the back of her neck with her palm and pulling the front of her blouse off her skin since they started their walk. She feels slightly delirious as they descend the stone steps in their sandaled feet. Her emotions have thawed, and they are raw now.

It's not such a bad idea. It will pass the time and tire her out for sleep. She peels down to her underwear. A hopeful desperate thought: *If Luciano knew, he would be jealous.*

She and Alex float on their backs in the warm water and stare at the stars. "A few years back my father took me to see the aurora borealis in Alaska. In springtime," she tells him. "It was fantastic. Flashes of green, red, yellow in the sky. Like shifting sand. Intensely bright in some spots and faded in others, and then it would change again. Wispy waves across the heavens like a big hand painting watercolors in the night sky."

"Glowing gases," Alex said.

"Charged particles from the sun," Sophie says, remembering her father's explanation of the northern lights.

"It must have been beautiful," Alex says, watching her closely. But Sophie does not hear him. She is thinking about how happy she felt during the night of the Rapallo festival and the following day, but since then, since then it's like a deep crevasse has opened up and she feels herself falling. She doesn't see this night she is experiencing now with Alex Colter.

She gets a great idea and she tells Alex, "Come, I'll introduce you to signor Girabaldi's younger brother. He's a fisherman." But she forgets the hour. It is late and when they get there one of the other fishermen tells her he has gone away. When they return Armande is seated alone in the kitchen.

"Nicola has gone to sleep?" Sophie asks.

"She returns to her *sorella,* her sister. In Verona," Armande says.

Her plane is due to leave in three days. And still no sign of Luciano. The pain is intense, the despair bottomless. When she goes for a walk along the cliffs with Alex Colter he orders her down from a ledge she has been walking like a tightrope, with arms extended outward. "Hey. What are you doing? Get down from there right now."

She doesn't answer any of her phone messages from Mr. Sherman. Instead she calls when she knows he will be sleeping and leaves a message saying she has been trying to reach him. She is so lovesick she can't eat Armande's savory potato-and-onion galettes, his Tuscan beef stew with mouthwatering tomatoes, garlic, and rosemary. She does, however, finish off Armande's private bottles of grappa at an alarming rate, bought from one of the five cities in Cinque Terre.

When she refuses his homemade *scaccia* bread, from his great-grandfather's recipe of fresh basil and plum tomatoes and Parmigiano-Reggiano cheese, he declares her gravely ill. Fortunately for Sophie, when Mr. Sherman calls the villa, Armande makes it known.

"Mr. Sherman, I'm fine. Just a touch of the stomach flu. I'll send the pictures shortly."

"But signor Armande says you aren't eating. I'm worried about you, kid."

"It's nothing. I had some clear broth earlier." Then in a fevered haste she asks, "Mr. Sherman, have you ever wanted to sleep all day?"

"Sure, kid. That's just the fever talking."

When Nicola returns from her visit with her sister, she is in great spirits. She sits on the terrace wearing a yellow dress that highlights the glow on her cheeks. She looks like a woman in love.

"*Bella,* you are finished with your picture taking?" she asks, squeezing Sophie's shoulders and placing her cheek next to Sophie's. "We shall miss you."

"Almost," Sophie says with a sinking feeling. "I leave the day after tomorrow."

"*Amor mio.*" Nicola kisses Armande on the cheek.

"Signora Girabaldi. Armande tells us you have been visiting your sister," Alex inquires.

"Ah yes. I returned to Verona. My sister Cecilia, she was able to get tickets. Last-minute for the opera. We went to L'Arena. They were playing *Carmen.* It was exquisite. Luciano was kind to pick me up at the pier." Sophie turns as the back door opens to reveal a smiling Luciano. His eyes scan the room, lingering for a moment on Nicola. Sophie's mind spins. Nicola approaches, her cheeks in bloom, and places an arm around Sophie. "I make up to you, *bella,* eh? Tomorrow we shop! Ha? Ha?"

Sophie giggles, confused yet happy to see them both.

Alex Colter makes an obnoxious comment as they splay the photographs Sophie has taken on the wooden table in the library.

"Crazy family, don't you think?" he asks underneath his breath, then turns a picture by placing his finger on one corner. "This one, I think." He pulls the picture of Nicola twirling in a rose-colored dress before a grinning Luciano; the lights from the lanterns are glowing, and there is an abundance of life going on behind them.

Sophie nods. "She's a little unpredictable."

"Her? He's just as bad, you know."

"Armande? He's the sweetest man," Sophie says.

"I'm not talking about the husband, poor sap. I'm talking about the brother-in-law."

"You don't know what you're talking about," Sophie says, standing immediately from her chair.

Alex looks at her stupidly for a moment. "You don't see it?"

"These people have welcomed us into their home," Sophie says, unable to articulate through her anger. "Good night, Mr. Colter."

Then a look of recognition crosses his face. "You're seeing him, aren't you? I'm sorry, I didn't know." In his face is a sharp look of disappointment that Sophie does not care to interpret.

In the afternoon, Sophie and Luciano have their first fight. On the path below her window she calls after him, her sandals crunching down on tiny wildflowers. He turns, bewildered to meet her. He is used to hearing a different voice call after him at this spot. The heat is soft. A time for lovers to lie in the sunlight, limbs intertwined. She thinks, even then, the hurt still tangible on her skin, that they might still lie together, could still work this out.

"Where were you today? Not that I'm spying." Why had she

used that word, *spying?* What was that? A movement from above? One of the windows?

He drags a hand through his hair. "I was working."

"It's just that I stopped by to say hello." She tries to place a hand on his shoulder. The whole time she thinks, *He will leave. Is leaving now as I speak.*

"I must report to you now?" A smile that borders on annoyance.

He listens to her explanation with a tight face and walks quietly away. She watches him go with terror. *Is this it?* she wants to scream. She wants to hit him with her fists and throw herself at his feet as she has seen Nicola do. Her mind races to take inventory. *What have I lost? Am I still a whole person?* She stands very still. Like a child playing hide-and-seek.

Alex Colter, on the other hand, though unwelcome in her room, decides it is different when the person who hates you is ill. In the evening he knocks on her door.

"Go away." He brings her water, slices of bread, the only thing she can stomach. "Do you think you could get one of Armande's bottles of grappa? He says I'm welcome to anything."

"No," he says without any apologies and stands with his hands in his pockets.

Sophie grudgingly lets him visit.

She finds her appetite, and Alex brings her the remainder of Armande's evening bouillabaisse. He watches her eat as he sits on the round-backed chair beside her bed. Opens his mouth, then shuts it again.

"What?" Sophie's eyes slide sideways at him.

Alex leans forward and clasps his hands together. "He's playing you like a broken record."

"I don't want to hear it."

"Why? Why can't you see that? It's a game he plays with her. Listen. Everyone's been on the losing end of a relationship at one time or another, Soph."

"Alex. Shut up."

Alex sighs and looks at her. She realizes with a start that Alex is good looking. How had she not noticed this? He sees her bemused smile and presses on. "Sophie, listen. I just feel kind of responsible for you."

"Well, don't. I can take care of myself. How is your article coming along?"

"Sophie, listen to me. Don't change the subject. One of these days Armande's going to wise up. He's going to walk in with a carving knife and it will be over. He'll serve them up to the guests in a nice quiche. Then tell everyone they ran away together."

"Don't joke."

"The whole town knows. I've been talking to people." He paces, hands in pockets.

"The three widows? They're gossips." She points to the door. "Out."

"I'm getting out. Let me know if you need anything."

She sits propped up on the bed, a perfectly healthy person except for her heart. Alex Colter, in his clean, worn jeans and T-shirt, with his short, messy hair, is someone her sister would have fallen for. She doesn't inspect her own feelings. Why she is fond of him though he irritates her no end. There is no way Alex can compete with the image of Luciano that Sophie has created in her mind. He is the one she shared the secret of her grief with. Her image of him has grown to major proportions, so that even Luciano himself cannot compete.

Later that evening she studies the stars through her telescope, hoping to discern a method to the chaos. Somewhere near the image of Cassiopeia she traces her mother, her father, her sister.

Imagine, people once looked at the heavens only with the naked eye. Chinese astronomers in the *Book of Silk* recorded twenty-nine forms of comets.

Luciano leans on his headboard. His body is a riot of grief, anger, self-pity. He has not touched Nicola. Not yet. Though she phoned him again and again from her sister's home. He has been walking in the gutters. Sleeping with the overeager woman from the Rapallo festival. The one Sophie saved him from.

He thinks of Sophie, and a wave of shame washes over him. Lovely, beautiful girl. Sophie is a fresh start. But he prefers to wallow in his own infested history.

This is the way Nicola finds him when she opens the door. He smiles, bleary-eyed, drunk on grappa; he knows she is real but his eyes are unfocused and he prefers to think of her as a hallucination. "Have you come to tear my clothes again?" he asks. "They are packed in my suitcase," he tells her. "I have turned into a hateful person."

"I do not hate you."

"Why should you hate me? You, who push innocent girls my way."

"I never meant to hurt her. I hoped the two of you would fall in love and leave me."

"I am leaving, in the morning. If you wish to come"—he struggles even then—"I shall be at the station."

"Take me with you," Nicola says. "I thought you would never return. And then I hated you for a long time when you did."

"You hate me still," he says.

"Love, hate. They are the same, aren't they?" she asks, laying her body slowly down beside him.

The moment ends too soon. As with an addict, the law of diminishing returns applies. Luciano's moment with Nicola fades too fast, followed by intense guilt. And if it fades fast now, what of the next time and the time after? It is not the same. His love for her is tainted by his love for Armande. She leaves his side before Armande can grow suspicious. He follows her out, and an hour later he sits on his rock and watches her shadow enter the big house to lie beside his brother.

Mad with jealousy, with guilt, he decides to go for a stroll near the cliffs to clear his head. He finds Sophie standing on a precipice, dangerously close, arms out, and approaches her slowly. *"Bella?"* he whispers. "Sophie?"

She turns to him; her eyes seem wet, but the salt water does that sometimes, and there is a chill in the air tonight. "Hello." She smiles and turns her back to the sea, to face him. She is standing so precariously that Luciano feels his heart flutter. He cannot read her face in the darkness. Again, guilt washes over him. "The other day, I said some things. Mean—"

"It's okay," she tells him and hops down, to his relief, to walk beside him.

Her presence soothes him, like the scent of lavender, clean and medicinal somehow. There is a healing quality about her. Perhaps it is just her youth, her openness. He could list a million things, he thinks, as he walks beside her.

On impulse, one he wants to believe in, he says, "I was hoping to find you."

She turns to him, hopeful. "You were looking for me?"

"In a way I was. Yes, I was in a way." His hands are in his pockets; he feels chastised by her wide-eyed gaze. How had he not noticed the caramel color of her eyes?

"What for?" When he stares blankly she shakes her head and rolls her eyes. "Why were you looking for me?"

"I—I leave tomorrow. I wish to know—" He is making this up as he goes along, but it feels right. Or at least he wants to believe it feels right. "I wish to know if you would like to go—" He clears his throat. "Somewhere."

"Where?"

"Anywhere. A trip. Can you take time off? Yes?" he asks.

"I might."

"Please," he says, and his voice sounds desperate to his ears. "Anywhere you wish." He shrugs. "Provence, Paris, the Pyrenees. Come with me."

She smiles broadly. Yet there is shyness to her body.

In a moment of boldness he holds his keys and jingles them in the air to tempt her. He is a fisherman, and this is his bait. "You can drive. Last chance. Please, Sophie."

It is the morning of Sophie's scheduled departure. Alex knocks on her door. "Not packed yet?" he asks.

"I don't feel so well."

"No?" He pulls the chair up to her bed and touches her forehead. She watches his face for signs of her illness, but he says nothing.

"What's going on, Soph?"

"It's just, I want to do the right thing."

"What do you mean?" Alex frowns.

"He's asked me to go with him."

"That son of a—I saw him go to her that night—" Alex is out of his chair and heading for the door.

"Alex." The ache in her voice stops him short. "I know. I saw them, too. But it's more than that. If I don't go . . . If I leave . . . If I go home . . . Someone might get hurt. I don't want to make the wrong decision. Not like the last time."

"Looks like you're the only one getting hurt." He paces the floor helplessly. "I don't understand, Sophie. What is it you're not telling me? Fill me in. I haven't gotten a chance to get to know you. You've been so consumed by this family. It doesn't make sense. You're the only one that's going to get hurt."

"I don't care about me," she says, sinking back into bed. "I don't care. Only, everything hurts. My skin, my eyes, the roots of my hair. It's like I feel everything."

He leans forward, elbows on legs, hands clasped. "Sophie," he says softly. "You're going to lose your job. You barely know this family. What do you care about them?"

"Please, Alex. Don't. I feel so dizzy. Leave me alone. Maybe I have vertigo."

"You haven't even sent your pictures in, have you?" When she doesn't respond he says, "I'll do it. Just—get up."

"Alex, I don't feel good. I swear. Really? You'd mail the pictures in for me? That's so good of you. I have the address. I'll pay you. Just let me sleep a little longer." It seems like all she wants to do lately is sleep.

"Oh no. I'm not leaving this room until you're packed." He fluffs a pillow, motions for her to get up, and eases it behind her back.

She sits up and leans back against the headboard, managing a smile for him. "I have to change into fresh clothes."

"Oh no. That skirt and T-shirt will do fine. You haven't complained, wearing it two days in a row. Come on. Up. Gather your things and I'll take the ferry with you to Rapallo and then we'll walk to the train station together."

It takes ten seconds to swoop up her belongings and drop them into her Samsonite. A sense of light-headedness overtakes her.

She is leaving another home again. Another family. A shaking starts at her ankles and ripples through her spine like a storm trying to pull a lamppost down. In two steps she is sitting on the bed. Alex gives her a look. "Get up."

Nicola is also packing when Sophie knocks to says her good-byes.
"You're leaving?"
"Ah, *principessa,* you depart now? My sister, she call me again."
"If you need a ride down to the pier, Alex and I can wait for you."
"No. No, do not wait for me. *Buon viaggio, bella, ah?*" She crosses the room to look into Sophie's eyes, holds her face in her hands and kisses each cheek. Sophie smiles and finds she cannot hate Nicola. That, in fact, it pains her to say good-bye to this woman who has brushed her hair each evening.

Sophie is gasping for air as she follows Alex. He turns, opens his arms, and hugs her, and in that moment, searching for selfish solace, she looks up and kisses him. A spark goes off between them but she buries it, and yet Alex's eyes linger on hers. Alex escorts her to the train station. He is friendly again, distant. Sophie wishes for a moment that he would be closer. But she is confused. The kiss was an accident, wasn't it?

Luciano is waiting at the train station with his suitcase. Her heart jumps. *He is waiting for me.* He turns as if not knowing what to expect and a smile dawns on his face. He jerks his chin up in hello to Alex, who just stares at him.

Both men wait to see what she will do next.

"Luciano, I can't come along. I have to return home," she says, nodding.

He nods, too; disappointment flickers across his face. A weight seems to descend on his shoulders. He asks, "Nicola. Did you see her at the villa? Did she say anything to you?"

Alex swears under his breath, but Sophie stays him with her hand.

"Yes," she whispers with a sad smile. "I saw her. She said not to wait."

Luciano searches her face, and she thinks she sees a spark of understanding. He nods and says, "Thank you, Sophie. Thank you." He kisses her hand and tries to shake Alex's, but Alex only turns away. Luciano nods again, scans the station one last time, and boards the train.

Alex will visit her in San Francisco, he promises. He will drive up from San Diego. He will introduce her to his friends. She thanks him quietly.

"You'll be all right," Alex says as she leans her head on his shoulder. He will not take advantage of the kiss. In fact, they act as if they had not shared one. "Next time you'll see it coming."

She ponders, on the plane ride home, the permanence and impermanence of things. Nicola and Armande and Luciano, a triangle spinning through space. Would their souls be born again someday only to repeat the cycle? Would Nicola be the man, and Luciano be born as the woman torn between the two?

She feels comforted by the fact that lightning will not strike twice. It had been the combination of the three of them: Luciano, Nicola, Armande, a hot spot of tension. Sophie had had the misfortune of being an orphaned star that fell into their orbit, changing the pull of gravity from Armande to herself, so that it became

Sophie, Luciano, and Nicola. Together they had formed a kind of fusion.

She will not let her mind drift to the last combination: Alex Colter, Sophie, and Luciano. She thinks of an article that had fascinated her as a child. A woman struck by lightning on her farm in North Carolina had lived, but for twelve months she had lost all sense of up and down. She could not walk. The woman had described it as feeling weightless. The way astronauts feel when they return to the earth's atmosphere. She'd had to relearn which way was up.

The sky turns gray, then purple as they progress through the air over St. Nazaire, beautiful electric slivers of silver white streaking downward through the sky and around the plane, followed by thunder. She falls asleep, a tiny star drifting over the Atlantic.

True to his word, Alex visits shortly after the *Cuisine* article runs. Their pictures and story complement each other. Alex brings along his younger brother, Ryan, the baby of the family. An exact replica of Alex but without the embarrassing memory of a shared kiss. Of a foolish heartache over another man. Ryan asks Sophie on a date, and she accepts. Two years later they will marry.

Alex Colter never mentions the kiss he shared with Sophie or that he thinks of her constantly, a constellation hundreds of light-years from his reach.

the BRUISER

"AND away goes trouble down the drain," he whistled and crooned the lyrics in his mind as he waited for the train. They goot in yer heid, those fuckin' jingles. Jeez, America, man. They thought ay everything. The images, too. It was no like ye were free from them either. That yin with the meaty detached hand in a white glove prancin' around trying tae sell ye on sloppy joes. That yin gave him nightmares fer a time. Fuckin' America, man. Ever' time he saw that commercial he wanted tae put the white glove in the microwave and watch it explode. Sing now, ye stupit fuck.

He shook his head and stepped ontae the train. And that, me lad, is why ye have tae take a holiday. Too many ay them jingles dancin' around in yer thoughts when ye should have lassies and ale, no some plump white glove dancin' and wigglin' its fingers. Bizarre. He looked left, then right and sat down in the back and lit a fag. In America ye couldnay smoke in certain public places. That's what he heard telt. Nay joke. Imagine that. People claiming the air around ye. He'd never make it there. He inhaled deeply and let the smoke oot through his nostrils. Worked like a charm in calming yer nerves. If he couldnay have a smoke at will he'd be a goner. Wound so tight ye could spin him like a top.

'Cause there were times, like searchin' fer the perfect word, when nothin' else will do ye except a smoke. Know what I'm sayin'?

He took another look around and sighed. He guessed it was too much tae ask that the AWOL would be on this train. Leave it tae the Man tae give him a screwin' jest as he's about tae take off on a holiday.

"Jest yin thing before ye go, Colin. I got a faver tae askt."

Ach, here it comes, he had said in his head. "What is it?"

"Ye know I wouldnay bother ye if it was no important."

"Let's have it then," Colin had said, rockin' back on his heels. That was his yin fault; otherwise he was a saint. He was an impatient bugger. Nay getting around it.

"I got two miner jobs fer ye since yer a-goin' there anyway." Pause.

And Colin had given him a look that said, Go on. I havenay goot all day.

"This bastard owes me a few quid."

"How much?" Colin asked, just tae keep it movin'.

"Well, that's no the problem anymore. The idiot jest left town withoot paying. So the money's no the problem. It was the problem, but no anymore. Jest bring him back."

"All the way back tae Glasgow?" Colin had exploded. "From Italy? And what about the Chunnel?!" He was no yin for explodin' on the Man, but even the Man knew he was askin' a wee much.

"Nay, nay. Jes give Ian a call when ye nab him and Ian will come down and pick him up at the station. I'll send Ian oot tae collect him. I jest can't afford tae have ye both so fer from me."

"Fair enough."

"Then there's another yin."

"Ah, for fuck's sake," Colin said.

"Come on. Just yin more. I'd be much obliged tae ye. I'll no forget it. Haven't I aye taken care of ye?"

"Let's have it then."

"This lass come around askin' me tae find her wean. A wee lad of six. Her husband took him tae Italy few months back. And the wean never returned. Word is he's staying wi' a certain fellow." Pause.

"Spill it."

"Well. Ye might run intae a wee problem. See, the auld man. Used tae be in the business. He's a rough yin. Won't let ye take the wean easily. Know what I'm sayin'?"

Colin had laughed then. "Yer fergettin' who I am, man."

"Nay. I'm no. I didn't name ye the Bruiser fer show. But don't get too comfortable when ye go tae collect the wee lad. The auld man might have somethin' up his sleeve yet. He was somethin' like ye in his day."

"A bruiser?" Colin asked. "Fancy that."

"No jest any bruiser. Yin ay the best."

"Well. Consider it done. I'm no seein' any unexpected setbacks. I should have 'em both tae ye by end ay next week. If ye say they're within close proximity tae yin another."

"They are."

"And I call Ian after I've located the wean as well?"

"Yes."

"And jest drop them off at the station tae gether?"

"Well, yes. If ye find them at same time. I'd be much obliged tae ye. Much obliged."

"Nay bother. Consider the transaction completed."

That was how their conversation had gone. So first things first. He had tae find the idiot who thought he could go AWOL on the Man. What a sorry fuck. Atrocious behavior. Ye make a debt. Ye pay it. Hear what I'm sayin'? Ye do no at all costs. Repeat: do no go AWOL on the Man. 'Cause he'll find ye. He'll send yin of his best mates. Like Colin. A.k.a. the Bruiser. The Man was patient to a fault. He'd let ye go on the installment plan if ye needed tae. If ye couldnay pay yer debt in yin lump sum.

Bad move. This lad was gony be yin miserable bastard when Colin was through with him. Colin shook his head. Fuckin' drainin' behavior. He would set aside a hidin' fer this bonghead such as the likes he'd never seen. These sometimers. Only come a knockin' on the Man's door when they needed a handoot. Didn't know how tae play within the rules ay the game. Tourists. That's what they were. As good as tourists.

Ah, well. Ye do yer job. Ye get it done. He would send someone ahead as well tae locate the woman's little boy so that it was a quick pickup. Then ye can start yer holiday proper. He was gony get one ay them foot massages at yin ay those beauty salons. His trainers had been bruising his feet ay late. But he was hard-pressed tae get rid ay the shoes. They'd cost him a pretty penny. Ferragamos.

"Well. Well. What have we here? A wee bit of action going on?"

He was watchin' an Italian kid across the aisle. Watchin' by no really watchin'. Ye stay in the game long enough, ye can't help but catch things. The kid was watchin' every yin. Good-lookin' lad. Countin'. Listenin'. A natural. Nay bad. There. He's made his target. Was he workin' alone? Colin doubted it. Kid was too clean-lookin'. No a bad technique. There were better ways to do it. Amateur. But no bad. He's seen worse. Probably gony get up any minute and notify the rest of his crew. Probably waitin' for him in the next compartment.

The lad stood and strode down the aisles tae the next compartment. Colin chuckled at himself. Ye've goot it like nay yin else has. Yer a natural, Colin Fergusen. Nay doubt about it. Ye can pick 'em a mile away. Like child's play. They probably owned these lines. Colin had heard about it. Rival gangs on the other lines. Bound to cross paths sometime. But that was no his problem.

The conductor came by and asked him tae take his shoes off ay the seats. Colin glared at the man, snorted, and took them off. The train had gone about two stops when the smelly curtains came undone and started smacking him in the face. Fer a second he snatched them in his yin hand. But the air was blowin' hard. It was too hot tae close the windows. All of them were open. He took a deep breath. Relax. Doctor told him in order tae keep his blood pressure down he needed tae practice anger management. Easy now. He breathed deeply and took out a small vial labeled *Inner Calm*. The Doc had suggested aromatherapy among his other alternatives. There ye go, Colin. Deep breath now, ay? Lovely. When he was through he screwed the cap back on and dropped the vial calmly intae his shirt pocket.

Then he unclenched his fists and took out his switchblade, cut both curtains down, and tossed them out the window. He looked around tae see if there were any protestors. Nay yin said a thing. A couple ay people got up and moved tae the next car. The next time the conductor came by he did a double take and Colin graced him wi' a beatific smile. He got off in Rapallo and went tae see about his target.

So this AWOL was known tae gamble in Monaco and hang out in the Italian Riviera. Particularly at a café in Rapallo. Standard practice when yer on the lam. Play in yin place, stay in another. Colin stepped down from the train. His trousers were sweaty from the ride. His suspenders hangin' down around his hips. His white shirt was goin' tae pieces. His fault. He'd gotten a little vain ay late. Dressing up like a dandy fer the lassies.

He studied his black hair in the shop window. Needed a trimming. The beard as well. Had tae go. The both ay them. He ran a hand through his thick crop ay hair. He could be startin' his holiday by now if it werenay fer this idiot he had tae track down.

Fuckin' annoying behavior. He'd topple him yin jest fer good measure.

The bastard's name was Eamon Thackeray. What kind ay name was that? Obviously his da was a dandy. His ma probably a good Scottish lass who got her panties soiled. Well, nay wonder the kid was daft. Bad start from the beginning.

Around about five o'clock Colin was gettin' a wee irked. Nothin'. Nay information flowin' from any source whatsoever. He was dyin' fer a lager, but he had a job tae dae. He called the Man. He whistled a tune as the phone rang. Oh, I wish I were an Oscar Mayer Weiner . . . He smiled intae the phone. He remembered that yin from when he was jest a wean. Clever people. Twenty years later and ye were still singin' the medleys in yer head. Instant craving fer a hot dog. Fantastic. It was like hypnotics.

The Man came on the phone. "Did ye find him this quick?"

"Eh? Ye kiddin'? I'm comin' up dry. There's nothin' tae be found here. Are ye sure he's been skulkin' here? Who's yer informant?"

"Thin Lizzy."

"Huh." Colin stuck his lower lip out and nodded. Lizzy was a good yin. Trustable. "Well. Either he's got wind ay me comin' or he's invisible. But I'll keep checkin'. Ye said Rapallo, right?"

"Yes."

"All right." He scratched his head. "I'm goin' tae put some food in my belly, see what I come up with."

"Colin, ye there?"

"Yes?"

"Look, if ye don't find him by sundown, go ahead and start yer holiday. I'll find somebody else tae look fer him. Jest bring me back that wean I ask ye fer. It shouldn't be too hard tae find him."

"Aye. All right then." He hung up and smiled. He was ready
fer his time off. Normally he would have fought it tooth and nail.
Nay. I'll hunt him down fer ye. Won't rest till I dae and all that
Hollywood bullshit. But nay, yer body knew when it was time
tae rest. Even bruisers needed tae rest sometime. Rejuvenate the
body. He was happy tae take a break. Let the fool Thackeray go
fer another few months. It was no like he was big-time. He was
jest a little fly in the Man's ointment. The Man would send
someone else tae capture him. Probably Ian. Aye, he would give it
till sundown. If he couldnay find him, then he couldnay find him
and all he had tae do was look for the wee lad tae send back.

He could dae for a lager and a hot dog. America, man. Get in
yer blood and stayed in. A million miles away and they had their
tunes chasin' ye halfway across the globe. They did have it all,
though. They did everythin' big, capital fuckin' *B*. Maybe no the
green green valleys, maybe no the pubs, but everythin' else. Casi-
nos in the desert. Polar bears in the zoo. Humvees in the inner
city. Lookin' like a lunar craft landin'. Outrageous the last. Vulgar
exercise ay coin. Was it really necessary tae have an auto that big?
Everyin' wantin' tae be like Mad Max. Like if there were a riot
ye'd be haulin' yer own private Humvee ower the bodies tae get
tae yer house. Was that it?

Could ye blame them, though? Producin' grade A movies like
Marathon Man. That stuck intae yer imaginings until ye were
Mad Max. Ye were the Marathon Man. Legendary. Colin had felt
a kinship with Hoffman's older brother. He was the shite. He
had a beef wi' the endin', though. He wouldnay have ended it
like that. The man was too good, he wouldnay have fallen fer that
"Come closer" bullshit from the auld fart and then the stabbin'. It
jest didnay wash. After he had escaped a car bombing. After
he had fought off that yin in his bedroom who tried tae choke
him wi' a wire. He was just gony fall for that? Nay fuckin' likely.

But he gave it four stars; would have been a fiver if nay for the botched killin' ay the older brother. It still gave him chills, that line, "Is it safe?"

He chuckled. Ower the top. Jest ower the top.

He passed by a dance-shop window and perused the exercise videos and training equipment on display. He'd been meaning tae take up yoga. America had a leg up on that yin. His mates had laughed at him when he mentioned it, but the hell wi' it. He was a believer. A month ago he had hurt his back during a wee game ay fitball. Jammed his spine right intae his hips. He was a miserable bastard sittin' on the sofa surfin' the satellite when he caught a bunch ay grown men proselytizin' on the merits ay the "auld art."

First testimony was from a marathon runner. It had improved his time. "Shut yer gob, ye fancy runner," he had shouted. But then that yin from an Ultimate Fighting Championship had sold him. A wrestler who looked every bit a strappin' lad. And Colin had thought, Huh, maybe. So when they flashed back tae the classroom instructions he had scoffingly tried some ay the maneuvers fer his back. He was sweatin' like a sow when he was through. And he would have easily dismissed it if no fer the next day, when miracles ay miracles. His backache was gone and he felt a certain flexibility and resilience to his spine.

The routine fit intae his plans. And that plan was called longevity. Let the cunts laugh. He'd be bringin' his toes tae his mouth like a newborn when they were auld in their bones like brittle toffee. See who laughed then.

"Can I help you, *Signore*?" a lass greeted him.

"I was lookin' fer yin ay them yogi mats."

"Yoga mats. Yes. What color?"

"Any color will dae, darlin'."

He was lookin' at the special bags fer the mats when he saw the lass was ringin' him up a canary-yellow mat.

"Ah, miss. Any color but that. Dae ye have something more manly? How about we go wi' the dark blue yin."

The lass shrugged. "That is why I asked. And you wish to purchase the bag, too?"

"Bag?" Colin asked, holdin' the zip-up container that looked fer all the world like a giant reefer carrier.

"Yes. It will keep your mat clean. You see? You fold sticky part of mat on the inside. Like this, eh? And then you put into bag to keep clean."

He shrugged, takin' down a black yin in his hands. If he strapped it across his chest he could look like those auld *Kung Fu* TV episodes wi' David Carradine. "Aye, add this tae the check."

When she brought out the wide-legged drawstring pants in his size Colin took yin look at them and decided it was time tae go.

He needed a lager and he needed yin now. He stopped at the nearest café. He couldnay get over it. In Italy the pubs were called cafés and the cafés were called bars. Go figure. Everything ending in *o*'s and *a*'s. Enough tae make yer head spin.

He belched loudly in the dark of the café. Everyone sitting outside under the umbrellas. He wasnay used tae it. All this sun. Some pretty lassies out here. He checked around once more, askin' all the right people. But nay sign ay yin Eamon Thackeray. The wee bastard took his AWOLs seriously. Fine with Colin. Sun was settin' in a few more hours. Probably around ten. What with the long summer days and all. He went tae see Thin Lizzy.

"Come back later and maybe I'll have something fer ye," Thin Lizzy had said. "I'll send some scouts out. Fact-findin' mission."

"Who ye got left tae ask? Maybe I could talk tae them."

"Nay, I'll do it. These three are tough ones if they doan like ye."

"Lizzy, man. That's what I'm here fer. Who're these scouts?"

Thin Lizzy seemed to blush down tae the roots of his hair.

"What is it?" Colin asked. "Who's yer reliable source?"

"Well. There are these three widows, see?"

The three widows stared at Colin like feral cats. They sat serenely on three foldin' chairs in front of the Hotel Rapallo. He wasnay fallin' fer that silver-haired yin wi' the sweet smile. "So, do ye have any information on a man by name of Roberto Romano? He drives the ferry. Ah'm an auld mate of his."

"Such a handsome boy, no?" the silver-haired yin named Clara, asked the other two.

"So ye doan have any knowledge of this man. That what yer sayin'?" He shifted uncomfortably. This one reminded him of his maw.

"Why don't you turn around for me, eh?" Clara asked.

"What?" Colin asked.

Clara gestured with a circle of her fingers. "Slowly. Turn for us."

"All right then," Colin blubbered. "I'll be back in a couple ay hours. On the off chance he may show." He straightened himself and walked stiffly away from the three women, tryin' tae keep dignified as they giggled behind him. He checked his watch. Six o'clock. He'd return around eight. If he hadnay found Thackeray by then he would wipe his hands clean ay it. He'd given it a good shot.

He walked back tae a beauty parlor he'd seen earlier. He felt like a dandy, but who gave a shite? These people knew what they were doin' in these fancy establishments. And it was no like he could go tae a barbershop and ask that they give his feet a rub-down. No like he would want yin from a man anyway. And he was no in the mood for yin ay those special places where the women came around in short skirts. He liked good girls. He liked tae eyeball the bad. But mostly, truth be told, he liked the good girls. Class act and all.

The establishment was called Molto Bella, and the door had a little cowbell above it so that it rung when ye walked in. He brushed his hair back and looked out from under his brows. There were some lovely lassies strutting aboot. Fancy-dressed clientele. He liked the place already. Long, tanned legs crossed, readin' magazines on their laps. Perfume jest waftin' in the air.

"*Buona sera, Signore,*" a woman greeted him at the door. "How can I help you?"

"Good evening. I'm in need ay a hair wash and a shave. Also I'd like tae have my feet rubbed. And maybe throw in the back fer good measure."

"*Sì,*" the woman said and gestured fer him tae have a seat.

He nodded and sat down. He crossed his legs like a man and wiggled his foot. When it was his turn a redhead came out and nodded tae him. A Scottish lass if he ever saw yin. Now if she opened her mouth and spoke in Italian, he'd fall head ower. Things were lookin' up already. She greeted him in perfect English. He supposed they'd sent her out special so she could speak tae him correctly. That's what he meant about these types ay establishments. It cost ye somethin'. But it was well worth the money. Safeguarded ye from any bad experiences. They did right by ye. All the fixin's.

"So they tell me you want a shampoo and a shave. And also a whole-body massage?"

"Nay. Ye got most ay it correct. But I'm partial tae jest my feet and my lower back. I get ticklish anywhere else. Can't explain it."

"All right," she said with a voice ay authority, checking off things on her clipboard and erasing others. "Come this way please."

Lass, I'd follow ye tae the ends of this earth. Yellow-green eyes. Even more strikin' if she would color her hair black. Set off the eyes even more. Listen tae yerself. Who are ye now that Scottish red's nay good for ye? Who are ye now, Elvis? Decidin' on a lass's hair color. That was a blunder, though, wasnay it? The black too black for fair Priscilla. Made her tae look like Elvira, mistress ay horror. Ye've got tae know when tae leave well enough alone.

But this yin before him. She was a nice sight tae follow. Mentally he was rubbing his hands tagether. Her arse left him gasping for breath. That was the kind ay arse he could give a good slamming tae. This was a nice development.

"Ower here?" he asked, pointin' tae a chair with a tilt back so that yer head laid nicely intae the washbasin.

"That's right."

"Where ye from, lass?" he asked.

"California."

"What ye doin' so fer away from home?"

"Exactly. Far, far away from home. Know what I mean?"

"Aye." He nodded. Broken home, probably. But he was no yin tae pry. He knew all about broken homes. His da, God rest his soul, was a wild yin. Always givin' Colin and his brothers a good hidin' when his mood gone sour. He once took Colin on a ride along tae give another man a hidin' fer directin' a few lecherous words at their ma. Fired a few shots at the man. The man got away but Colin's ear had been so close he heard a ringin' in it fer months after. And at first he kept thinkin' it was the phone and he had kept pickin' it up. They thought he had gone daft, but as it turned out he'd only gone temporarily deaf.

"Where you from?" she asked, then laughed. "Lemme guess. Scotland?"

"No much of a stretch, eh?"

"No. I had a boyfriend from there once. Half Scottish, at least. I see him every once in a while, but he's not marriage material—know what I mean?"

"Aye."

"Eamon's father's English, though."

"What was that?" Colin almost sat up, but she pushed him down gently and threw a cloth around him. Was this some kind ay joke?

"You're going to get all wet."

He opened his eyes tae have a look at her. Tae gauge if she was joking. Make sure she wasn't up tae any tricks and liable tae slit his throat. But nay, she was just chattin' along wi' her mate beside her, washin' some other lass's hair.

"So Eamon has not called?" the lass next tae them asked. *Tsk. Tsk.* "Bad man. You must not be so kind to him when he returns. You always take him back." The woman waggled a comb as she told her client tae sit up and began combin' through her hair.

Maybe Eamon was no so stupid after all. Maybe he had goot word ay Colin lookin' for him. But this quickly? Or maybe the Man was not pleased with his work at all and he was settin' Colin up tae finish him off. Finished by a girl. No likely. Colin snorted. That would never happen. He was the Man's right hand. Still, he couldnay help feelin' like he was on *Candid Camera.*

Had Eamon Thackeray's girl just fallen right on his lap? Work, man. It bloody followed ye everywhere. Ah, well.

"So yer no seein' this man anymore?" Colin asked, givin' her the auld twinkle wi' his eyes. He could turn on the charm when needed. Had a lass in every port, like that Ricky Nelson song. *And in every port I own the heart of at least one lovely girl.* He was no yin tae brag, but he'd been told a time or two that he was no hard tae look at. So he turned it on a wee bit when it served his purpose. Other times he could make a man feel like the devil himself were after him. It all depended on who was on the receivin' end ay the party.

"No." She blushed as she leaned ower tae shampoo his hair. God, but her fingers felt good goin' through his scalp. She was workin' them in wee circles, gettin' his lather up. Her chest just inches from his face. A little tae the right and with a heft from him she could be lyin' on top ay him. When she finished shavin' his beard and trimmin' his hair down tae a decent length, she took a step back and grinned.

"Well, what a surprise," she said. "You didn't tell me you were halfway decent looking." But her face said he was more than halfway. More than half. Ye still got it, Colin.

"Maybe we can skip the foot rub and I can take ye tae dinner?"

"Maybe you can take me to dinner and I'll give you the foot rub after." She smiled.

Colin grinned. Dubious man. Dubious if it werenay so coincidental. Too easy. He might be able tae mix business with pleasure yet.

After an expensive dinner and two bottles ay nice Italian wine, it was easy pickin's. Ye just line 'em up and shoot 'em down. She told him everything. She was prime for it, though, bein' as angry as she was. A boozer in waitin'. Eamon had pished his chance away the other evening. She'd caught him romancin' a brunette in Monaco. So she'd left early. It was no as if she'd caught him in bed—he'd only been talkin', but same difference in her book. He was due back tonight. He always came crawlin' back with presents galore. Colin almost wished he had more time with the lass. He was no one tae take advantage ay a drunk. He liked his women sober, so they were part ay the action and no bystanders. He bought her another bottle fer good measure and took her home.

He sighed and looked at her smilin' face. He could jest sit down and pretend she'd no told him any ay it. Temptin'. Temptin'. He could take her somewhere else and they could live happily ever after. At least fer the duration of his one-month sabbatical. Och, shite. He could no do it. That was why he was so good at his job. He told her tae rest, sang her a little melody, and gave her another glass until she was down fer the count. The two ay 'em would wait for Eamon. Surprise!

He was watchin' television when the latch turned. Colin put on his knuckles. He could fight bare-knuckle, nay problem. But he had his long-term plans ay stayin' in the business tae consider. So the thought had come tae him earlier this year tae start lookin' out fer his hands. Necessary precautions. Fer longevity. If ye were a lifeguard, ye put on yer sunscreen, right? If ye were a welder, ye put on yer mask. If yer business was bruisin' people up, ye wore yer knuckles.

The first thing that came in the door was a present wrapped in a blue ribbon. Colin shook his head on the other side ay the door and waited fer the idiot tae step in.

"Love?" asked the voice.

Colin almost tapped his foot. Let's get on wi' it, ye stupit fuck.

The guy obviously heard the television and stepped half his body intae the room. Colin slammed the door on the first half ay him, then pulled him in by the jacket collar. Nice leather. And shoved him against the dresser. "Nice ay ye tae stop by, Eamon." He had to laugh. The bastard had red hair, jest like his lass. They must have made a pair, the two ay them.

"What have ye done tae me lass?" Eamon looked quickly tae the bed, where his lass was conked out.

"Never ye mind. Have a seat."

"The bitch. She set me up."

"Are ye no hearin' correctly?"

Eamon took a desperate look at the door. Colin shook his head and smiled.

"What are ye wantin'?"

"Aye, isn't that a kicker? Do ye honestly think yer in a position tae ask? Ye take things from the Man. Ye approach him like a dimwit wi' yer hand out, he blesses ye wi' his generosity, and then ye skip town on him? And ye have the gall tae ask what it is I want?" At the mention ay the Man, the lad started tae shake.

"The Man? He sent ye?"

"Nay, Santi Claus sent me. I'm jest usin' his name in vain. Have a seat, ye idjit."

"What dae ye want?"

"Ye know the score. I'm tired. Gather yer things. Yer goin' home."

The bastard made a break fer the window. Colin rolled his eyes. Och, ye could almost call it. It happened ever' time. He let the man get tae where he was hangin' by his hands, his foot above the fire escape, and then he held ontae one hand and banged the window down several times. Loud yelping ensued. "Ye comin' up or will ye be leavin' yer fingers behind?" Colin asked. He had been a wrestler in school and it came in handy lots ay times, the good grip.

"Up. I'm comin' up."

"Really? You'll no be hangin' out for a wee minute longer?"

"Nay. Let me up."

"All right. No that I don't trust ye, but I'll just be holdin' this blade ower yer hand fer good measure till yer nice and settled in. All right? Try any funny business and yer hand gets shanked. Got that?"

"Aye."

He tied the man up and called Ian on the phone. "I've got Thackeray. He tried tae make a break fer it. So I cracked a rib. But he's a yelper, so I doan think the train is such a good idea. He's no gony come along quiet, like a man. Know what I'm sayin'? Better ye send someone over tae pick him up. And leave the girl alone. She helped me out. What's that? Aye. Thank ye. I'll be enjoyin' it soon as I finish this yin last favor. Tell the Man he owes me a foot rub."

the three widows of signor alberto moretti

afteR the reading of Alberto Moretti's will, each of his three widows reacted differently. Nenette took an extra-long swim at the bottom of the lake. Clara took to her bed, and Anna Margareta laughed hysterically.

They thought nothing of Alberto's request that his will be read in public. He had been something of a show-off, and so the three women dressed in their best designs and appeared at the local courthouse to hear the reading. To see who owned what and who would have to be dealt with if one received a possession that the other wanted above all else. The evening before the trial—er, reading of the will—Clara dreamt that everything they owned was to be sawed in three parts and in the end they would have nothing. She went to the courthouse riding beside her two rivals, ready to do battle but outwardly demure.

Alberto, of course, split his three estates and his grand mansion above Rapallo evenly among the three women, and each was more than satisfied, but he had one last request before each could claim the designated property. He challenged his three wives to produce a new design *collezione* superior to the ones found in the Museo del Merletto and to be housed eventually in the mansion they currently inhabited, which was to be converted into the Museo Alberto in honor of his memory. His wording to the grand turnout of one hundred local residents was such: "And so, dear friends and neighbors, for many years of your loyal business and friendship I give you something to remember me by three years from hence. Your very own lace and design museum. The Museo Alberto."

The audience, of course, clapped and whistled, but they walked away whispering, "What did he mean 'your very own'? We already have the Museo del Merletto!" Still, they were eager to watch the friendly competition between the three widows and to see what the talented women would produce.

The widows seemed relieved by the request. "Even in death he thinks of us," Clara said to her neighbors, though her smile was strained.

"Yes, how kind," Anna Margareta retorted.

Nenette, the most voracious reader of the three, exclaimed, "Why, it is like one of those Poe novels. A wish from the grave!"

With brave smiles they left the courthouse and returned home immediately to begin their new designs. Each one tried to rally some form of teary determination, the kind one gets when saluting the flag or hearing the national anthem. But nothing.

Each morning in the riviera town of Rapallo, Italy, the three widows make their pilgrimage arm in arm from their mansion in San Michele to the Hotel Rapallo below, to sit on the front deck and watch life as it passes in front of the turnaround.

On this morning, Clara, Alberto's first wife, waves at the hotel manager, Romeo senior, as he greets them with a *buon giorno,* then brings a hand quickly to her mouth as an impolite burp escapes her lips. *"Scusatemi."* She blushes at her two companions. "I am not quite myself today. My stomach pains me."

"I am experiencing the same thing. Is it a rolling type of cramp?" Anna Magareta asks. She was Alberto's second wife, named like the Swedish-American actress with the same strawberry-blond hair, though it is colored now, and the same pointy breasts, though it takes heavy-duty support to keep them up.

"No," Nenette, the French Senegalese and third wife, answers, averting her eyes and cringing inwardly. She hadn't meant to poison them. She loved them best, above all, but at times she was overcome by such a wave of compulsion she could not control herself. Last night when the cook had turned his back she had snuck into the kitchen and sprinkled the concoction over their evening meal.

At the last minute she had held back from the amount necessary to make the ingredients fatal. She could not go through with it. She always held back and always felt guilty. As a penance she had matched them almost bite for bite. If they were to die from her hand, then so should she. These women were like her sisters. Even if she wanted desperately to be free of them. Sometimes the strongest prisons were the ones created by the people you loved the most.

Today they sit beneath the orange trees and wave to signora Pucci. "*Buon giorno,* Elena, how are you today?" the angelic Clara asks.

"With such a beautiful day as this, who can be unhappy?" the woman asks.

"Oh, was I not just saying that very thing?" Clara asks. The other two widows give patronizing smiles and wait until the young woman is outside hearing distance before they start in on her person.

"Her hair is thinning. I can see her scalp. Did you see?" Anna Margareta asks.

"Bony hips. She has a boy's body. Really, she has nothing to keep her husband with," Clara agrees. "Poor thing."

Nenette simply grunts.

They point these things out though the young woman has perfectly fine breasts and naturally healthy hair. They continue to poke fun at her face, her bowlegs, and her lack of style until their next victim approaches. The three of them are inseparable. Surprising, really, when you consider that they are the bitterest of enemies.

Though signor Moretti has long since kicked the bucket—or, as signora Clara likes to say, "gone kaput"—they are still in competition for his attention. For just a little way east, in the Parco Casale, stands the Museo del Merletto—the Lace Museum of Rapallo—within which resides over fourteen hundred rare and precious handmade laces, alongside donated *abiti da sera,* evening gowns made of organza, silk, and satin, from wealthy families dating from the sixteenth century through the twentieth.

Also included are some of the widows' finest works, created for signor Alberto Moretti's lace shop, the Manifattura Moretti, during its heyday. The *collezione* is truly a sight to behold. The townspeople assume it is a grand accomplishment for each of Alberto's widows to have her designs displayed in such a manner, but the three widows think this an insult.

"The thought! Of having our designs stuffed in a little museum among lesser works," Clara said when the museum first opened. She was greatly offended.

"I could make a finer tapestry than that court-jester amateur scroll," Anna Margareta said at the reading of Alberto's will. She was referring to the *Commedia dell'Arte,* housed within the *museo,* though truthfully she wasn't so sure. The delicate lace panel, measuring approximately eight feet by one foot, was spectacular, with its comedic scene of court life, kings, noblemen, and ladies-in-waiting. The minute she made that declaration, a ten-ton weight descended on her chest. Often she finds herself wondering why she had boasted such a thing, and in front of so many people!

"Do you remember how bitterly we used to compete for Alberto's approval?" Nenette will ultimately ask. And the three of them will laugh as if it were so long ago, when, in fact, the rivalry is more potent now than ever.

For two years they have been creating designs to rival and surpass those housed in the museum. Or so they say. Some have been more productive than others. Their unified goal has been to show the entire community of Rapallo the talent of Moretti's three widows. Individually, secretly, their goal has been to outdo one another.

"It shall be my final tribute," Clara said, "to *my* Alberto's memory."

Since the public reading of his will, the townspeople have been waiting with bated breath for the grand opening of the first wing of Alberto's own lace museum. Today as they sit beneath the shade of the Hotel Rapallo's generous awning, the *polizia* signor Vespucci and his young wife approach. "*Signoras,* how goes the new *collezione?*"

"Patience, patience," Clara answers, but once the Vespuccis are past hearing distance, she turns to the other two widows and asks, "Do these people have nothing else to look forward to?" Though she would be offended if they did not ask with such anticipation.

Anna Margareta has retreated into herself; the thought of competing with the eight-foot panel at the Museo del Merletto winds around her neck, threatening to choke her with its scenes of laughing characters. Still she manages to throw one stab in the couple's direction. "It is about time he let her out of the house. She is as pale as a ghost!"

"Yes, he'd do better to take his wife out more often than spend his day harassing the poor ferry driver around town, waiting for him to slip up," Nenette says. For she is very fond of their ferry driver, though he is an ex-convict. She knows he takes sole care of his grandson and always has a kind word for her, though Clara orders her never to return his greeting of hello when they board his ferry to Portofino.

Nenette has become the spokesperson of their group by default, because Clara and Anna Margareta grow shrewish early in the day from answering the various inquiries by tourists regarding the direction of the old *museo*. She points them down the pier, adding, "But return in a year and we will have a finer *museo* for you to visit. Remember the name: the Museo Alberto."

The early evenings are reserved for the variety shows in the hotel lobby, where the night clerk serves them grappa from the adjoining restaurant. The three sit before the television and giggle and shout to the man who resides in the television box. They love to watch the host of *Viva Italia*—a takeoff on American shows like *Lawrence Welk* and *Hee Haw*. Various women parade around in scant bikini-type clothing and bend over to allow the host to smack their rumps.

Clara, of late, once the conservative of the three, has been overcome with such passion at the sight of the host as to throw off her shawl and shout lewd, inviting comments, followed by a jiggling of her meager breasts. In her mind the host of *Viva Italia* hears her wolf whistles through the glass screen, and blushingly his eyes tell her, *Later, Clara, save that for later* as he unflinchingly continues with his banter to the live audience. She likes to blame her actions on the grappa, but the other two widows know better.

The show's host is named Giuseppe, a twin to Fabio, the same Italian whose image has graced the American romance novels that Clara loves to read but vehemently denies, though they all know she stuffs the books beneath her mattress.

The three widows gather and giggle around the television set, oblivious to any of the hotel guests waiting impatiently for the Internet, which cannot be plugged in while the television is on. "Only one plug," the night clerk, Romeo junior, usually tells the guests. "The *signore* are watching the television. They are guests here, too. I have no control."

But the truth is, they are not guests. And the two night clerks, the young, handsome one, whom they like to make blush, named Romeo, and his father, Romeo senior, continue to perpetuate the lie, for they are quite fond of the three widows, who flirt with them both unmercifully.

"Ah, what I would not do to place kisses along his chest," Nenette sighs.

"Who?" Clara asks, winking at the young clerk. "Giuseppe on the screen or Romeo?"

"You are bad, Clara." Romeo junior shakes his head.

On Thursday evening behind the Guardia Banco, just off of the main boardwalk, the Piazza da Mare, which by day is filled with shoppers, has shut down to host a live band. The three widows walk down the street, blocks from the hotel, shoulder to shoulder, handbags swinging from their elbows, to the plaza. They sit in the folding chairs and watch the young and old alike dance beneath the stars, and together the three take a simultaneous sigh and remember Alberto.

"Alberto took me to many of these soirees. And the *abiti da sera* he designed for me with the long trains, and the others that showed off my delicate waist"—Clara holds both hands to her waist, mindful not to dig her hands in too close or hold her breath too long—"placed me above the rest."

168 / Tess Uriza Holthe

Clara was the first wife. She was Alberto's first seamstress, and the lace designs she hand-sewed were beyond compare at the time. This was before Anna Margareta, but more of that later.

Clara was the daughter of Alberto's rival, signor Torino. Alberto searched far and wide for someone with Clara's talent to produce his precise designs, but there was no one. Only Clara, raised by nuns in hallowed halls, could replicate with austere elegance the delicate strands of flowered borders that Alberto drew: the kerchief of oleander trees, the scroll of roses, tablecloths bordered with magnolias, and the napkins finely stitched with lavender bouquets and scalloped edges.

He met her quite by accident on a walk up to San Michele to clear his head. He had his hands behind his back and his mind in the clouds, cataloging his various designs as he trudged uphill, following the paved road along the coastline.

Clara spotted him immediately as she descended the steep hill and decided the walk was a ruse just to meet her. There was no sidewalk along the other side of the street, and so she stayed her course and decided to face the thief. She had seen Alberto studying her father's designs at their store windows five days in a row, and on the sixth day, when he had not come for a visit, several choice pieces had been stolen overnight. As Alberto soldiered up the hill, his brow dotted with sweat, without (so he said) seeing her, Clara's blue eyes narrowed and then rolled with exasperation.

"Who does the buffoon think he is fooling?"

If he wanted to bump into her, she would give him a bumping into he would not soon forget. At the moment that Alberto made contact with Clara's left shoulder he was contemplating a pinwheel design in his head. No one had yet created such a design, and perhaps each panel, if he broke it into quarters, could depict a different season. With trees. Yes! A tree of life with . . . but the idea and the following conclusions flew from his mind like a bird of paradise, never to return, the moment Clara swung her shoulder so hard he fell into the nearby bushes as she kept walking. "Help!" Alberto shouted, thinking he had been apprehended by thieves. When he realized it was merely a woman, he stood and flicked the branches from his coat. "Not even an 'Excuse me'?" he sputtered, grabbing on to the offending bush for support. Clara turned on him, her eyes full of contempt. "It is you who needs to apologize for bumping into me and for stealing my father's designs!"

When the halo of stars around his eyes cleared, Alberto beheld the foolish woman in a haze. "I excuse myself? For *your* clumsiness? And what is this about stealing your father's designs? Do you know who I am?" He fixed her with a glare. "I am Alberto Moretti, you churlish—" His sight stabilized at this point. "Oh, signorina Torino." He blinked at the sight of her.

"Hmph." She folded her arms and tapped her foot, taking his measure with one eye closed. She tried not to notice how dashing he looked, standing slender and dark-haired before her, his face full of apology.

"Truly my apologies," he said. "Have I hurt you? May I take you to lunch?"

"No."

"My house, it is just up the way. A refreshment perhaps?"

"No."

"Please. What can I do?"

Ordinarily, Clara was not this rude, but since she was certain Alberto was a thief, albeit a good-looking one, and since she was not used to cursing, she said, "You can stuff your hand up a pig's behind, you pig!"

He blinked. "A pig's behind?" But she had called him a pig. Did she then mean for him to stick his hand up his own behind? In his confusion he thought perhaps she meant a type of exercise she herself performed to ease her tired hands. She was, after all, a seamstress of the highest caliber, and with genius came a few eccentricities. He had a few of his own. "Is that what you do?" he asked in awe.

"Animal! You are not getting your hands on my body or our designs."

A fixation with the hands, he thought.

She was about to stalk away with much-affronted indignity when she slipped on some of his sketches, which lay scattered on the cement. Fabulous designs were picked up and swirled suddenly by the ocean breeze and over the cliffs. She watched in horror as the designs flew away, then she lunged here and there, only to catch a corner before it slipped from her grasp. She dropped to the ground, hands splayed to save what she could, and he shouted in alarm. Whatever happened, he must care for her prized hands, which would bring his designs to life.

"Your designs," she stuttered.

"Your hands," he answered, and noticing her concern he saw a means to gain sympathy and took it. "I was working on one in specific when you—when I bumped into you. I may have lost the idea forever." He gave her a troubled frown of despair. They were indeed beautiful designs but replaceable, for Alberto had a million in his head. He noted belatedly that she was possessed of the blackest head of hair and very pretty. She had an entourage of suitors following behind her at a respectable distance. When he glanced at them, they studied the oak trees, or their shoes; one gazed out to the port; one even went so far as to lick his finger and raise it, as if gauging the temperature and direction of the wind.

Clara was horrified. She knew what a designer's sketches meant to him from her father's own rantings, and tantrums, and she began to weep. At least ten designs had flown into the sea; three were ripped to shreds beneath her shoes; and five more had been stuffed slyly into the pockets of her suitors—for sale, no doubt, later, on the black market.

"I am so sorry," she sobbed. After all, the stolen pieces from her father's collection had been mediocre at best. Those she'd glimpsed as they flew away were masterpieces.

But Alberto was not concerned. "Your hands, my dear. Your hands." For her hands were scraped, and her pointer finger already swelling. He scooped her up as she protested and carried her the rest of the way to his villa.

"But your designs," she said, looking over his shoulder.

"To hell with them," he said as Clara made the sign of the cross.

At his home with the bay windows and views of the port and the town of Rapallo below, he laid her carefully on a soft sofa of tan suede and maple and proceeded to carefully clean and tend to her cuts. To Clara's astonishment, which was great already, he disappeared for a moment into the next room and returned with a blue bottle of French lavender oil and proceeded to massage each hand. She felt twenty years younger (and she was only twenty-one). She fell asleep, and when she awoke she was in love. And so was Alberto, with her hands.

The love for Clara as a person came much later for Alberto. After he had watched her stitch the borders of lilies and bougainvillea, the rectangular tablecloths for a proper Italian table, the handkerchiefs and veils. She had such a pure, clean form that his designs took on a different texture, a higher level through her hands. Always he insisted that she keep to the sparse, traditional form of white on white, unless he specifically designated color. It highlighted her talent, he explained. None of that newfangled colored thread for his Clara.

They married, of course, and he was never more in love with

Clara than the day he met his second wife. Anna Margareta was a bombshell in her youth. Redheaded, dressed in her own designs. When Clara first saw the woman, she knew she was in trouble. But her memory of the younger Anna Margareta is jolted as the present-day Anna Margareta rises from her chair and bolts into an alleyway.

"Anna," Clara calls after Anna Margareta. "Where are you going? Come see the Chef Girabaldi and his wife. They approach and oh! Here comes her lover, her brother-in-law, Luciano, across from us, sitting contented as a well-fed cat. Why, I almost expect him to lie on the ground and stretch out his belly."

"How can you know for sure if they have slept together?" Nenette asks, skeptical of Clara's gossip. For she knows that more often than not the stories originate from Clara herself. And the most frightening thing is that usually the stories come true.

"How can you not see it? Luciano is younger, handsomer than his brother. How can Nicola not have an affair with him? And besides, Nicola once belonged to him. Anna, you are missing everything," Clara barks.

"Just a moment," Anna Margareta calls out in the alley, stuffing her bra with two of her powder puffs. Anna Margareta finds it harder and harder to keep up with the younger upstarts visiting the Thursday evening dances. So she always brings along a little help. When she's done she shoves her way through the crowd to sit beside Clara. "Where is she?"

Clara looks at Anna Margareta's bust. Is she crazy? A portion of her pink powder puff peers out over her bosom like a gopher from its hole. *Tsk, tsk,* she thinks secretly. It has come to this now. Her once resilient bombs have become like mush. How the mighty have fallen. Clara shakes her head as Anna Margareta claps her hands in delight. "Oh, there will be such a row tonight, to be certain. When signor Girabaldi sees the way his brother has been eyeing the *signora* . . ."

Clara meets the eyes of the other women seated beside them. Have they caught Anna's runaway appendage? She is oblivious to the bets going on behind her about when she, Clara, will stop holding her breath and let her real waist melt into the puddle she carries around every day. A diet of cannoli filled with crème had widened her waistline to the size of the Colosseum.

"Do you remember when Alberto first took me to this very spot?" Anna Margareta asks.

"How can I forget?" Clara asks. "It was the week of our one-year anniversary." But what Clara remembers the most is the first time she ever laid eyes on Anna Margareta. It was just after the Second World War, at the grand ball of signor Puccini in San Michele, just at the point where the hillside dips downward into Santa Margherita. Clara herself was dressed in a pale blue dress that matched her eyes and set off her black hair, which Alberto insisted she tie in a bun. He believed that looks must never interfere with showcasing the design. *Long, clean lines* he extolled at all costs.

Which is why it was such a surprise when Clara set eyes on Anna Margareta. There was music involved, and Clara was in her element.

"Alberto, you have outdone yourself," his friend General Ackerman, a French-German aristocrat, announced. And the general's comrades agreed, with claps to Alberto's shoulders.

"It took me three days, no more." Alberto rolled his mustache between his index and thumb as he admired how his design flowed like liquid over Clara's body.

The general's men laughed, for they had meant Clara and not the gown; the gown was only an afterthought. Any one of those men would have loved to have been attached to the severe Clara, but the stars she saw revolved only around Alberto.

Over and over out in the terrace, in the garden filled with white magnolias, Alberto heard compliments about his design and

Clara, but suddenly at eight o'clock all talk ceased. A wildfire went through the crowd about a new designer who had just arrived. The man had both designed *and* sewed the piece worn by a voluptuous redhead. Alberto went to see what all the talk was about.

He felt sick when he saw the design. It challenged every belief he had. The concept was wild. It was an incredible copper organza piece with an embroidered pattern of fuschia bougainvillea climbing up from the woman's waist to lick at her perfect breasts like flames. He took it all in with one fell swoop, including the woman with her hair left down in large curls and green eyes; everything about her was blatantly loud. "Disgusting," he whispered under his breath to Clara. "It is a masterpiece."

Alberto took the sighs from his friends to mean the gown, which was, in fact, better than any he had created. But again he missed the fact that they were sighing for the opinionated woman beneath the gown and not the design itself.

To his utter disbelief, Alberto learned—and almost fainted at the knowledge—that the woman wearing the gown was none other than the designer herself! Preposterous. Magnificent. He had to have her. In a trance he left Clara's side and asked Anna Margareta to dance in front of a gawking crowd of several hundred people. The band was playing a lovely Italian sonata.

Anna Margareta looked at him with lazy-eyed amusement. "No, I have come with my lover."

"But I do not see him anywhere," Alberto begged. "Surely he won't mind one dance."

"You do not see him, because *she* is standing right beside me." Anna Margareta took the woman's hand and kissed it.

Alberto stepped back to gain a better perspective and tried a different approach: "*Signorina,* I am Alberto Moretti, a lace-and-clothing connoisseur, and I stand in awe of your creation. May I please have this dance to bother you with some questions? An apprentice speaking to a master?"

Though he never stated who was the apprentice and who the master, Anna Margareta, for her part, was confident she was the master and, furthermore, she understood the sincere fascination for another's design. Hadn't she herself been in the throes of it herself at various times? She inclined her head and allowed herself to be escorted onto the dance floor.

Within a week Alberto had charmed her with his talk and ideas. He propositioned her with flattery like a whore on a street corner. He would provide for her lover as well, if she would only marry him. This was something Anna Margareta could not refuse. True, she was more talented than Alberto, but also true was the fact that as a man he was paid more for his talent. So why not ride the fool's coattails?

She accepted his proposal despite the snakes and foul concoctions Alberto's first wife slipped into Anna Margareta's sheets and drinks each night. Truth be told, Anna Margareta thought the striking and severe Clara incredibly beautiful and highly corruptible. She was not, but Anna Margareta managed to squeeze in tight against her whenever she could. She also took great delight in personally waking Clara in the morning, in hopes of seeing a stray thigh or creamy breast from the ice queen. If only Clara would let Anna Margareta's red hair melt her inhibitions. But Clara never did. The influence of the nuns was strong in her veins.

Anna Margareta and her lover moved in immediately with their meager belongings. They looked around the great mansion with unimpressed faces—"I suppose this shall have to do"—but behind closed doors they squealed in delight at their good fortune.

After Anna Margareta and Alberto were married, he moved out of Clara's room and relocated down the hall, where he had the wall broken down between two smaller rooms to make a new master suite. That night Clara made her most incredible design of all. A white-on-white (for she never used colors) tapestry of a tree of life with falling leaves that looked suspiciously like tears.

As a consolation present, Alberto gifted her the next day with a set of ornate sewing scissors and a maple box to carry her various needles and thimbles in. "I shall care for you if you let me. There is no question of divorce. Why bother with such trivial details? I would be honored if you remain as you are," he said with a bow. What could she do? Who would take her now? She accepted and plotted all three of their deaths: Alberto's, Anna Margareta's, and her lover's.

In the evenings, after Anna Margareta finished her beautiful designs of colored threads on white, Alberto would join his new wife in their rooms, and Clara would hear Anna Margareta's moans down the hall. So the fool had somehow converted her. Clara would have been comforted had she known that all Anna Margareta allowed him to do was massage her hands in Bengal spiced oil and that is what produced her moans of ecstasy.

"Has it started yet? Has Girabaldi seen his brother's look of longing?" Nanette takes a seat between Clara and Anna Margareta; in her hand is a plate of spicy *penne arrabiata*. She takes one look at Anna Margareta and exclaims, "Your puffs are getting away from you."

Anna Margareta, red-faced, gives Clara such a look that Nanette feels it as it crosses over her chest. "Why did you not tell me?" Anna Margareta asks.

"Why do you bother with such things?" Clara asks.

Nanette giggles and shakes her head. She is the youngest of Alberto's three wives. African and French, with mocha skin and gray eyes. Alberto found her on the streets peddling incredible designs of laced seashells on a turquoise background, golden threaded stars on a midnight-blue sky. She made cheap but striking gowns stitched with sea and sky themes always on a dark linen canvas. He took her home, gave her the right materials in backdrops of indigo organza, periwinkle satin, slate silk. With the three of them, his designs became world-renowned.

Alberto Moretti married each of his wives for their designs and sewing abilities, yet each was lovely in her own way and so it could not be said that he had poor taste. He was a man of impeccable taste. Each of his wives was ten years older than the previous one, and each Alberto had married directly after dispensing with the last. But to Alberto, dispensing simply meant moving the woman to the next room. He was vehemently against divorce, and so when he wished to remarry another woman he simply did so, without informing the church that he was already married. Instead of divorcing the previous wife, he cared for her like a favorite heirloom.

Once he finished with a woman, he stayed true to the next. It could never be said that Alberto was a two-timer. He never slept with the previous wife once he was done with her, despite any sly plans she might have had for getting into his bed at night. When he was done with one, he was done.

The three of them each call it an early night and retire to their separate rooms. This night Clara waits until Anna Margareta and Nenette are snoring evenly down the hall before she lights a candle and pulls out the designs from her desk. "Ah, when the people see my amazing work they will know which one of us three you favored the most, Alberto, and why."

As Anna Margareta lies in bed feigning sleep, she can hear Clara banging her design drawers busily in the next room. She counts knowingly as Clara pulls out each thin drawer. "One, two . . . twelve." She cringes in dismay, thinking, *Clara has created an entire roomful of designs. Whereas I . . . I have created nothing but grand expectations.* The panel she had promised the townspeople would be far superior to the one in the Museo del Merletto is only a sketched edge of butterflies' wings. How silly. The beauty of the *Commedia dell'Arte* is in its ability to tell a story. What story is she telling with insects copied from a picture book, and of American butterflies and not European? Somewhere along the way she has lost her inspiration. What story did she mean to tell?

She waits until Clara is snoring before she sneaks into her room to view Clara's progress. She creeps up steadily on bare toes and almost falls over with horror when she lights a tiny candle to view Clara's work. Why, the images were not Clara's usual white-on-white austerity with perfect stitches of fig trees, climbing roses, and lilacs. These are explicit sexual scenes of the kind found in the book *Arabian Nights,* which Clara has been hiding beneath her pillowcase. Anna Margareta cannot understand the need for secrecy—this is the twenty-first century, after all.

She looks from Clara's serene, lax face back to the lustful designs of men riding women and women riding men on all fours and laughs in relief. Better to have no designs at all than such repressed ones. *The people of Rapallo will think Clara mad.* She laughs, then falters: *or a genius.*

The next day as Clara and Anna Margareta go for their standard walk to the Hotel Rapallo, Nenette begs off, saying she is feeling a touch of the stomach flu and will catch up with them later. Once she hears the front door close she hurries to her own desk. She broods over her many creations. They are nothing like what the townspeople expect. Instead they are sleek runway designs like those found in the many *Vogue* and *Elle* magazines she has hidden under her desk. Each time she starts her day she begins with the thought of creating something for the lace museum. Something that will make Alberto proud. But when her pencil touches down to paper she finds herself drawing evening gowns, casual wear, lingerie.

It takes all she has to drag herself out of bed each day. What is the use in living when life is a prison? A motor starts, then stalls. She can hear the dogs barking and the engine wheezing, trying to catch, but nothing. When she pushes open the double windows she sees that the chauffeur is now supine under their fancy car. He has started the car but is looking for more signs of trouble, she supposes.

"Clara will have such a tantrum if she sees that the car is not working," she mutters. But as she watches the chauffeur's feet twist and turn underneath the car as he works in the confines of the open garage, she feels a sudden elation and runs down to see him.

"Giovanni," she says, kicking at his shoe.

"*Sì, Signora,* you are ready to go to town?" he asks, sliding back out from under the car. "I shall ready the Audi for you," he says, wiping his hands.

"But the Audi is dirty." She folds her arms.

Giovanni winces at the insult, for they both know that he had just washed the car the evening before. "But, *Signora*—"

"Please take it out back and wash it again."

"Of course." He bows curtly and walks to the back.

When he is gone she starts the car engine, shuts the garage door, and slides inside the car. She sits in the driver's seat and inhales, happily drunk with exhaust. *Now I will be free,* she thinks. But then the thought of how angry the local residents will be at the unfinished museum and how the weight of it all will fall to Clara and Anna Margareta changes her mind and she opens the garage door and leaves. *What is wrong with you?* she asks herself. *Yesterday you decided at the last minute that you wanted to kill off everyone to set yourself free. Today you decide only to do in yourself, and even that small task you cannot do.* She shrugs and staggers back to the house. *Coward,* she declares to herself as she places a cool hand to her aching head. She does not notice Giovanni running back to see what the smell is about.

At midnight, when Clara and Anna Margareta return from their walk, Giovanni is parked outside the Hotel Rapallo, waiting eagerly in the Audi under a palm tree. When he catches sight of them, he flicks his lights on once, steps out of the car, gives a curt little bow with a smile in his eyes, and holds the door open expectantly.

"What are you doing here?" Clara asks Giovanni. "Is something wrong with Nenette?"

"No, *Signora.* I simply thought since it is twelve o'clock..." Giovanni holds his cap in his hand as if in supplication. His eyes fill with adoration for his Clara. The expensive cologne that he'd bought and wore especially in hopes of impressing the beautiful Clara has long ago perspired from him. Despite the evening heat, Clara is a stickler for tradition, and expects him to wear the black chauffeur's suit, boots, and cap.

Clara shrugs. "So it is twelve o'clock. Well, we are not ready to go home yet," she says. "The nerve," she says to Anna Margareta. "I will decide when it is time to go home. And why are you driving the Audi? What happened to our Mercedes?"

"Come now," Anna Margareta says. "Don't be so harsh. You know how he dotes on you."

"He is a pervert. Incapable of hiding his lust." Clara straightens her skirts and crosses her feet at the ankles as they watch Giovanni, with rigid back and red taillights, drive away. She misses the raised brow that Anna Margareta, with her new knowledge of Clara's perverted designs, gives back in return.

Anna Margareta is tired, and she had been so happy that Giovanni had had the foresight to pick them up, seeing how they called him every evening at exactly midnight. She watches as Clara regroups and bats her eyes at the evening clerk Romeo senior. "Another grappa, Romeo." She holds up her small tumbler.

Anna Margareta rolls her eyes.

"Will you have another?" Clara asks.

"Why not?" she asks in boredom.

It takes all of five minutes for them to be served and for Clara to make intense eye connection with the blushing Romeo senior. "I bet you have quite a few vacant rooms tonight, eh, signor Pucci?"

"None, *Signora. Tutte al campleto.*" He opens his palms like a benevolent priest explaining to the congregation, when there are only two drunk biddies in front of him.

"But surely you have an empty closet or two?" Clara laughs lecherously.

"Clara, enough," Anna Margareta says.

"I was only joking," she says, her eyes moving up and down the length of signor Pucci's trousers as he goes about clearing up the plate of olives they have left untouched and the small crystal glasses he had brought out especially for them. "Anna, call Giovanni now."

"But you just sent him home."

"To teach him a lesson, why else? Now we need him back."

When Giovanni, prompt as ever, appears ten minutes later, Anna Margareta is so annoyed with Clara she says she will walk. "It is a lovely evening; I need the fresh air to clear my head."

"Suit yourself. I suppose it is just you and me, eh, Giovanni?"

Poor Giovanni. Anna Margareta shakes her head, chuckling to herself as she watches them go. *Clara cannot see the love he has for her. Clara has gotten worse since we started this ridiculous collezione.* Anna walks with head bowed. It is only when she nears the top of the rise to their house that she looks up to see their neighbor signora Rossi in her front garden.

Her eyes lit up. "Signora Rossi, pruning so late?"

"I heard a noise. I thought it was that stupid creature digging in my yard once again. These damnable creatures are eating my grapes."

"Ah, I have a remedy for that. I once had a vineyard myself. My family farm. I used to come home with my fingers red from the berries," she says wistfully.

"Would you like to come in for a drink?" signora Rossi asks. "You can tell me your remedy beside my electric fan."

Anna Margareta looks at the woman's trim figure, her lovely dark green eyes and midnight hair. How she longs to comb and plait the exquisite raven threads. She is quite a gardener herself. Her first lover, signorina Constantino, and she used to spend endless hours caring for their roses, but that was so long ago. Alberto had cured her of those "vagabond tendencies," as he called it, when he married her.

"A drink?" Anna Margareta asks. "Oh, but it is late. I couldn't bother you," she says, gravitating toward signora Rossi's open gate.

"Anna, is that you?" Clara bellows from the topmost window. "Come quickly. Nenette is feeling ill."

Anna turns apologetic eyes to signora Rossi. "Some other night perhaps," signora Rossi says.

"*Sì, signora Rossi. Buona sera,*" Anna sighs heavily. "The warden calls."

"*Ciao,*" signora Rossi answers, and the informality of her last words do not go unnoticed by Anna Margareta.

Clara is livid when she shuts the bedroom window. "A bit old now for that kind of thing, aren't you?" she asks Anna Margareta when she reaches the top of the stairs. For Clara is afraid to have Anna or Nenette wander from her. Together they are the three widows of Alberto Moretti. Without them she truly does not know who she is.

"Too old for what?" Anna challenges. Anna is fifty years old, but she feels as if she were eighty from the way she has lived since she met Alberto, and now that he is gone, she feels married still to her two companions.

"You know," Clara says. "Besides, I saw that you haven't even created a decent design for our grand opening next week. You had better get to work."

"And Nenette? Is she truly sick?"

"Of course. She tried to inhale the exhaust today. As if pretending not to poison us all the other evening was not enough."

"What is wrong with her, do you think?"

"The same thing that is wrong with all of us. The same thing that draws you to those irregular desires for signora Rossi. We all miss Alberto."

The two widows go to see their third sister and pat Nenette as she lies in bed, her eyes fevered. "Poor Nenette. Do not worry. We can postpone the opening of the museum until you are better." At Clara's words, Nenette wrenches herself forward in bed like a body possessed. "No." Then, more gently: "No. I will be fine."

They tiptoe around one another, unable to accept the hard fact that if they do not complete the designs, they will shame Alberto's memory. And, more truthfully, without a museum they will have nothing to show for the youth they gave up and devoted to Alberto each time he abandoned them for the next wife.

In the morning after she finishes with design number twenty, Clara replaces her reading-stitching glasses with her Perfect View contact lenses. When she can see correctly, she notes through her window that signora Rossi is once again tending to her garden, and an idea takes hold. Within seconds she is walking toward the woman.

"Signora Rossi, how are your plants faring?"

"Ah, well, as I was telling Anna Margareta last evening—"

"Well, yes. Let us get straight to the point. I do not appreciate your making eyes at my lover." Clara almost chokes on the last words.

"You and Anna Margareta?" signora Rossi asks, astounded.

"Yes. What did you think?"

"I am so sorry, Clara. I had no idea. I would never move in on another woman's partner."

"Yes, well. So now you know. So stop your drooling every time we pass."

With that Clara turns her back and returns the fourteen steps to their house.

Anna Margareta is up and having an espresso. "What did you say just then to signora Rossi?"

"Ah, well. Can you imagine? After trying to come on to you last night, she made moves on me! That woman has no decency. She will sleep with any woman. Any woman will do. Really."

"Did she do that?" Anna Margareta asks forlornly. For her confidence had been given a small jolt last night when she'd found that she could still be attractive to another woman. After all the time Alberto had spent in convincing her that such attractions were only for the youthful and searching.

"Yes. Nenette," Clara says as Nenette walks into the living room, still sleepy-eyed. "Make sure, when signora Rossi comes on to you—for surely you are next; as I say, any woman apparently will do—make sure you tell her to stop pawing at us."

Nenette looks from Clara's stiff-backed posture to Anna Margareta's defeated one and sighs. She turns on her heels and goes straight to her room and shuts her door.

"See what you have done?" Clara hisses.

"What I have—?" Anna Margareta frowns.

Nenette locks the door and takes the ten-foot table runner she has designed from underneath her bed. She bundles the heavy silk to her chest with the rest trailing behind her as she walks to her closet.

"The two of them, Clara and Anna Margareta, fighting like two chickens, the grand opening in a few days, and neither I nor Anna Margareta have completed any designs." And what's worse, she had snuck into Clara's room the other evening, and what a surprise that had been. Clara was not the prude she wanted them to believe she was. They were all so depressed. She wished they would agree to see Dottore Toscana, as she had pleaded with them to, but they refused.

Nenette drags a wicker chair to the closet and steps up with the tablecloth, threading it through her chinning bar, where she did her daily exercises, and wraps the rest around her neck. Then, with a "God forgive me, again," she kicks the chair from underneath her. Her eyes bulge immediately as the tablecloth tightens, choking off her air, then slips through the amateur knot. She falls to the floor with a loud crash.

"Nenette! Open this door. What has happened to you?" Clara shouts.

"It is nothing," Nenette coughs. "I simply fell as I was doing my exercises. Leave me alone."

When they set out for the Hotel Rapallo that morning, signora Rossi turns her back and concentrates on her flowers. Anna Margareta turns the other way. *So it is true. Why, she cannot even look at me. Going after the both of us.*

Clara stifles a giggle. *It is working. I have divided them before it can start.* She asks Anna Margareta, "What did I tell you?"

Nenette thinks, *How beautiful signora Rossi's garden is. I wonder if she has something poisonous I can consume.* On the way down she thinks of ways to throw herself from the cliffs before the others can reach her.

It is the day before the grand opening of Alberto's *museo,* and the owner of the Hotel Rapallo invites the townspeople to celebrate this joyous occasion. Truthfully, the woman who owns the hotel is an absentee landlord who lives on a private island in Bali, but the hotel clerks Romeo senior and Romeo junior had agreed that it would be a nice gesture and that their employer would never know.

Up above in San Michele, as the three widows sit meditating over their creations, a brass knocker clanks outside their door. Nenette, who has stayed up all night and once again created haute couture when she had intended nothing more than a wall tapestry for their *museo,* sighs and gets up, thankful for the reprieve. "I shall answer it. Do not worry, Cook," she urges as Giovanni, the chauffeur, makes his way from the kitchen, where he is preparing breakfast. When he is in the kitchen he becomes known as Cook.

It is signora Rossi with a bouquet of flowers. "Good morning, Nenette. I wanted to wish you all a good show tomorrow. Will the three of you be walking down to the Rapallo for your celebration soon? I thought to join you."

"The other two will leave in a few minutes. I have a few things to complete before I can rest. Let me show you to Anna Margareta's room."

Up in her room Anna Margareta is throwing a silent tantrum. She has laid the lace panel she created on the floor and out of hysteria lies down with it, clutches the edge, and rolls herself into a mummy. Three years and she has created nothing but a design of Alberto hotfooting it through hell. She cannot possibly present this tomorrow at their opening. They are stuck, the three of them, with this abominable Herculean task. How can they face the townspeople? "We have disgraced Alberto's memory," she mutters.

This is the way she looks when Nenette leads signora Rossi to her room, leaving signora Rossi with a backward glance and a faint "It has been nice knowing you, signora Rossi."

"Anna, what are you doing?" signora Rossi asks.

"I have nothing to live for. Nothing to show. You wish to see the grand *collezione* of Alberto's second wife? Here. I shall show you." She unwraps herself by propelling her body the other way, revealing the lace panel, then she bursts into tears.

Signora Rossi takes one look at the design and laughs. "Why, that is the most truthful depiction of Alberto I have ever seen!"

"You do not think me mad?" Anna Margareta sniffles.

"For agreeing to take on this task, yes. You've let this man rule half your life and you allow him to do so even now, after he is but dust!"

"But the townspeople. They expect—" Anna sobs.

"Ah, well. I am not the one to ask. As you know, your Clara has done everything possible to make them ostracize me. So I am not the one to ask about what they do or do not care about because I do not give a damn."

Her words touched an old feeling in Anna Margareta. They could be her own words many years ago, before Alberto had stolen her confidence.

"I do not wish to do things in his name anymore." A chuckle escapes Anna Margareta's throat.

"Who can blame you? What person in their right mind would? Will you still go on with this debacle?" she asks, kneeling closer to inspect Alberto's grimace, which Anna Margareta has captured to the last detail. "Come, let us think of a plan." She offers Anna her hand.

In her room Clara has every intention of continuing with the grand opening. In fact, she scrutinizes each design, admiring the numerous love poses she has conjured by hand. Fifty-eight in all. She lives through these creations. She inhabits their world because hers is already spoken for. "Fifty-eight designs for you, Alberto," she declares. "I have made enough for the three of us." With that she blows the entire *collezione* a kiss and goes down for her morning walk and grand reception at the Hotel Rapallo. She is very angry to see signora Rossi draped on the arm of Anna Margareta in the foyer, but she holds her tongue. She will think of another plan to separate the two.

Two hours into the festivities, with the locals turning out to present their own amateur creations on tables and in sketches, Nenette has not shown up. It is only when the smell of barbecue from above starts that Anna Margareta gasps.

"The mansion is on fire!"

"But where is Nenette?" Clara screams. "Giovanni, hurry. The fool has tried to smoke herself to death."

The four of them pile into the Audi, while the hotel clerks call the fire department.

Nenette is walking through her room in a smoky daze. Because of her lack of sleep the previous night she has dozed off atop her designs with a cigar in her mouth. She has plans to cook herself in the wood oven after tomorrow, but not this. Not to harm someone else's hard work. She woke to find her room burning. "Ah, they will kill me," she sobs, trying to gather Clara's designs.

It is then that the door breaks open and Giovanni rushes in to sweep her up. "No, Giovanni, let me stay. I must gather everything. Help me. For Alberto's memory."

He brings her safely to fresh air as Clara claps in joy and throws her arms around the big man. "Signora," he says, "I could only save her and not your designs."

"Who cares about the designs as long as my Nenette is safe?" Clara declares.

As they wait for the fire department, the house slowly begins to crumble and the three widows proceed down the hill. Yet when the first truck arrives the fire has not fully consumed the house and their designs might still be saved, so Clara waves them down frantically and points them in the wrong direction.

"What now?" Anna Margareta asks.

"Now we go down and celebrate the closing of Alberto's *museo*." Clara smiles.

"And I shall tell them of all the lovely designs I witnessed this morning." Signora Rossi squeezes Anna Margareta's hand. "How sad. But the three of you are so heartbroken now. You could not possibly re-create such a feat. It will go down as a legend. The *collezione* that lived for only a day."

These days, whenever anyone asks about the two lace museums, the widows point and tell them, "Ah, you are mistaken. There is only one *museo*. The quintessential Museo del Merletto. You must go to see some of our old *collezione* housed there, among lesser works."

In the evenings the three widows watch the variety shows together at the Hotel Rapallo; they are the best of friends, sisters really, and inseparable. It is only when they retire that they part from one another to the privacy of their own homes: Nenette to her design studio, where she is fast making a name for herself as the premier fashion designer Nenette Moretti; Giovanni with his new wife, Clara; and signora Rossi with her new wife, Anna Margareta.

the ferry driver
of portofino

THE WHOLE town of Portofino knew that the ferry driver was an ex-convict who had once killed a man and some felt that he did not deserve the love of the beautiful woman or the little boy, but the convict did not care and he was not sorry for it. He was fifty-five years old with tattoos on both forearms and along the right side of his neck, which kept him from many jobs except this one, which he valued tremendously, almost as much as he valued the boy. Though nothing could surpass the latter.

His route is simple. Each day he starts from Portofino, where he cuts across the rich blue ocean to Rapallo; from Rapallo he turns back to Santa Margherita, then back to Portofino, where he begins again. Three ports of call. One can see the change in wealth from charming Rapallo to secluded Santa Margherita, with its fancy hidden hotels upon the hillside, to luxurious Portofino. The distance is only fifteen minutes by ferry. The boats that dock in Portofino are giant yachts with names such as *Viking* and *Tigre d'Or* and polished streamlined sailboats of the racing class.

The townspeople like to encourage their guests to select Roberto's ferry without warning them. Then, after their guests have returned from the ride, they like to ask, "So what did you think of our ferry driver?" They take the pleasure that zookeepers do in sticking a broom into the cage of a dangerous tiger in front of paying customers, as if by doing this they go into an equitable battle and there are no bars to keep them from harm.

"Did he scare you? He is quite harmless, I assure you. It has been a long time since he killed a man." Their talk belongs to braggarts who don't know the true story or the fact that it has not been such a long time since the ferry driver killed a man.

"How goes it, old friend?" young signor Toscana will usually ask. Without a social drink in hand signor Toscana, like most of the businessmen, feels awkward and frightened in the ferry driver's steady presence. It is worse when the ferry driver wears his aviator sunglasses. The businessmen try in vain to read him, but see only their fool selves reflected back.

Usually the pleasantry will fall away into an uncomfortable silence at Roberto's silent stare. He learned in prison that too much talk reveals too much. And friends create obligations, and obligations in prison are something one does not want to owe.

There are others who do not care that he is an ex-convict. These are the ones Roberto needs to watch out for. They are un-impressed that he is an ex-convict. "Well, he's a ferry driver now and he'd better not look at me sideways," the men like to spit off to the side as if in challenge.

In prison, Roberto would never allow this. In prison, he would strike immediately if an apology did not follow a slight and the people would know never to humor themselves at his expense. But he values this job tremendously. It allows him to care for his grandson. So he eats his pride. The women find it hard to look him in the eye. They think him a savage. Though when his back is turned they stare.

Robert knows this, their fear. He can smell it. Small fear, he thinks. Nothing like the big, raw animal stench that reveals itself in prison. He extends nothing to change their view of him.

He was not always this reviled. Roberto Romano had been but a boy of seventeen who had combed his hair and left his house with a kiss from his mother to attend a simple school dance, which would take him on a hazardous route by night's end. He returned very early the next morning, brittle, bloody, and hand-cuffed by the *polizia,* and was told to gather his parents together and a change of underwear.

Both Roberto and the other boy had been showing off the entire evening for the attention of a girl. It was a benign sort of showing off, and they were even in everything. It came down to switchblades. Neither intending to use theirs. In fact, both were very much all talk and filled with the light-headed excitement of youth. Both a little worried about breaking a nose or cutting their knuckles open. They could easily have been friends.

But they each had their own group of friends, consisting of jealous boys envious of Roberto and the other boy's popularity. The goading built to a frightening hum during the evening. By night's end Roberto and the young man found themselves crashing through a window. When Roberto's knife spun out of his pocket during the fall, his opponent immediately went into a panic and pulled his knife out, at the advice of his friends.

Roberto's friends then shouted, "Watch out, Roberto, he means to kill you." So Roberto struggled, wrenched the knife free, and the next thing he knew there was blood on the floor and they were slipping on it. His frightened opponent fell chest-first onto Roberto's hand, extended to deflect the boy from falling atop him. He had forgotten that the same hand held his knife. Roberto remembers the smell of fear that encompassed them both. Swallowing them in a sweet, pungent texture that seeped through their pores.

It is the same scent he excreted when he met the old-timers in prison. He had cried then. He is not ashamed to think of it. He is a different man now. He was just a boy then. That boy is long dead.

He served two months before he refused to be bullied and truly killed a man, and then another, so that more time was heaped upon his sentence. He was beaten past death on two different occasions, so that he earned the name Devil in prison. He had guards place bets and wake him in the middle of the night for some dogfight with another convict. He has learned that the biggest men are not always the best fighters and sometimes the smallest ones are the scariest because they must use subterfuge in their fighting to balance the scales.

He lost his ability for tears, and in that time he watched his life move before him like a mute moving-picture show. His father's last dime was spent on bribing an official, and after thirty years Roberto was let out, in time to care for and watch his father as he wasted away.

For a time after he was set free he was like a rabid creature. He could not function in social settings without exploding into a fight. Every word he took to have second meanings. It has taken six years for him to trust that he will not be blindsided. And two more to swallow his pride so that he does not get sent back to prison.

The jobs he has held since then have always involved roughing people up. Sometimes for a crooked *poliziotto,* sometimes for a group of hoodlums. His only requirement was money. It was only by luck that he attained this job. Through an old friend of his father's. Luck and possibly for God's own amusement.

"Nonno," Grandfather, the boy of six says, tugging at his folded jeans, and drops a squirming worm onto Roberto's white tennis shoes.

"What is it, *nipote?*" he asks, getting ready to jump ashore to anchor the ferry. The boy is not his but somehow showed up on his doorstep a year ago. "Who are you?" Roberto had asked.

"Your grandson, your *nipote,*" the little voice squeaked. The child had cigarette burns along the insides of both arms, a rash on his neck, and hopeful eyes. Later Roberto would find that the boy also came with an endless supply of nightmares and a bottle of calamine lotion for his rashes.

"But I have no son or daughter, so how can you be my grandson?" Roberto asked, touching a lock of the child's tight curls, wondering if the boy had lice, and searching for a resemblance of himself in the tiny face.

The little boy, a mulatto, said, "My papa tells me you are his papa and to stay here until he returns." It was possible. Roberto had been quite the ladies' man in his youth, before his life swerved into the gutter.

"What is your name? Who is your grandmother?"

"My name is Claudio, but you must call me *nipote* because that is what I am. Your grandson." The boy claimed he had never met his grandmothers. Roberto thought that surely the boy's father would show up by night's end and he could clear up the matter of whether he had fathered a son. He let the child stay on the front steps in the hot sun to play by himself. That was a year ago.

Others have shown up as well, as if God decided to amuse himself and supply Roberto with things he had been robbed of in his lifetime: a beautiful young woman, too young he thinks, and his own private *poliziotto*, Marco Vespucci, who watches Roberto like a favorite television program.

"I know who you are, Roberto Romano. You belong in the cages with the riffraff. Slip up once and it will be my duty to throw you back in."

Let him, Roberto used to think. *Who is he trying to scare? I have seen it all.* But since the arrival of the boy this has all changed.

—◊◊—

"Nonno!" Claudio stomps his foot. He is wearing cuffed jeans and white tennis shoes like Roberto's.

Roberto continues to look toward the dock. "What have I told you about that type of behavior?"

"It shall get me nowhere."

"And so?" Roberto asks, his face straight behind the sunglasses.

"And so I am stopping, Nonno. Please just put the worm on the hook and I shall leave you alone for the rest of the afternoon."

"And how do you plan to do that when we are both on the same boat?"

"There are ways of making oneself invisible."

Roberto keeps his face straight, but inside he is laughing. He wonders sometimes if he has not been had. If the boy's true parents live nearby but cannot afford to care for him. Or if the child is an orphan who decided to approach a lonely man the way a stray dog finds someone to feed him. Or a circus midget. The latter probably. His grandson who is not his grandson is a circus midget.

"Look, Nonno, the pretty lady approaches." Claudio breaks into a broad smile as they prepare to dock at Portofino for their second run of the day. Roberto nods, watching her from the corner of his eye. She is hurrying past the *ristorante* Delfino, with its blue awnings, squat round-backed cherrywood chairs, the small boats covered with blue canvas, and waving to make sure they see her. He continues to avert his eyes. He looks from the yellow to the peach house settled in between the palm trees and tall, rectangular fir trees above the different shops. The buildings stand shoulder to shoulder, tall, with the green-and-white awnings stretching out like skirts below them. The Hotel Nationale, Timberland, and various boutiques.

Above and farther behind, where the road slants upward, the large stone house with its mustard-colored awning displays its clothesline of bed linens and pillow cases drying in the morning heat. The lovely horizontal-striped church of sage-and-white, with its circular window, sits elegantly in the jungle of trees.

Roberto's heart wrenches when he sees her. The sound of her sandals slapping the stone floor shaped like a jigsaw puzzle, beat a rhythmic grace that lulls him as he waits for the sleepy-eyed passengers to board. She gets in line behind three of Roberto's regular passengers—the three widows of Rapallo—as they bid good-bye to their cohorts, setting up shop and unfolding chairs beneath the shade of the orange trees to sell their embroidered linen tablecloths.

Claudio waves at her, and she waves back. A slip of a girl no older than twenty-five and absurdly pretty. A tall reed among the tourists and workers. Inky black hair and eyes. Italian with a touch of, what is it? Persian in her eyes? Her hair reaches to her waist, lifted now and then by the breeze like a lazy lover's touch. The construction workers, their naked chests glistening with sweat, wipe their brows, pausing from their drilling of the cement road to give the ferry driver an envious look and shake their heads, asking, "What does she see in the brute?"

"Roberto." She waves. "Help me up, Claudio." She extends her hand.

At fifty-five, Roberto knows he is fitter than most men, but he is twice her age and will not entertain it. He will not steal her youth as his has been stolen. He knows nothing much of her, but he suspects there is an absent father involved and possibly too many immature boys fawning over her, performing stupid antics. And so the infatuation with him.

"The next ferry comes in ten minutes, *Signorina*. I have to make a stop in Santa Margherita on an errand, before Rapallo,"

Roberto says gruffly, ignoring her outstretched hand holding the ticket. "You shall make better time waiting for the next boat." He lets the next passenger by as the girl stands off to the side in confusion.

"I am in no hurry. I do not need to be at work for another hour yet. I made a large sale two days running in the clothing shop, and my boss has given me the good shift."

They look at each other. Inside Roberto feels as young as she looks. Inside he sees himself as a young man slightly older, looking at a smiling girl. And when he was younger he could have won her easily. But outside he knows he is no longer this boy, and simply because she offers him flattery he will not let himself take advantage. She should be with that boy there on the lawn with his shirt off, wearing short pants and bouncing the soccer ball from his knee to his chest to his friend.

He presses his lips together in acquiescence and she walks past him to lean over the railing, her dark blue peasant skirt lifting to show sandaled feet and slender ankles.

Claudio brushes past his grandfather to follow after the girl, his man-sized fishing pole banging against the railings. "*Signorina,* please, can you string this creature to my hook?" Claudio asks.

Roberto watches as she laughingly makes a face and holds the worm between the very ends of her fingers and bravely plunges the hook through.

"Claudio, what have you caused me to do? The poor creature."

"He doesn't feel it. Nonno says they are used to it."

The girl looks at Roberto, and he turns away. He would lie to keep his grandson from worrying. To keep him from being a ninny.

"*Signore,* how are you this morning?" Roberto asks the three widows as they file past him. They always pretend not to hear. Which is why he asks. Although the eldest of the three usually arches her back as she passes him, as if to display her wares. He once heard the youngest ask, "Why can't I say good morning to him? It's ridiculous. We see him most every day!"

"He is of the bad sort," the eldest widow said.

As he steers the ferry away, he glances over to confirm that the girl is beside Claudio. Roberto feels a happy excitement at her presence, as if he will suddenly show off somehow. In what way he knows not. If he had known three weeks ago that she would be boarding his boat and dropping her packages and that he would be the one to help her, he would not have shown up for work that day. She has appeared each day since then. He asks himself a million questions. If she were ugly, would he be as flattered? Would she then feel like some cloying presence?

She could wear a sack over her entire body and she would still be lovely. *There is a brilliance to her that is more than surface.* Such answers annoy him to no end. What is the problem, truthfully? There must be some flaw that keeps him from accepting her friendship. Perhaps his instincts are telling him not to. It cannot simply be from strength of will that he repels her attraction. Maybe she is mad? He looks at her. She glances back clear-eyed. Was there ever a more fresh-looking being? She is translucent. She is trouble. And trouble is something he cannot afford.

It is difficult to ignore the slender, perfect breasts, the prominent shoulder blades, the long line of her back. The stringy arms he could hold in one hand. A dancer's body. What would be the harm? Perhaps he should let go of his worries and accept the girl's attention. Perhaps he, too, is deserving of love.

"Claudio," he calls.

The boy hears him but refuses to answer. Roberto repeats the call, so that the girl straightens from looking over the railing and turns to lean on it instead and look from Roberto to the boy and back to Roberto.

"*Nipote,*" Roberto finally says, quietly.

"Yes, Nonno?" Claudio turns, full of fake innocence.

"Oh, you hear me now, do you?"

"Yes, sir. When you call me *grandson* I hear you."

"Show the *signorina* your new favorite spot." *Away from me.*

Claudio takes her by the hand and leads her to the upper deck, where he has been trying to fish. Even though the hook as it drags barely skims the water. Roberto watches them go. Perhaps he is fooling himself. Perhaps she simply wants a friend, thinks him safe, and enjoys visiting with Claudio. Yes, that is it. To be clear-minded again, he sighs. But then she gives Roberto one last look before following Claudio up the stairs. And in that look there is such a pureness, a pressing curiousness, that it threatens to devour him. When she is out of his sight he can breathe.

Five minutes into the ride the seagulls that perch regularly on the rails fly away squawking, and a hail of grape seeds drop down. Roberto knows without seeing that it is the three American boys with their backpacks, and, of course, their bag of grapes. He asks his assistant to watch over the steering and goes to the top deck. He tells himself he is searching for the boys, but his eyes do not listen and immediately seek out the girl. When he sees her, he sees the three American boys. Roberto watches from the stairway as the three boys cast furtive glances toward the girl. Showing off and ribbing one another.

The Japanese one takes a mouthful of grapes, chews, and says, "Watch this. Thomas, watch, dude," and catches an unsuspecting pigeon on the side of its head before it flies off. They laugh, slap hands in the air above their heads. Roberto waits for the tallest of the three, the blond-haired one, to fill his mouth with grapes before he approaches stealthily and grabs him by the scruff of his shirt. The boy almost chokes, and the three drop their hand fulls of grapes.

"Not on my boat."

"Yes, sir," the blond one says. "Sorry."

"Clean this up." He points to the grape seeds on the floor. "If someone should fall," Roberto says.

"Dude," the first boy says. "I told you to quit messing around," and they shove one another slightly as Roberto walks away. *"Signorina."* Roberto nods to the girl. Below, he curses himself. *Stupid. Stupid. You, too, were showing off for the girl. You know better than to handle these tourists. It only takes one phone call from an angry mother and you lose your job and therefore lose the means to care for your grandson. Do not be so stupid next time. See how she clouds your thinking? You would never have done that before.*

They dock in Santa Margherita, and he cannot get off the boat quickly enough. He ties the boat to the dock and walks behind the passengers as they depart on their various sightseeing excursions, for their day jobs and their breakfast meetings, pulling out cell phones as if on cue.

"Roberto," the girl calls out from the top deck.

"Nonno," Claudio echoes, leaning precariously forward. Roberto is unfazed. He has taught his grandson to swim like a fish in the last year.

"Stay on board. I shall only be a moment."

At Santa Margherita, the morning sun is still soft, but the pavement is already soaking it up. He deposits the package of supplies with signora Carey, the brown-haired *americana* whose husband has just opened up a plate shop among the excellent *ristoranti* lining the small port. He looks at her fancy yellow dishes painted with black olives and lined in blue trim. On another shelf she has various bricks of soap in different shades of green. And throughout the shop more plates, hand-painted in coral, blue-gray, red.

He feels a sudden urge to swing a bat through the store. Is this

202 / Tess Uriza Holthe

now what is to become of Santa Margherita? A waterfront of fine tourist boutiques someday? Though he has nothing against the Careys, he hopes not. There is already Portofino for that.

"Roberto." Signora Carey smiles broadly, mischievously. Her lipstick is on her teeth. Roberto relaxes. He eyes her up and down. Though he has no interest, this is something he has no qualms about. When the *signora* is bored and wishes to have fun, they make arrangements. They are close in age. They have done it before. Non *problema*. Nothing against signor Carey.

But today when the woman leans close to him to accept the package he suddenly feels repulsed. "Would you like to carry this to the back for me?" she asks.

"Not today, *Signora*. I am behind schedule," he says.

Perhaps it has something to do with the fact that when she is not interested in him, she orders him around like a servant in front of the customers. As if she would not dare get even the hem of her skirt dirty by brushing near him. Just a week ago she went to the back room on the pretext of yelling at him in front of the customers, only to pin him against the packages as he carried them in.

"Nonno." Claudio rushes in. "I thought we had lost you."

Roberto looks at the boy.

"We?" the *signora* asks, still smiling.

"*Buon giorno, signora Carey.*" Claudio bows. "*Sì,* the *signorina* and I." He reaches for the girl's hand and takes it reverently.

The girl floats in on light feet full of charm as she walks alongside Claudio.

Signora Carey's body goes rigid. "We're not open yet," she says, though it is obvious the girl is with them.

The girl nods. "Claudio, let us not bother your *nonno*. Will you come with me to look at the shop next door?"

The boy immediately sees the situation and waves good-bye to signora Carey, who stands beside Roberto, stunned.

"Why, she is just a baby! You should be ashamed!" Her eyes are hard, wicked.

Roberto shakes his head. "There are many things I should be ashamed of," he says. *"A domani, signora Carey,"* he bids her until the morrow, as he takes his leave. Knowing full well he has not satisfied her silent questions.

As he waits outside for Claudio and the girl, Roberto sees his very best enemy approach, the *poliziotto* Marco Vespucci. *"Signore,"* he says.

The police officer is always unhappy to see him, yet he follows Roberto like a shadow. "Taking an extended delivery break, I see. Does your superior know of this?" The policeman slaps his baton into his open hand. "Another package for signora Carey, eh? Signor Carey has been gone for quite some time now. How many months has it been?"

Roberto shrugs at the insinuation. He saw many men like this in prison. Usually they were under the protection of a beast. It is no different with the *poliziotto* who scrutinizes Roberto's every movement. He is protected by his uniform.

"Where is the brat?"

"My grandson is next door."

"He should be in school."

"I intend to send him to school next year. I have been reading the exercise books with him. I have spoken with a teacher. They agree it is in his best interests to spend time with me this first year without his parents." Roberto knows enough of this man to be accommodating. The man is looking for the slightest thing to send him away.

"Nonno," Claudio shouts. "Look what the lady bought me."

Roberto stiffens. He knows simply by looking at the *poliziotto*'s eye that the man sees the girl. A glazed look has overtaken the *poliziotto*. And Roberto witnesses this with a sinking heart. Whatever benign harassment the *poliziotto* has given him, the tide has now turned into a deeper meaning for the unhappy police officer.

"And who have we here, Claudio?" he asks.

The officer always speaks kindly to Claudio. He looks down at him now as if he were listening to his own son brag about his day at school. The *poliziotto*'s eyes take on a wistful smiling quality before he turns them, harsh and scrutinizing, to Roberto. Roberto marvels that even of this, the man is jealous. The *poliziotto* wishes Claudio had shown up on his doorstep instead of Roberto's. Claudio disentangles himself from the *poliziotto*'s petting of his hair and hides behind the girl's skirt. "I don't know her name," Claudio says.

Roberto braces himself. He had hoped to never know the girl's name. That way it was easier not to think about her. She was intangible. A part of the wind.

"Anna Lisa," she says. "Anna Lisa Rouhani."

So he was right. A Persian father, an Italian mother. Roberto pictures the girl's mother fleetingly.

"Bellissima." The officer kisses his finger and looks her up and down.

She does not blush or smile but looks the officer in the eye until he is the one blushing.

"Your mother works for the embassy, yes?"

She nods, listening. Watchful of the *poliziotto*.

"And your father the doctor?"

Again she nods, without offering anything more in return.

"You look like your elder sister," the *poliziotto* stutters.

"You know everything about me, *Signore*," she says, putting a hand around Claudio's shoulder. "Come, Claudio, let us board the boat." And with that she walks by the two men.

Roberto stands stunned. She has a father. A doctor, at that!

She comes from an educated background. She has a mother and a sister. It brings to question now her interest in him. And further confirms that her attachment to him is trouble. He thought surely an absent father was involved. He thought her a naive young girl, and yet she did not look in the least naive staring down the *poliziotto*. He scratches his head and looks at the *poliziotto*.

"So you are in the business now of rescuing young children and seeing young women," the *poliziotto* says.

"I have nothing to do with her. She appeared on my boat three weeks ago." Roberto shrugs.

"If anything should happen to the girl," the *poliziotto* warns. "By the way, I've come to tell you, now that simply because your friend has appeared don't think you can start trouble."

"What friend?" Roberto asks.

"What friend." The officer looks at him. "Do not get smart with me. At the first sound of any disruption in my neighborhood you shall hear from me."

"Roberto, come see the fish Claudio has caught," Anna Lisa calls from the ferry.

Roberto suddenly feels old and tired. The girl's perfume is too intoxicating. Her step too light. Why, she could be sister to his grandson. "I have business to attend to, Officer Vespucci," he says, excusing himself from the *poliziotto*. This news from the officer saps his strength. Roberto has no friends. Who is this person the *poliziotto* has described? His instincts rise up and tell him to take his *nipote* and run away. *Ahh. You think life revolves only around you and the boy. Did I not warn you not to grow so attached to him? Look what you have become. A straight man. So straight you are like a starched shirt from the cleaners.*

You worry too much that you are the center of the poliziotto's existence. Probably the poliziotto has many such lowlifes as yourself that he visits. You know him by now. He likes to instill fear in the few places that he can. He cannot physically beat you, so this constant harassment. Of course he doesn't want your nipote. What would he do with a little boy? You put too much on yourself. The man's only interest is to harass you all day. Nothing else.

In Rapallo, Roberto docks to let passengers off and on. Then he turns and motors his ferry past the orange umbrellas of the Hotel Riviera, with a square cable of buoys marking off the safe swimming area, and heads back toward Portofino. Above are cliffs and pale pink houses with red gabled roofs nestled into the mountains, a three-story mustard castle with turret, a stone church with horizontal stripes of sage green and white and a circular window. Trees and more trees. Everything so green and the sea so calm. Church bells ring from up high. Roberto breathes deeply of the Mediterranean, letting the Italian Riviera soak into his blood.

At noon the *poliziotto,* Officer Marco Vespucci, returns home for a meal prepared by his wife and for a siesta. His young boy, about the age of the ferry driver's grandson, approaches him with a toy. "Papà," his son says.

But Marco Vespucci is distracted. He brushes the boy away. The child is too sickly and soft for his liking. He follows behind his mother's skirts. His skin is not at all brown, like the ferry driver's grandson's, and there is no light in this boy's eyes. He is not daring, too afraid to stick even his hand over a ship, much less lean his whole torso over the railing as Marco has seen the ferry driver's boy do time and again.

"Papà," the boy says again.

"What is it, Amerigo?"

"I—"

"Helena," he bellows over the boy's words.

His wife materializes like a ghost from the shadows of the

dark kitchen, with a hot plate of fish and potatoes. Marco brings a hand to his chest, startled by her appearance. "Why is the house so dark? It is like a dungeon in here. It's no wonder your boy is so pale."

Helena says something, feebly tugging at the curtains. Marco tires of her presence, of her constant bruises and black eyes, which he has given her, and immediately swings the curtains apart with a loud swoosh of his arms. His wife cringes. He treats them as if they were servants, a cook and her son. Nothing in his manner aside from the abuse says that they are his. He regards them both with annoyance. What a disappointment they are to him. He has done everything in life that he wished to accomplish. These two have no dreams whatsoever but to scurry between shadows.

His wife folds her hands and seats herself opposite him. Her face is too longish, like a horse's. Often he wishes to joke at her and ask, "Why the long face?" It is a joke he once heard an American tell about a horse that walks into a bar, and he thought at that moment how perfect the joke was for his own wife's face. He stabs his fork into the meal she has checked every ten minutes, then every three minutes before his arrival to have the sole baked just as he likes. It is perfect today. One of her best. He realizes this and yet he says nothing. Too lazy to extend the grudging compliment. Besides, too many compliments will make her lax in her duties. He eats noisily. And tells her about his day so far.

"I have a good mind to report both that ferry driver and the teacher at the school. He is neglecting that child. The boy should be in school. Why, soon he will be illiterate if he doesn't get the proper care. A child must be nourished from the start. And did I tell you? Now he has as part of his entourage a young woman. Wait until her father hears of it." He takes a sip of wine and does not mention that the girl in his story takes his breath away, makes him forget he has a wife.

"A girl, you say? Appeared from where?" she asks.

Marco has not heard her. He glances at her to make sure she is listening. "And then a friend comes to visit. The man asks at the station where this ferry driver lives. As if we are the information center. Pass me the salt, Helena. Next time a little more salt, eh? Is too much like paper."

And on he goes, never asking her how her day is. How their child is doing. He will leave and she will spend the next half of the day preparing and waiting for him to speak similar words to her until bedtime, when he is asleep and the day is finally over and she is safe.

The *poliziotto* leaves his home thirty minutes earlier than most workers. He is rabid about the girl he has seen today. Prettier than her mother or her elder sister. When his wife calls after him about leaving too early and adds timidly that he should take a proper siesta before going back to work, he answers, "You know how hard I work. Why do you ask such things? I have paperwork to attend to. What a stupid question."

How unfair it is, he repeats to himself after he checks in at the station and is instructed to roam the train station for an hour. There has been another bomb threat. He is like a sewer rat forced to live underground while the ferry driver basks in the sun and spends his time ferrying the rich and beautiful from charming Rapallo to luxurious Portofino, in the company of the smart boy and beautiful girl. How unfair life is.

He can see it. The girl's infatuation with the ferry driver. But what he is not sure of is whether the ferry driver is interested in the girl. Marco will watch the ferry driver carefully over the next few days. If he shows the slightest bit of interest in the girl, Marco will have something over him. Surely her father, the big surgeon, and her mother, the smart embassy woman, would like to know of this louse's interest in their smooth-skinned daughter.

Ah, but to have the girl look at him in the same way she looked at the ferry driver today. To have the boy admire him like he does the ferry driver. The *poliziotto* has secretly bought sunglasses of the type the ferry driver wears and has stood in front of the mirror a few times to mimic how the man stands with feet apart or positioned on top of the railings as he waits for the passengers to board. The *poliziotto* thinks over and over again, as he searches for possible suspects that have been described over the radio, that if the ferry driver were gone, somehow he would acquire the boy, the girl, and the job.

The *poliziotto* has waited and waited for the ferry driver to slip up. But the man is practically a saint. He would rather let the passengers assault and humiliate him than lose his job or the boy. But the *poliziotto* knows that no one is a saint and soon the ferry driver will slip up.

Colin Ferguson propped his feet up on the next seat as he sat under the awning ay the Caffè Delfino and admired his recently purchased Baume & Mercier. He was anxious tae start his holiday. But there was this yin last job he'd promised the Man. Tae find this woman's wean and send the tot back home. It was hot, but he lit a fag. He hadnay wanted yin until the man beside him had lighted up. He went back tae studyin' his watch. Black leather, rectangular, gold-framed. Something tae be said fer understated elegance.

Twelve noon, the watch read. The ferry driver was an easy yin tae find. His contact had located a man and child fittin' the description Colin had given them. The ferry driver would dock in an hour and Colin would nab the boy, send him back tae Scotland, where the boy's maw awaited, and then he, Colin, could finally start his holiday. He pulled oot his recently purchased Frommer's guide tae Italy. Fuckin' brilliant. Everythin' broken

down fer ye. What eating establishments, lodging, the whole pro-
duction. Priceless. He was already attached tae the thing. The
pages already dog-eared and underlined.

He raised his hand tae order a coffee. A nicely shaped hand
for a bruiser, with one ring on it, his da's. He took care ay his
hands. A regular massage and manicure. The boys back home
liked tae tease him, but let them. He hadnay the common com-
plaints and ailments they had from their line ay work. He didnay
need tae soak his in hot water after giving someone a hiding. Ye
had tae protect yer investments.

"*Signore?*" the waiter asked.

"*Un caffè.*" He tap-tapped the side ay his thigh, doin' a rhythm
wi' his hand. He had trouble waitin' around fer things. He was
an impatient bugger. He sang a wee bit ay the BoDeans track tae
amuse himself. When he was a wean his father would sing tae
him. From then on it stuck. Didnay matter where he was, if he
got impatient he sang. "As I write . . . I watch the night go down.
And I see the lonely, twinkling lights of town."

He flipped the pages. Cinque Terre had been a letdown. He
had started backward at Riomaggiore, the ugliest ay the five cities,
as far as Colin was concerned, and gotten disappointed, aban-
doning his plans tae see the other four. He wanted tae book a visit
tae Abano Terme in Veneto, where there was a famous spa. Tour
the shops in Milano a bit. Buy more clothes. Maybe find a pretty
lass and take her tae the opera in Verona. He hadnay realized
how fun it could be spendin' all his hard-earned money. A person
could go soft from it. Och, then there was the fur coat he had
promised his maw. He pulled out his cell. He'd better phone her
and settle it now.

"Hullo," she barked. He could hear the Hoover he had just
bought her. Top ay the line wi' all the trimmings.

"It's me, Colin."

"Eh? I'm no interested." She hadnay heard him.

"Ma!"

"Aye? Who is it?"

"It's me, Colin. Turn the vacuum off fer a moment."

"Colin?" Her voice turned sweet. He could almost imagine her ears pinning back the way their dog Rosco's did when he was happy tae see ye. "Ye all right?"

"Aye. Fine, Ma. How's Grannie?" He was beatin' around the auld bush, he knew. He wasnay afraid ay any yin, but angerin' his maw was another thing all the gether. A war ay attrition is what she fought, until ye were knackered and just beggin' her to let off on the ears.

"She's fine, Colin. Cranky as ever but fine. I'll give her the phone?"

"Naw, Ma. Listen, I've been thinkin' aboot that fur coat ye've been asking fer."

There was a pause and then a quick intake ay breath. "Have ye found yin already? Wait until I show Alice. She'll drop dead on the spot wi' envy. Showin' off her rabbit's fur like it was something. And in the hot weather. I wouldnay take mine oot until it was proper cold. What's it look like?"

Och, hell. He gripped his face in his palm and moved his hand up and down. He wasnay yin fer workin' up tae things. "A dead animal's what yer askin' me fer. The hide ay a dead animal. Ye doan see anythin' wrong wi' that, Maw? Ye doan think Rosco looks better wi' his coat on than off?"

"He's a dog, Colin, fer cryin' oot loud. Ah'm no askin' ye fer a dog's fur coat."

"But still. Can ye grasp what Ah'm saying? How'd ye like it if someone were tae wear yer skin around? Tae a fancy gatherin'?"

"Have ye gone daft? Doan be cheeky. Ye asked me what I wanted fer me birthday. Lord knows ye've goot the quid. But if ye cannay be bothered, than ye cannay," she sniffed. "I doan see what all the hubbub's aboot." Another sniff and then a long pause. He wasnay gony fall fer it. Tears, man. They did just the opposite fer him.

"Jest because I asked doesnay mean yer gettin' it. It jest means I asked. How aboot a diamond? I'll get ye yin bigger than—"

"Doan want a diamond. I want a fer coat. If ye cannay get it fer me, I'll save up fer it myself. I'll wear yin when Ah'm Grannie's age. Ye'd like that, wouldnay ye?"

"Och. There's nay talking tae ye, is there? I'm off," he said and hung up on her. Fuck it. The auld cunt. He was gettin' her a diamond. And she was gony like it. Nay animal fur. Disgustin'.

He clenched his fists, then shoved off. Well, he had chanced a call and she hadnay been in a good mood. It was always touch and go wi' her. Ye never could tell. And that was comin' from him, Colin. Her favorite. He counted out a tip and placed it beneath the ashtray. "Thank ye," he said, noddin' tae the waiter.

The ferry approached on time and he went tae greet it. So Colin had found out a few things about this ferry driver Roberto Romano. Thing number yin, this man was quite a bruiser himself in his heyday. Killer instinct and all. Ye cannay make a bruiser out ay some yin simply from tryin'. Ye could have yerself some yin big enough and smart enough but if they didnay have all the qualifications they were nay good tae any yin. Ye have ta have it inside ye, innate, zero remorse, whatever the job needed. Ye couldnay go soft from anythin'. Thing number two, ferry driver stays tae himself (fair enough) and until the boy he was a very lonely man. Interestin' pieces ay information.

He thought ay his maw again. Aggravatin'. He shook his head and propped a foot on a step and lit another fag, outwardly oblivious tae the smiles the Italian lasses gave him in passin'. He didnay have the time. When he was on the job Miss fuckin' Universe could walk by bare-arsed and he wouldnay blink. He'd stay the course. That was why he was such a success in his job.

He waited until all the passengers had filed out and hopped ontae the boat. "Robert Romano?" he asked the driver.

"No." The man shook his head. "Is his lunch hour."

Colin frowned. Why hadnay he thought ay that? His maw, she twisted his mind sometimes. He never made slipups like this yin. It was this whole bein' on break, but no. It was screwin' wi' his heid. He wasnay sure tae twiddle his thumbs or get tae work. His thoughts in disorder. "When will ye be expectin' him tae return?"

"Tre." The man held up three fingers.

Colin nodded. He had time.

The ferry driver received a call from his coworker, Stefano Bertolli, the man who covered his lunch breaks. Roberto had given him money as an incentive a year ago, asking the man to let him know ahead of time if anyone came looking for him. Stefano wanted him to know that a man was looking for him on his boat. Roberto had a sad feeling. There was no doubt what this was about. He had been living straight for some time now. When people show up and don't leave their names, when they look for you at a police station as if they were your friend, something was amiss. This had to do with *nipote.* Most certainly.

He was giving up on God. God was playing games with him. Giving him one thing that he treasured, only to take it away. He had grown so attached to his *nipote.* He did not think it possible, but the little boy's laughter gave him hope.

"Nipote, come here," he said to Claudio as the boy stood transfixed beside Anna Lisa before the rows of candy at his favorite confectioner's shop in Rapallo.

"Yes, Nonno? Are you done with your espresso?"

Roberto palmed his grandson's head. His eyes shone. The boy's face was radiant. The rash on his neck was completely gone. This life they shared together suited them both. "Your *mamma*. Did you tell me the truth about her?"

"Yes!" Claudio instantly began to scratch his neck.

"Nipote," Roberto said, again stopping his hand. "This is different. Listen carefully. Can you do that?" The boy nodded. Roberto knelt down to his size. "Before, I asked because, and I am being honest with you, I asked because I did not know you and I wanted to send you back. Now I ask because someone may want to take you back if your mother is alive. Though you tell me she is not. If she is alive, you must tell me. If I hurt someone to keep you from going back, I could go to jail. Tell me, is she alive? It shall be a secret between us."

"Un segreto?" Claudio asked, peering at Anna Lisa, who was perusing the rest of the window of sweets.

"Sì, between us only," Roberto answered gravely.

"Yes, Nonno, my *mamma* is alive." The tiniest of whispers. Roberto already knew the boy would say this. But he had to hear it for himself. His heart twisted. *"Nipote,* then I cannot fight. I must send you back."

The little boy began to sob. His words jumbled together. "Please, Nonno. I know that I lie sometimes," he sobbed. Then, at his grandfather's look, he amended, "All the time. But I am not lying about this. See?" He pointed to all the cigarette burns along his arm. On his back. Scars Roberto has already seen for himself. "My *papà* is truly away. He is not bad, but he cannot take care of me. My *mamma,* she is bad. She did this to me. That is why my *papà* took me from her. And my limp." The little boy's face twisted, his eyes overflowing.

"Enough." Roberto held the boy against his leg. He knew when someone was lying, and the horror in the child's face and voice were not fake. He did not doubt that the woman had done this to her own son. He knew because the boy did not miss his mother in the least. And because the boy cried out, "No, Mamma," from time to time during his sleep.

"I shall protect you with my life, *nipote,* but promise me you are not lying about your mother's treatment."

"I would never lie about that, Nonno. I would rather die than see you hurt."

"Okay. There are a few things we must do then, and they must be done quickly. You must go away for a while. Do not make that face. It is only for a few days."

They parted with Anna Lisa, and she asked if it would be okay to fix the two of them dinner that evening. Roberto agreed, too distracted to argue with her. What he needed to do was take his *nipote* and leave town this very moment and see who showed up in their absence. But then would he always run? Better to stay now and face this danger, no? He refused to acknowledge what was burning in his heart. The fact that if the girl were not present he would have left immediately. But perhaps we can stay and think of a plan and have the girl in our lives, too.

"Roberto," signora Donati, his landlady, said curtly as Roberto held the low iron gate open for his grandson. "Your friend from Scotland came to visit today."

Roberto's stomach turned. "I have several friends from Scotland. What did he look like, *Signora?*"

"Look like?" She continued to sweep, and Roberto herded Claudio ahead of him. Sometimes the old woman would say one thing and end the conversation as if she realized as an afterthought that she was talking to dirt. "He was not so much your friend as a friend of little Claudio's mother."

"Ah yes. Now I remember him. He must be quite tall by now."

"No, you don't remember very well. He is no taller than you. But very wide in the shoulders. Like a rock."

"Thank you, *Signora*."

"Also, the young lady claimed to be your friend. So I let her in, too."

"Too?" Roberto asked with a sinking stomach.

"*Sì*. The man, he has come and gone and come again. They are both inside waiting for you."

Roberto listened to this with his head turned and his hand resting on the doorknob. Before he could react, Claudio ran past him into the house, shouting, "Anna Lisa!"

When Roberto stepped in he saw a stricken Anna Lisa, her bag of groceries still full, seated at his small kitchen table with her hands folded. Beside her stood Claudio, unmindful of the danger, and in front of the stove, next to the box of knives, a well-dressed raven-haired young man.

"Come on in, Robert," the man said. "If I'd have anticipated ye were throwing a party I might have brought ye a jug ay wine. Things bein' as they are"—he lifted his shoulders—"I'd like tae get this ower with quickly."

Arrogant, like Roberto used to be when he used to do the same line of work. You had to be. It threw the opponent off guard. Roberto studied the size of the young man. He was compact but, as signora Donati had said, big just the same. Without thinking, he cracked his knuckles, and the man's eyes went immediately to his hands. Roberto remained silent.

"Surely ye knew I'd be comin' fer the wean someday, eh?"

"His mother is a bad woman." Roberto was stalling for time. He needed more to assess this man. To assess the situation. It had been at least two years since he had fought. He was afraid of letting his grandson see the beast inside him. When he opened that door, which had remained closed for some time now, he was not sure what would come out or if he could control it.

"That's no my problem." The man was unbuttoning his shirt cuffs and folding them up slowly, revealing big forearms, and all the while watching Roberto. He stepped up and to the side, where he could still watch over the girl and the boy; then he stepped toward Roberto in one fluid motion. So fast it made Roberto's mind spin with fear.

"I don't want to go home to her," Claudio suddenly sobbed. Anna Lisa shushed him, taking his chin in her slender fingers.

"I came to prepare a dinner for you and Claudio. I did not know. Do not worry, Roberto. He has not hurt me," she said in Italian.

"*Signorina,*" Roberto said in apology as he lunged toward the man.

The *poliziotto* was walking quickly to the ferry driver's house. He could not be more happy. The ferry driver's landlady had called him. There was some noise—she was certain it was fighting—going on at the ferry driver's home. *Finally, finally I have him,* he thought. *I shall throw him in jail and then both the girl and the boy shall be free of him.*

When the *poliziotto* arrived, the landlady was waiting outside Roberto's apartment. "There, in there," the landlady said. "The walls are shaking."

The *poliziotto* pulled out his gun and kicked the door in, though there was no need to, for the door was already unlocked.

In the corner of the room the girl was holding the boy as the two men squared off. It was the same Scottish man the *poliziotto* had spoken to the day before and the ferry driver, standing toe to toe, each swaying a bit. A table was overturned. A bag of groceries scattered across the floor. The ferry driver's lip was cut and bleeding thick sap onto the floor. The skin over the Scottish man's eye was swelling to the size of a walnut.

The ferry driver had just finished wiping his lip with the back of his hand and spitting blood when his opponent charged him again and the ferry driver propelled him back with a series of jabs. The younger man staggered back, then smiled, his jaw impervious to the blows.

"That's enough. You are both under arrest," the *poliziotto* said, aiming his pistol.

"Aye, mate, that's a hard yin. Seein' as I'm no goin' naywhere but on my way. And I'm no goin' naywhere without the wean."

"Just the same. Put down your weapons."

"What weapons, ye stupit bastard?" the man asked, still eyeballing the ferry driver.

"Stop or I shall shoot," the *poliziotto* said.

The ferry driver felt his breathing tighten. Anything but that. If the *poliziotto* shot this man, their troubles would be bigger. Whoever sent this young man was bigger and stronger and, judging by the dress of this young man, obviously richer. Rich people scared Roberto. They were ruthless. If something happened to this man, bigger fish would come after him. The boy and he might not matter. They might become liabilities. There was only one way out for the bruiser, and Roberto knew that he blocked the entrance.

It was too late to stop the *poliziotto* from firing, so he did the next thing he could think of. He turned quickly on his heels and butted heads with the *poliziotto,* wrenching the gun from his hand. Then he went for the bruiser.

"Anna Lisa, take Claudio," he shouted over his shoulder, sending the Scottish man against the stove with a series of punches. He waited until she was safely out the door before he let loose on the man.

When the *poliziotto* awoke there was blood on the floor. He did not know who had hit him. The girl, the boy, and the Scottish man were gone. Only the ferry driver remained, unconscious beside him. "What happened?" he asked.

"Did she get away?" Roberto demanded, coming slowly to his senses at the *poliziotto*'s question.

"Where is the girl?" the *poliziotto* asked. "I will have you thrown in jail," he said. But there was nothing he could prove.

The next day, when the *poliziotto* found that the family he had thought the girl belonged to did not know her, Roberto was somewhat frightened, but he believed she would show up the following afternoon. There was also nothing the ferry driver could do, for the boy was not really his and so he could not report the missing child or the missing girl to the *poliziotto*'s superiors. They were both at a loss. All Roberto could do was wait. She was keeping his *nipote* safe, he told himself.

For two days the *polizia* questioned the ferry driver, but he had no answers. For two days Roberto waited for Anna Lisa to return his grandson or to send notice to meet him somewhere, but no notice ever came. On the third morning he went to the shop where he had seen the girl working.

"*Buon giorno.*" The saleswoman smiled at him.

"*Buon giorno, Signora.* I am looking for the young saleslady."

"Bah, she is gone. She left two days ago in a hurry. Just like she appeared three weeks ago. In a hurry to find a job."

Roberto's head began to spin. How had he fallen for her tricks? The girl was obviously in cahoots with the man sent to retrieve Claudio. She'd probably been sent ahead of time to locate the boy and ensure that he was truly the one they were looking for. And Roberto had helped her confirm this. He bowed his head and thanked the woman, walking out of her shop. His mistake had been letting his guard down. Of wanting more, when he already had his little *nipote*. His mistake had been in believing that crimes such as the one he'd committed in innocence would not go unpunished. His mistake had been in believing that he, too, deserved the luxuries the people of Portofino received. He should have left town with his *nipote* the moment he'd found out that someone was looking for him. But he had dared to believe that he, too, could find happiness.

After the third week he told his boss that the job reminded him too much of his *nipote* and he turned in his resignation. He would go back to fighting again. He would hunt this bruiser down, though he knew in his heart he would never find his grandson again. He packed his bags and turned in the remainder of his rent for the year. He looked to the heavens for an answer, but the only one he could come up with was that the boy and the girl had only been on loan to him. Roberto knew now not to trust and that to love is too much of a gamble. His eyes, which were once open to the boy, are now shut to the rest of the world.

The *poliziotto* Marco Vespucci spends most of his days searching for hidden bombs. Now and then his mind wanders to where the ferry driver might be.

tHe Last BULLfiςHt

tHey had seen him, he knew, but he kept walking. He lifted a newspaper from one of the stands and boarded the train. July 18, the paper read. GianCarlo could feel his eldest brother, Angelo, bearing down on him from behind, so he picked up his pace, walking through the train, shoving open doors, and moving from car to car. In the sleeping quarters as the train went through the tunnel, Angelo caught up to him and shoved him into one of the empty compartments.

He went headfirst, hitting his lip against the rubber armrest, and felt it pucker immediately. He wiped at the cut and looked up at his two older brothers, Angelo and Marino.

"Enough, enough," Marino said, putting a hand through his hair. "Gianni, where have you been?"

"*Stronzo*," Angelo hissed. "First you disappear for two days and then you have the balls to ruin our mark? We spent the last hour tracking that woman. She was distracted—it was perfect."

"She was in tears on the train. Mamma used to say it was bad luck to hurt someone injured. Do you wish the bad luck to transfer onto us?"

Angelo threw his hands up in the air. "Pah, what do I care for those old superstitions?"

"Anyway, we were to stay on the Italian lines," GianCarlo spat. "That was our agreement. Especially now after that incident with the dead American. Or have you not learned your lesson yet?"

"So you are to teach us lessons now? Who are you supposed to be, the *Rom baro*? Why did *you* get off?" Angelo demanded.

"Because I saw you had picked her out."

"And you never announced your presence to us? You think this is a game? That American game . . . that hide-and-go-seek?" Angelo said.

"It is not I who thinks this is a game," GianCarlo said evenly.

"Enough." Marino pounded his fist against the compartment. "Gianni, I asked you a question. Where have you been?"

"I went to see the bullfights."

"The bullfights," Marino said with a bland look.

Angelo scowled but held his tongue. GianCarlo could see he was about to have a tantrum, so he sat down and lit a cigarette. Marino shook his head and roughed up GianCarlo's hair and took the pack of cigarettes from GianCarlo's hand. "Enough anger. God bless your feet for walking you home safely. We have not eaten for two days. That is why we were following the woman. We are desperate."

"Desperate is not the way to make a good mark." He heard the lecture in his voice and felt instantly bad. "I am sorry."

"Is okay," Marino said. "But we must make a mark today. Otherwise—" He lifted his shoulders.

"I have some money," GianCarlo said and pulled out a roll of bills he had lifted from a shopping woman on his way back. The woman had a gold necklace and a fine red dress and he'd decided she would not miss her purse.

Angelo quickly snatched up the euros and counted them out. GianCarlo's eyes narrowed on Angelo's bruised face. "What happened to you?" he asked. Angelo's eye wore a purple halo, and his neck was bruised.

"Ah, you should have seen the size of the Scottish man who hit brother," Marino said, waving the match in the air to put out the flame. He inhaled deeply of the cigarette and let the smoke out through his nostrils and slapped his palm to his own brow. "The man was giant. Like a boulder. I told Angelo it was not an easy mark and to choose another, but he thought the man a sissy because he was well dressed. A big gold ring. New watch." Marino's gestures were exaggerated, pointing quickly to his own wrist, his ring finger. "Carrying all these packages like a woman. Marino held his arms out to his sides like an ape. "But he was fast. When we came upon him it was like fighting the wind. Our hands grabbing air. Brother took the brunt of the punches." Marino winced, looking at Angelo.

"He surprised me, that is all," Angelo said, his eyes sulking as he looked out the window.

Marino raised his brows. "Ah, but the moment we tried to take the wallet. The Scottish was so quick. He grabbed me and shoved me against the wall, where I bumped my head, and then he grabbed brother by the hand and twisted it. It took two of us to keep him at bay." Marino chuckled. "And all the time he kept smiling at us. It was frightening. Only when he appeared bored did he stop. I think the man was in the business. I tell you that man knew we had marked him from the very start. He simply wanted to see how good we were.

"I tell brother we should go to Scotland; perhaps the take is bigger there, by the look of that man's clothing. I hope we never see him again. I thought he was going to kill brother. Lifted him up with one hand by the neck." Marino chuckled. "It took all I had to wrestle the arm free and then he kicked me so hard here. Look." Marino pulled his pants down to his hip, where a bruise in the shape of a heel print shown an angry blue-black.

GianCarlo whistled.

"It wasn't that bad." Angelo crossed his arms.

"Brother, it was bad. It was very bad, brother. How can you say it was not?" Marino nodded gravely. "What a story to tell the others, eh?"

"Tell others. Who is there to tell?" Angelo asked, excited again.

GianCarlo looked down at his hands. He had not meant to stay this long. He had meant only to gather his things. Leave a note of farewell. But seeing his brothers like this. Starved without him. "Let us go eat and then we can think on what to do while our stomachs are full," he suggested.

"Perhaps we can eat in Cannes?" Marino said sheepishly.

"Che fregatura!" A rip-off, Angelo said, throwing his hand in the air. "Those prices are for movie stars, not for one who wears tattered clothes."

Marino looked down at his clean trousers, striped burgundy and blue, tight and ending at the ankles. He felt suddenly like a court jester at Angelo's words. At least his clothes were clean. And what to expect with no women to wash for them? His gaze drifted down to his knees—patched over twice with a floral pattern, which had seemed flamboyant at the time—then farther, to where the hem hung frayed. "Surely there is someplace not so expensive." He turned one foot over to inspect the hanging rubber heel he had mended with copper wire.

"What have I just told you?" GianCarlo asked. "We risk the wrath of the French ruffians. We must stick to our Italian trains. Leave the French to theirs. Why tempt fate when there is room for us all?"

At this Angelo snickered, "How noble. From you, who has been eating well." He placed a hand on the glass partition and leaned against the door, looking out into the walkway. His other hand, GianCarlo noticed, lay flat across his stomach. "Try to talk sense into Marino. He has become crazed over a *gadji*."

"A girl?" GianCarlo grinned. *"Non c'é male,"* he said. Not bad. For his brother Marino was not one for romance. "Is this true?"

"Sì, a beautiful girl."

"A stinky *gadje.* She will infect us with her uncleanliness," Angelo said. "And more importantly, she shall get us killed."

"A *gadje?"* GianCarlo asked. His people, the Romany kept to themselves. Anyone not Romany was a *gadje,* an outsider. Though it is something their mother never kept to, which is why she broke with her family when she married their father, an Italian, a simple *gadje.* It amuses him that his brother is following in her footsteps. Someday their bloodlines will have almost no traces of Romany. Which is what the rest of the world wishes, is it not? To purge itself of their kind? "A *gadje?"* he repeats.

"Sì, the heart knows no divisions. Romany, *gadje,* what does it matter?" Marino gestured into the air.

"It matters, *stupido,* when the girl belongs to one of the French ruffians!" Angelo threw his hands up. "Talk to him, GianCarlo. He thinks I am being strict. It is true I do not like the *gadje;* they are like dogs. But must you choose the very girl of one of theirs?"

"What does she look like?" GianCarlo put an arm around Marino and punched his shoulder to cancel Angelo's bad mood from affecting their conversation.

"Che bella." Marino grinned, punching him back.

"Che bruta!" Angelo contradicted. "She has no teeth."

"Only the front two are missing. Otherwise she is *perfetta.* Her hair, golden. Like spaghettini. So slender, her dress floats behind her like a ghost." At his description GianCarlo and Angelo both laughed.

"Brother, your poetry is pathetic," Angelo said. To GianCarlo he joked, "He thinks he is like the poet Papusza now. Take care you do not meet the same fate as she did."

"So be it. For this woman I would disown myself," Marino said.

"I agree with Angelo. Your poetry is pathetic," GianCarlo

chuckled. "But truly, Marino, we must talk about your infatuation with this girl. It can come to nothing. Why anger the others?
There are plenty *bellezze* in Italy."

Marino scoffed, "Have you forgotten my face? It is a wonder
this one even looked my way."

"Let us discuss your *bella ragazza* later," GianCarlo joked.
"We eat now."

They ate a big dinner in Verona, Angelo insisting they order *vino
da tavola,* cheap table wine, so as to stretch the money out longer.
GianCarlo noted that Angelo did not return the money to him
but put it in his own pocket. If it would keep them from fighting,
he would allow it.

As they sat filling their bellies they watched an old woman
with two dachshunds; with her tattered cloak, she looked as if she
had stepped out of an ancient play. Her hands were gnarled, and
she had a crooked nose. Her spine formed a frail hump, and she
walked with a cane to keep her head up. One step for every
painstaking five minutes. The dogs grew so tired of her they kept
from matching their steps to hers. They would wait then, as the
end of her cloak brushed past them, scurry forward a few steps to
catch up to her, then stop, holding a paw up to wait again.

"I cannot stand to watch this." Angelo's face twisted in frustration. He wiped his hands on his pants and leaned straight back
in his chair to watch her. Then, shaking his head, he attacked his
steak with a knife.

"This is true," Marino said. "I wish to pick her up and carry
her to her destination."

"Yes, but probably then she would turn and head back the
other way to spite you," Angelo said.

GianCarlo smiled inwardly at his brothers. They fought all

the time these days, and he hardly recognized them from the boys they had been when their mother, rest her soul, had been alive. But at this moment, eating, they were happy. One could not tell from Angelo's frown and Marino's protruding cheekbones, but he could see it in their chatter.

As they went through the crowd on their way home, Gian-Carlo bent to place a coin in her cup and the woman grabbed his wrist. "Leaving again?" she asked. "Do you think you can return and find things unchanged?"

Her words shook his composure, and his brothers clapped him on the shoulders. "We are leaving, now. *Buona notte, Signora,*" Marino said. When the woman would not release Gian-Carlo, Marino said again, gently prying her fingers, "Good night, *Signora.*"

GianCarlo had ordered a big meal, much more than he could eat, enough so that he could bring the leftovers to the young orphan boy who slept on their doorstep without angering Angelo. But when they arrived home, the little boy and his mat were gone from the front landing.

"Where is Pietro?" GianCarlo frowned. The landing looked much too clean. The boy had showed up on their doorstep a few days ago. He was running away from his mother. He showed them his cigarette burns. GianCarlo doubts that the boy's true name is Pietro. At times he has had to repeat the name before the boy's head snapped to attention. They asked if he had no other relatives. A grandfather, he said. "But they would hurt him if I returned."

"They?" GianCarlo asked, but the boy refused to speak any further.

Usually the mat where the boy lay was rolled up and neatly placed in one corner, if he was still out begging on the streets. He preferred the neighborhood or inside the courtyard in front of

L' Arena, where the *polizia* did not bother him and the opera patrons dropped coins into his paper cup, for he was only six years old. "Where is his mat?"

Marino looked at the ground and scratched his head, then glanced at Angelo.

"I told him to go. There was no food." Angelo's voice picked up volume.

"There was no food and we told him he was better to beg on other doorsteps until your return," Marino said.

GianCarlo knew that Angelo had chased the boy away and that the orphan would not return for fear of GianCarlo learning the truth and fighting again with Angelo. "He is an innocent in all of this. How could you—" GianCarlo could feel a hot anger burning up his back. "He has no one. We have one another."

"Gianni," Marino said softly. "We had no food. Whether we chased him away or not. We had no food even for ourselves. Better he lands on another doorstep, eh?"

GianCarlo nodded. "Is this what you tell yourself? At our doorstep the young one was under no obligation to give anything in return. On other doorsteps . . ." He let his silence fill the air. "The simple act of allowing him to sleep under our care kept the wolves away from him."

As he lay in bed that evening, GianCarlo let go of the false smile he had worn all day. It was good to see his brothers, even Angelo, with his sour face. There was no question they loved one another. But though his brothers did not see it, GianCarlo had been changed by watching a simple bullfight. He was different. Well, not simply because of the bullfight but because of all that had occurred. He knew without a doubt if he did not leave now he would lose his soul for good. He would become like that bull, performing for the entertainment of others. To the death. He had discovered a violence within himself when he had picked the pockets of the audience in Pamplona as they had cheered on the matador encouraging the poor creature's death.

He had always been the coolheaded one, but now he felt an uncontrollable rage coming from within him; that was what he had aimed at the barbaric crowd that night. And the most frightening thing was that it had not left him the next morning, this anger. Instead it had burrowed deeper into his being, so that every day he felt it building. This life he was leading was eroding his soul. He did not know how to harness this monster. He wished to lash out, and he had never felt this way before. He recognized it as the same force that looked out from Angelo's desperate eyes, and this terrified GianCarlo more than anything. There was barely any hint of his mother's goodness left within him. So faint was her voice. He knew that the only answer was to leave. To find work somewhere far enough so that he could not return to his brothers when his resolve grew weak. It wouldn't be easy, but it would be harder for Marino and Angelo. And maybe he could enroll somewhere in school. Learn to read. The whole world seemed closed to him when he saw people reading the papers.

Learn a trade. Any trade, though the thought of metalwork, of working with his hands, appealed to him. Many a time he has admired the handiwork of the ironsmiths in the imposing gates and terraces of large houses. In the blue patina, copper, or black wrought iron. He has fingered the intricate designs of ivy, poppies, sunbursts, and medieval shields in the ironworks of these houses. He would like that.

But now is not a good time to leave, when you need to convince Marino that this girl may cause more trouble than she is worth.

GianCarlo dreamt he was in a smoky tavern, his lungs choking, filling with dark, tubercular laughter. When he woke it was pale gray daylight and Angelo was smoking a cigarette over him.

"What is it?" GianCarlo asked.

"We must collect Marino. He has gone to see this girl again."

Cannes was six hours away by train. "Are you sure? Perhaps he has just gone for a morning walk."

"He sneaks away when he goes to see her because he knows how it angers me."

GianCarlo sat up in bed and gestured for a cigarette. Angelo slapped his shirt pocket, looking for his pack, then found the cigarettes bent in his trouser pockets.

"I know he went to see her because the bathroom smells like cologne."

"When has he ever worn cologne?" GianCarlo scoffed, trying to make light of the situation.

"Yes, when?" Angelo gave him a pointed look and brushed an impatient hand over his head. "The other evening he walked into the fragrance shop and the woman gave him a handful of small samples. Now he tries a new one each evening." Angelo looked like a parent whose child had failed to obey him. First GianCarlo had wandered and returned to the fold, and now Marino was gone.

GianCarlo sighed and pushed his legs over the bed to pull on his trousers. Another setback. He had wanted to sit his brothers down this morning and speak to them with a cool head to tell them he was leaving. He didn't know if he could stand a minute more. The longer he stayed, the more he could feel himself taking root. The stronger the hate inside him grew. He wanted to be on the road. Making a new path for himself. He wanted the countryside to blur past him from the window of a train into a new country.

The neighborhood Romanies sneered at the two of them when

they stepped out into the courtyard. Even signora V, who used to play cards with their mother. She turned her back when Gian-Carlo raised a hand in greeting.

"What has happened since I left?" GianCarlo asked. "I've been gone three days and I come back to find Pietro evicted from our doorstep"—at this his voice could not fight off the irritation in him, ready to explode like dynamite—"and now the neighbors are looking at us with evil in their eyes. Is it safe to walk our own neighborhood?"

Angelo stuffed his hands into his pockets and continued walking.

"Thieves." Signora V spat on the ground as they walked by. "You give us a bad name. As if we do not have enough trouble landing on our doorstep, you must bring the *polizia* closer our way. If your mother could see the three of you now. This was never her wish. What if they riot and burn our buildings?"

Angelo kicked her wash bucket filled with water aside. "Shut up or I may be the one to burn your building down. To quiet you."

"Angelo," GianCarlo said, placing a hand on his brother's shoulder.

"Ah. Hear how he threatens me? Did everyone hear?" She put her hands on her hips and threw her head back to shout at the neighbors. Her turquoise kerchief, folded over her head and tied at her chin, strained with the veins on her neck as she shouted. Windows opened and shut. People stuck their heads down to look at them. To GianCarlo, she said, "Two days' pay my husband wasted because of you. Two days they questioned and questioned him. And signora P, too. We thought a mob would ensue. What have we ever done to you? My husband is a hard worker. Never will we be free from persecution. Gypsies they call us again. When it was becoming Romany. You have slid us back down the hillside into the mud."

"Brother, tell me what has gone on in my absence," GianCarlo pleaded as they continued to walk, leaving the shouts of the woman behind.

"Someone told the local *polizia* that the thieves who hurt the *americano* lived in our apartment building."

At this GianCarlo said nothing. He did not wish to get into it with his brother about how the famous American had died and what part Angelo had truly played. "And what happened then?" GianCarlo asked.

"What happens every time one Romany in a thousand commits a bad deed? The authorities and the community become like a mob. They harass the other hundred living in the neighborhood. One officer took signora V's grandson Emilio in his arms and rocked him in front of her. Brother, I thought he was going to throw the infant down. 'How light he is,' the officer said without a smile. 'So small, so easy to slip from my grasp. Now, tell me. What do you know about the *americano*'s death?' I was so frightened for that baby."

"Were you questioned?"

"No," Angelo said, refusing to elaborate.

On the train to Cannes, GianCarlo thought about his mother. Signora V was right. His mother had had other plans for them. She had brought them up intentionally keeping them from her family. She did not want them to learn to be part of the ancient tradition of blacksmiths, horse traders, auto traders, musicians, basket weavers—good trades, and yet she had wanted nothing that had to do with being a Romany. Because she had believed it would be a mark against them in life. Weren't they already doing much better than her own family since she had married their father, an Italian? she'd asked.

GianCarlo had sighed. He supposed, he'd told her, if working in a fruit-preserves factory, the five of them, twelve hours of bottling and packaging for the entire family, was considered better than any of the other trades. Trades he thought more noble than putting fancy fruit in jars for *gadje*. She'd taught them a lesson here or there to supplement the missed schooling, though she herself had nothing more than an eight-year-old's education.

But it had made his mother happy to leave her Romany blood behind and work side by side with their father. She was Italian now, too, to whoever asked. Then their father had caught a bad virus and died within two weeks. Their mother, like a true Romany, had been afraid of becoming infected not by the disease but by an inoculation needle tainting her body. In that she was still a Roma. Distrustful of having a foreign instrument put into her blood. She believed in absolute cleanliness, and she still believed in her soul that the *gadje* were unclean. So she had followed their father. And after she was gone, the boss had turned the remaining three of them out of a job.

"Is nothing personal. You are good boys. Didn't I give you all work?" he had said. Even though the three of them had been inoculated, he turned them out. But they knew. They knew it was because of the whispering of the workers at the factory. Gypsies, they called them. Filthy. GianCarlo had been twelve, Marino fourteen, Angelo sixteen. "I cannot risk an outbreak. An infection into my product. You understand?"

"May we come back after a few months?" Angelo had asked. Angelo was still soft then. There was still a tenderness in his eyes. He still trusted in goodness. Still fresh from their mother's influence.

But the boss had shook his head and shut the door on the three of them.

Most people would think they had been stealing for years. That it was a tradition passed on for generations. Such a lie. Such an untruth. They had learned to do it, to survive, they had been taught the tricks of the trade from a *gadje,* no less! Any orphan would have done the same. The learning they had had to do. The beatings during a theft gone wrong. Once Marino had gotten cornered and his head kicked into confusion. GianCarlo had had his hand crushed. Which is how he became their point man, as his hand healed.

They had forced themselves to learn after they were refused job after job, *e così via,* after their mother passed. Angelo refused to have the three of them separated. If they kept paying the rent, the landlord never mentioned that there were three minors under his roof. He did not ask how they found the money. Or what part of their soul they had to give up in attaining it.

Their mother. How GianCarlo missed her. Her friendship. Her smile, the way it could fool him into thinking all would in the end be all right. She with her quirky ideas of what was Romany and what was *gadje* and confusing them at times by choosing which traits she wanted to keep. She wanted to pretend she was not Romany, and yet how she despised some of the *gadje* traditions. They had nothing left of her but the Romany wedding picture she had persuaded their father to take. It hung on a corner wall near the bathroom. She smiled down at them with her post-photography-colored lips. The only bright portion in a black-and-white picture.

My God. GianCarlo shook his head, smiling at the memory. She'd even refused them keeping a dog in the house because the animal was unclean. She thought *gadje* ridiculous for allowing such a thing to live with them. In the end she had been deluded. They could act and pretend they were *gadje.* She could marry one and they could be half *gadje,* but the Romany part of them always seeped through.

It was as his grandmother, his mother's mother, had once told him. She'd said, "It is as if we have an invisible mark pasted to our foreheads that tells the *gadje* we were once slaves. And once a slave, always a slave. Never have I known their treatment of us to be better than that given to serfs."

And everything bad about the world the *gadje* laid at their feet. Even to go as far back as blaming them for making the nails that had crucified Christ.

In Cannes, GianCarlo asked, "And where does this woman live, Marino's girl?"

"Here," Angelo replied.

"Where here?"

"In the train station," Angelo replied.

GianCarlo looked around the station and shook his head. It appeared safe enough for tourists. The weather was warm, the palm trees danced in the small breeze. Except for the occasional theft, they were safe. But for him and Angelo there were different rules. The French gang that claimed the French lines would spot them immediately. One always recognized one's own kind.

"I thought for a moment you said—"

"I did."

"Inside the trains, you mean?" GianCarlo asked.

"No, brother, why is it so hard to understand? They live *in* the station."

"But where do they sleep?" GianCarlo spotted a young blond boy a few years younger staring at him. Possibly twelve, maybe fourteen. Something funny in his angelic face.

"How should I know? I've only been here once to collect Marino from the girl. It is as if he is intoxicated when he is with her. You will see how ridiculous he looks."

Twice, GianCarlo thinks but does not say. *You have been here twice. Once more for the American who was killed. That you killed? Brother, what truly happened that night?*

"How will we find him if you don't know their hiding place?" GianCarlo asked, watching the French boy whistle low as he kept walking.

"Sit here," Angelo said, motioning to a tiled wall where at the bottom a six-foot-long bar ran, enough to put their small buttocks on. "That one, he is part of their group."

"That one?" GianCarlo asked in surprise. "If his hair was any longer I'd think him a girl. He is so attractive."

Angelo looked from side to side. "He has seen me once. He will notify the rest of them."

"And how is it the girl's boyfriend allows brother to visit her?"

Angelo shook his head. "They don't know who we are. They think, for the moment, Marino is simply a customer."

"A customer?"

"Yes, brother. I told you she was unclean."

"A prostitute?" GianCarlo asked in disbelief. "I thought you meant she was a *gadje*."

"She is that, too."

GianCarlo tried to understand what Angelo was telling him. "Who is their leader, then?"

"I have yet to see him," Angelo said.

The next thing GianCarlo knew a group of eight or ten such children appeared. All fair-haired, light brown, blond, white blond, blue eyes, green, hazel. "My God, in white gowns they could sing in a choir."

Angelo snorted. "The church would crumble if they set foot in it. See the littlest one? With the scar along the back of his neck that goes down into his shirt?" At GianCarlo's nod he said, "He fought a man twice his size. And I can only tell you he won."

"How do you know this?"

"Marino told me. Watch now. They have made their target. See how they work. Different from us." Angelo's face lighted with fascination.

THE FIVE-FORTY-FIVE TO CANNES / 237

A young girl was in their group. She wore a small pink shirt and blue skirt, her outfit completed with a beaded blue cap. She could have been a young tourist wandered off from her parents. Except for the fact that she hung with seven boys, all of whom could have been her brothers.

The young girl was holding a puppy. She cooed and petted the puppy. She sat alone and smiled. "Would you like to buy a puppy?" she asked the tourists. And GianCarlo became fascinated. She was his equivalent. She was the scout who picked out the target. Of course the tourists could not bring a puppy across the seas. No, they told her time and again. But they could not resist petting the animal. Taking it in their arms as the puppy licked their faces.

"Why can't you keep him?" a woman asked, rubbing the puppy's ears as she knelt down, oblivious to the young boys jostling past them as they kicked a soccer ball beside her.

The young girl shouted at them to watch out. "You will hurt my puppy." The boys responded by laughing. It was a canned act, GianCarlo could see, but to someone outside of the business it was ingenious.

"My mother," the girl said. "Maman will not allow me to keep another puppy. I have given all of them away. The entire litter but Brigitte. Each day it grows harder and harder, for she follows me everywhere. I hate to give her up. But Maman insists."

"I wish I could take her. But I don't live here," the American replied, holding a map, wearing a baseball cap that read *S.F.*

"Non?" the young girl asked innocently.

"Non," the woman replied. "Isn't her accent sweet?" the woman asked an onlooker. The woman stood, beaming down at the little girl, while unbeknownst to her, her entire purse had been picked clean. The young boys reported twenty feet away to the one with the scar and were putting on her watch and already trying to hock it to passing customers. "Well, I hope you find a

238 / Tess Uriza Holthe

home for her." The woman waved to the charming young girl as she boarded the train.

"Perfetto, eh?" Angelo shook his head.

GianCarlo shrugged; he'd grown tired of waiting. He was highly competitive and he thought the job amateur but did not wish to dwell on it if he was planning to leave. It was tempting to discuss what the ruffians could have done better. He went upstairs to buy a sandwich and espresso. The young one with the scar followed him. But GianCarlo pretended not to notice. He was descending the stairs, pulling the thin French bread with salami and cheese from its clear plastic container, when he saw Marino strolling toward Angelo with a smile across his face. He looked well rested. His hair was a mess. A thin twig of a girl followed behind him. Marino placed an arm around her possessively. The girl stood before Angelo and flipped her hair with disinterest.

"Who is next?" she asked.

Angelo shook his head, red-faced.

"You?" she asked as GianCarlo approached. GianCarlo choked on the bread, and Angelo had to slap his back hard to dislodge the food. The thin boy with the scar hung off to the side, watching GianCarlo closely. The girl looked at GianCarlo's piece of bread and salami strewn on the floor.

"Henri." She motioned to the boy. "Fetch me something to eat."

The boy approached just as GianCarlo offered her his sandwich. She took it and thanked him with a leisurely smile that studied the length of GianCarlo. He shifted uncomfortably.

"I know you," Henri said.

"Yes? Where?" GianCarlo asked.

"Somewhere. I have seen you before."

GianCarlo shrugged. "Yes, possibly. What of it?" He didn't

like the boy's stare. It felt like the stare of a rabid animal. Then just as quickly the boy smiled an eerie sweet smile and took off running with his pack of look-alikes.

"Marino, let us go from here," GianCarlo said impatiently. "There is much to discuss."

"*Sí, andiamo.*" Marino leaned over to kiss the girl. She let him but was busy counting the money he handed her. Marino added an extra ten of GianCarlo's money from the other evening. "Buy yourself something beautiful."

"With ten euros?" the girl scoffed, snatching the bill. "*Oui,* I shall buy myself a new dress, a manicure, a car." She was still laughing as she walked into the crowd, and then she was gone.

"*Che bella.*" Marino shook his head, his eyes shining with love.

GianCarlo looked from him to Angelo, whose look seemed to say, What did I tell you? "Come, Romeo, there is much to discuss." When Marino still stood there, watching where the girl had disappeared, he asked, "What is her name?"

"Georgette," Marino said, pronouncing the name as if it were a rhapsody.

"And her boyfriend's?" GianCarlo asked, watching Marino carefully.

A frown crossed Marino's face, knocking him from his cloud. "Jean-Louis."

"Such a precious name," GianCarlo scoffed. "Is he as pretty as the rest of them?"

Marino led the way to their train. "Prettier," he said with disgust. "All right, brother, I understand your point. She has a boyfriend. But what is to keep her from falling for me?"

GianCarlo remained silent, and Marino laughed at his own words. "What indeed," he joked. "Signore Empty-pockets." He turned his trouser pockets out. "I gave her our last euros."

"We noticed," Angelo said. It was said gently and seemingly

with understanding of Marino's swollen heart. GianCarlo marveled at how now and then the old Angelo seemed to resurface from the deep. It made him sorry he was to tell them he would be leaving.

He blurted it out the moment they sat down. "I am leaving."

His brothers said nothing for a long time. "It is how I imagined," Marino said. "You would never have stayed away for three days. Didn't I tell you?" he asked Angelo.

GianCarlo looked at Angelo, ready for a fight, but Angelo continued to stare out the window. "When you were gone, it gave me time to think. It is time for us to part. Ordinary men, they grow older. They leave, they find one another again. And then when Marino found this girl I realized he wished to leave, too, and neither he nor you were doing it for spite."

"Never for spite," GianCarlo said, his heart bursting with relief and love for Angelo. "And we will find one another again, as you say."

Angelo simply smiled out into the darkening sky. "Perhaps."

"When do you leave, youngest?" Marino asked.

"Tomorrow, at the earliest. The longer I stay . . ." He stopped; the words were difficult in coming out. "The longer I stay . . ." He felt immediately bad at the ease of how this had gone. A deserter: that was what he was.

As if reading his mind, Angelo said, "In war a deserter would be shot."

"Brother," Marino said to him, "what did we discuss? If Gian-Carlo wishes to leave, let him go."

Angelo nodded. "So be it."

"There is something else we must discuss. Marino, you cannot continue to visit this girl. What if they find out we run the Italian lines? They will cut out your heart for walking into their territory."

Marino just shrugged. "They will not find out."

GianCarlo saw at that moment that Marino would not listen. He had found some form of happiness, and nothing they could say would cause him to stop seeing the girl. Except for the girl telling him to stop coming, and why would she do that? But this was not his concern anymore. The more he concerned himself, the more he would find cause to stay, and he needed to leave first thing.

They rode the train lines and made their marks, one after the other. With GianCarlo in the group things went quickly, almost breathtakingly so. GianCarlo could feel the blood and the quick excitement racing through him, and again this strange violence that had taken up residence inside him building and building, so that he jostled their marks as he left. He shouldered people harder. And when he selected the mark, he no longer worried about anyone's welfare. He picked out the elderly, whereas before he would only have done so if they were desperate. By the end of the day, as they counted the take, he was sweating and fevered. "I cannot stay," he said.

In Verona they walked home with heavy hearts. "Do you remember when Mamma used to take us to the *museo*?" he asked.

Yes, his brothers nodded with smiles on their faces. "And her book lessons?"

"Yes. I never had the heart to tell her I was no longer learning." Marino smiled. "'Good morning, brown cow.' Remember that one?" Marino laughed, shaking his head.

"Or that signora V's five-year-old grandson could read the entire book better than me," GianCarlo laughed. "But it was nice to let her think we were like our neighbors."

"We *were* like them then," Marino said.

"No, I don't think we ever were," Angelo said.

They drank and talked long into the evening and before bedtime they shook hands without speaking words of good-bye. He knew that he would wake and in the morning his brothers would be gone. It was easier that way.

In the morning it was as he had predicted. Angelo and Marino's beds were straightened, the sheets tattered but tucked in the way their father used to do. He went and stood over each bed: "God watch over thee and bless your legs to walk you safely home and your minds to think clearly."

He gathered his two pairs of pants; his sweater for winter, for soon it would be turning cold; his one pair of shoes. His nicer pair he left beside Marino's bed, for him to wear when he visited his new girlfriend. And as an afterthought he unzipped his duffel bag and left Marino a red silk shirt that Manuela had given him for Christmas; he knew Marino had admired it very much. On Angelo's bed he left his part of the take from the previous evening. These served as his good-bye letters, for the three of them could neither write nor read.

In his backpack he found Marino had given him two cologne samples and that Angelo had placed their mother and father's wedding picture, wrapped in newspaper. He unwrapped the wedding picture and replaced it on the wall beside the bathroom to look after his brothers.

When he closed the door to their apartment the first thing he saw was the French boy Henri speaking to their neighbor signora V. "Yes, can you imagine? The *poliziotto* came here inspecting each one of our houses for the death of the American from Cannes. How they traced it back here to our piazza in Verona, six hours away, is beyond me. But, ah." She shook her head. "Those three boys. Those boys. Somehow I know they are involved."

They met eyes over the old woman's rantings. And then the French boy was running and GianCarlo took chase. If the boy got back to his French gang and told them that his brothers were more than customers, that they were also thieves crossing into the French lines and had killed the American, whether by accident or not, they would hurt Marino and Angelo.

GianCarlo caught up to him at the train station but the boy wriggled out of his grasp. In that instant, however, he saw that the boy's eyes were dilated. No doubt from inhaling glue, as Gian-Carlo had seen them doing yesterday. Handing small brown paper bags to one another. They were running at full sprint, leaping over parked suitcases, past passengers who shouted after them. GianCarlo could feel the anger building to an explosive point inside his chest. Pounding to get out.

He could hear Angelo's voice from the previous day. "That one. The one with the scar. He killed a man twice his size."

He won't do that to me. I have twice his heart, GianCarlo promised himself as he followed the boy onto the Ventimiglia line. He thought he had lost the boy until he saw the white shirt through the crowd in the sleeping quarters. GianCarlo parted the doors and followed him down the hallway. A little surprised to find the boy seated and waiting for him in the last compartment.

GianCarlo stepped inside and looked at the boy, Henri, who smiled at him.

"What is it?" the boy asked.

"You do not think I would let you run back to tell on my brothers, do you?" GianCarlo asked. "It was an accident. They were not trying to cross into your territory that day."

The boy propped his feet up on the opposite seat. "And you think this is why I have come?"

GianCarlo's eyes narrowed. He was a little winded from having to run through the station with his backpack full. "Why, then?"

"Your brothers are harmless. We knew immediately it was the two of them who hurt the American. They are sloppy."

At his words GianCarlo reddened. The description was accurate.

"And the romantic one. He talks in his sleep to my sister when he lays with her. They are brainless. Who do they think our leader is? He doesn't even know he lays with her each evening. The one I heard you call a prostitute is our leader. My sister. But the three of you are so arrogant.

"And you are good at what you do. But only you. Without you they are like a chicken with its head cut off. I didn't come here for them. I came for you. You are the brains of the organization. Without you, they are nothing. Without you, they do not interfere with us."

"Well, you'll be happy to know I am leaving. I was leaving today. So leave them alone." It took all his pride but GianCarlo added, "Please."

The boy laughed. So sweet his face looked like a golden-haired child laughing with delight. "No. You are not leaving. You are not going anywhere. And your brothers, the stupid ones. They will think you far away and never know our sister has ordered you killed."

At his words GianCarlo saw movement from behind him. Eight or nine, he couldn't count the small ruffians lining the corridor outside the compartment. One by one they slowly let themselves in. Boys, fourteen and fifteen in age. All holding weapons. GianCarlo could feel the rage build up in him. Closer and closer they moved. He put his bag down slowly and looked for the one with the biggest blade and charged forward.

HOMECOMING

ON the train ride over, she dreamt she had dropped the urn. Does one ever plan to make such a trip? Her arms are bare as she steps from the train into Ventimiglia Station. The tropical heat does nothing to take away the chill that nests inside of her. She rubs her limbs with a fierce irritation until she feels her blood circulating. She is still nauseated from the plane ride. Claudette Dumont has a fear of planes, an even greater fear of gathering her husband's ashes.

A deep breath. *You can do this.* She seeks out the women's toilet, pushes her sunglasses to the top of her head, and cups her hands to douse water on her face. The coolness is a balm to her swollen eyelids. She stares at her lavender eyes, prodding the puffy purple skin around them with her fingertips. Her eyes suffer horribly whenever she cries, the surrounding skin swelling to gigantic proportions.

"What does the other girl look like?" her husband, Chazz, always jokes after she has had a good cry, pretending she has been in a fight. *Used* to joke. How long will it take before she grows accustomed to the past tense? How sad when the time comes that she accepts her husband as deceased. She hates the sound of the word. So close to the word *diseased*. But she equally despises the words *passed away, dead, mort*. There are no good words for death.

When she emerges from the toilet, the station is empty. She reaches a hand to the back of her neck to rub away the sudden prickling of her skin, turning just in time to see two gaunt-looking men following her. She picks up her pace. The underground is a maze; she needs to get upstairs. She can feel the trains rolling above as they arrive. Big metal wheels grinding to a halt on iron rails. The sound loud enough to drown out any cries for help.

Where are the stairs? *Merde.* She hurries down the white-tiled corridor toward what appears to be a dead end but continues on as if this is where she intends to go. The door to the men's toilet opens and the nice young man who helped her with her suitcase appears, wearing his yellow backpack. He looks from her to the men following her. "GianCarlo," she says, a bit too loudly. Her voice ricochets from the cement floor to the tiled walls.

The Italian boy comes to her and takes the handle of her suitcase. *"Signora,"* he says, his eyes never leaving the two men, almost as if he recognizes them. "Let me help you to carry this. Is not a good station to be alone." The two men following stop to let them pass, and Claudette feels her heart thundering in her throat. She thinks she may burst into tears. Instinctively she places her hand on GianCarlo's arm and keeps pace with him, fighting the impulse to look over her shoulder.

"Thank God," she says, placing a hand to her chest as he leads her through the labyrinth and up the stairs.

When they are aboveground she takes deep gulps of air. The relief of seeing other passengers waiting for their trains washes over her. "I went to use the toilet and found everyone gone!"

"Yes, *Signora*, this is not a good station to be alone."

"It is not as I remember," she says. "I lived here once. Not here, but in Cannes. I find it changed." The boy nods. Whether he understands or not, she cannot say. He is a handsome boy. Curly black hair, dark olive skin. Fifteen, sixteen? She once wished for a young brother such as this. With caring eyes and bashful demeanor. He reminds her of another boy she grew up with. "Will you sit awhile with me, GianCarlo?" she asks.

"Sorry, *Signora,* I have somewhere to be. But come, see those women there?" He points to four women chatting happily on a stone bench. "They wait in front of your Cannes line. And see there"—again he points—"a conductor. You will be safe from those men, *Signora.*"

"Yes, of course. Forgive me. I am a bit nervous. Jumpy. *Comprendez?*"

"*Sì,*" he answers. "Be careful on the French lines as well, *Signora.* There are a group of men. Same as these. They ride the lines back and forth."

"*C'est vrai?*" she asks, hoping he will understand her French, for she is too anxious to think of the appropriate words in English.

"*Sì,* I do not lie."

"It has changed since I last visited."

"If for some reason you find yourself alone, scream. Give them your money. That is all they want. But try to stay with people at all times. *Capisce?*"

"*Oui, merci, GianCarlo.* God bless. You are like a guardian angel." She tries on a smile, and it wavers.

The boy looks at the ground. "*Buon viaggio, Signora.*" He waves as he boards the train, heading back in the direction they have just come.

Claudette takes a seat beside the women on the stone bench and wonders if she has confused him somehow. She tries to warn him as his train jolts, then starts, but he waves. She shrugs. Perhaps he was cutting class and simply riding the lines.

The women seated beside her stand, and Claudette checks her watch and follows as they board the five-forty-five to Cannes.

248 / Tess Uriza Holthe

Chazz's father had suggested they have his ashes sent home. "It can be arranged quite quickly, I assure you, Claudette. You may find things very different without Chazz." She had bowed her head, realizing that he was for once trying to extend some form of kindness her way.

"Thank you, but I would like to bring him home myself." She hadn't added what has haunted her for weeks now. *I am, after all, to blame.*

When his father said, "Damn him for leaving," Claudette remained silent during the tirade. "Another one of his spur-of-the-moment grand ideas. What was he thinking, going to Cannes?"

She did not say what she was thinking. She did not say, "He was running, of course. From my decision." The night she was to tell him whether she wished for a divorce or not, he had impulsively bought a ticket to Milano to avoid her verdict. She flinches from the thought, though she knows it is true, that if she hadn't been selfish, hadn't thought only of her own well-being, he would be alive today.

So sad, she thinks at a distance from herself. Like a bird circling from above, looking down at her physical self seated on the train. How sad that when Chazz was alive she refused to return to Cannes. "But, Dettie, that's where all your memories are. All our good ones. Don't you want to go back to them?" he had asked.

And she had said, "No, my memories are here with you now, Chazz," and felt disingenuous. She remembers the day. It was raining on the Golden Gate Bridge. The sky around them and the cement walkways on either side of the bridge were a wet charcoal gray, the rust-colored bridge like slick clay. And Chazz, as he drove, remarked on how he wished they were in sultry Cannes.

"Besides, I'm afraid I will find it different somehow." What she meant was, selfishly, that Chazz was different. He was diminished from his illness, and she did not want to return with that Chazz. She did not want to ruin those perfect memories. The one of the confident Chazz with the spry step, his smiles reflected in the people he passed. And lastly, she did not want her old friend Justine at La Croisette to see how changed he was. He was not the Chazz they had vied for that day.

"See whom he asks to serve his table," Justine had said, her voice giddy as she deposited a plate oiled from a *niçoise* salad into the plastic tub in the kitchen. The plates had clinked with the forks and spoons. And then Justine's disappointment a few minutes later when Chazz, the man on sidewalk table five, had spoken directly, unmistakably to Claudette.

"But then how would I ask you out?" he had asked, fluidly in French, after overhearing Claudette wishing all the impatient Americans back home, where they'd come from.

She could have flown direct to France, but she wanted to follow the route he had taken that night. So here she is staring out at the same sights, perhaps on the same train, in the same seat. She knows one thing. That he had boarded the five-forty-five to Cannes that evening from Ventimiglia Station. The beginning of the end for him. There had been eyewitnesses from the moment he stepped down from the train. After which he had disappeared into the crowd until a few moments later, when he was hit by the taxi.

It was always her fear that he would call at some frightening hour and she would walk barefoot across the cool wooden floors of their San Francisco Victorian to the phone and find that something bad had happened. She hadn't counted on someone else calling because he wouldn't be able to.

What about his fear? What had he felt, running alone through the terminal? Which one of his demons had chased him into oncoming traffic? His thoughts of her leaving? His fear of his anxieties returning? His nightmares about his old governess? Which of his extremes was he riding that night, depression or mania? Paranoia or melancholy? Words that Claudette, as a young bride, had grown all too familiar with.

She shakes her head. How to get the images of his smile, his laughter, his sadness, his tears, which shot like sunlight through the window, from her mind? There was no one to help shoulder the weight. She would not humiliate his memory by confiding in his friends about his troubles. She would not taint Chazz's memory that way. Let them remember him as golden. If that was all there was left of him. The way he looked that first year they met, with his skin, his smile, his hair, the aura about him like sunshine. So capable. Claudette had always felt cushioned by his care, wrapped in the fine blanket of his love.

The least she can do is carry the burden of his sadness like a grown woman. Hadn't she done so throughout their toughest times? *Normal* for a wife. Didn't she owe him that much?

"What did you see that last evening, Chazz?" she whispers, touching her fingertips to the glass. She slips her foot from her thong sandal and scratches the back of her calf. Her feet are sticky from the heat. She traces a stray hair behind her ear. She has cut her hair again. Even shorter this time. For a moment the thought *What will Chazz think of my new hair?* wafts through her mind. Those were the sneaky ones. The ones that slipped by her resolution to accept his death. He is dead and yet she finds she has to murder his memory as well in order to move on. "What were you searching for, *mon coeur*?" she asks.

"Mademoiselle? Are you all right?" A gentleman across the aisle extends a tissue. She thanks him, surprised that she has been shedding tears again.

"Merci," she says, lifting the tissue up slightly with her hand.

He shakes his head. *"De rien."* It's nothing.

Her body falls easily into the feel of the train. So familiar. It reminds her of day trips with friends. Of skipping school and going to St. Tropez to hunt for the wealthy celebrities. She'd had no idea then she would marry one of them. She never mentioned this to Chazz. She feels like an imposter. So many things Chazz did not know about her. Things she thought she would tell him in time. But in time his illness took over. In time there were other things that would occupy their minds.

Her silly crushes and girlhood dreams seemed so trivial afterward. From the moment they met, Chazz's world eclipsed hers, so that Claudette herself became a vague memory. It was addicting to have someone need you so completely. There was only the Claudette that began the moment she met him.

So she never told him about her engagement to another. How she broke it off the moment she fell for Chazz. How she planted herself there at the restaurant when she learned the precise hour he liked to take his lunch. How she heard he was a wealthy man.

She is touched by the newspaper picture of Chazz posted on the lamppost in front of the station, with candles and flowers at the base. A very American gesture. Someone has taken the time to honor him. She stares at his face, the studied studio smile familiar, and at the same time not. When he smiled, it was not controlled like this. It was wide and expansive and it pulled you into him. She bends down to place the bouquet of roses purchased across the street with the few others. She touches the ground with her fingertips. Black tar, sticky, dirty; small pebbles stick to her fingertips.

She feels for a moment as if she will lie on the ground to be near him. She has begun to cry again, silent tears without the sobbing. People are watching her. She stands abruptly and gives the area one more look. Then turns her back to the terminal, as if she is Chazz that night, about to cross the street. Only Chazz had been running.

The police report said that the moped that gave the beep of warning as he stepped into the street came from the left. So he must have looked this way, over his shoulder, even as his body

252 / Tess Uriza Holthe

propelled him in the opposite direction. There had been two men chasing him or running with him, and then he had looked to the right; she turns her head, and the next thing he knew . . .

A taxi pulls up to the curb, startling her. She gasps so loudly that more people glance her way. Her hands are shaking. She feels self-conscious and, again, thickheaded, as if she will faint. Her face feels parched from shedding so many tears. She does the only thing she can think to do and steps into the taxicab. As they drive away, she turns one last time to look back at the train station. This is not at all how she pictured her visit to the spot where Chazz fell, but the taxi is now moving, the tires spinning away from where her husband died.

After a moment the driver says, "Mademoiselle."

"Rue Bivouac Napoléon," she answers. She will visit the bookstore they used to frequent so Chazz could buy his American books, though he was fluent in French. He insisted that the language translated differently. This was what one did after the death of a loved one, wasn't it? Visit all the places and remember?

There would be time to inspect Chazz's château and get the update from the real estate agent on prospective buyers tomorrow. It is her decision to sell the house. The driver, not wanting to get stuck in traffic, drops her off at the end of the street and she walks toward the bookstore with the confusion of someone who has just woken from a heavy sleep. But once she reaches the store she can only look through the glass.

"*Pardon, mademoiselle,*" a woman says.

"Oh." Claudette steps to one side. She has been blocking the door. She turns and hurries to La Croisette, to see her friend Justine.

Justine ushers her in after a shout and a tearful embrace and leads her to a corner booth. It is just the two of them. People will not be seeking dinner until seven. And most wish to be seen dining outside in their fancy clothes, so the two of them have the interior to themselves.

"I saw him that night, you know," Justine says before Claudette can spill her own story that is dying to be let out.

"The gendarmes told me," Claudette answers. She does not describe the sterile typed reports of the accident relating how the *victim* ran to this spot. Two men accompanied the *victim* where he fell at such and such a spot. Where the *victim* was fatally hit by an oncoming taxi.

"I tried to speak to him. I called his name over and over again, but he was with two friends. He ignored me. I was a little insulted." Justine dabs her eyes and chuckles. "But I thought to myself, perhaps it is business and here you are in your silly uniform calling *Monsieur Jorgensen. Monsieur!* Like a simpleton. Me in my silly uniform. Probably he was with business associates. Ah, so stupid. I have been unable to sleep. I keep remembering. How stupid I must have looked. He must have been embarrassed."

"Oh no. He would never be ashamed of you, Justine."

"So amazing that you two found each other. Imagine you were just a worker such as me. We worked here side by side. And he chose you." Justine smiles. "And soon you were wearing fancy dresses. Fancy clothes." Justine's voice trails off; she sighs.

Claudette studies her hands folded on the table.

"Do you remember? The day I pointed him out to you?"

"I remember," Claudette says.

"But that night when I saw him on the train. He was so changed. His face. And his clothes. I almost did not recognize him. Still, it was him. He recognized me. But it was as if he could not speak in front of his associates. The next day, I was so ready for him to beg my forgiveness for the snub. You know how he can charm. And then I found the next day that he had . . . you know. I

254 / Tess Uriza Holthe

am so sorry, Claudette. But why were you not with him? The two of you. So in love. He was such an angel. Perfect." Justine crosses her arms and shakes her head. *"Pauvre Chazz."*

And all the things Claudette wants to confide to her friend slip away. She will not have Chazz remembered badly. She leaves, promising to spend more time in the next few days with Justine.

The two men again. Who were they? Where had Chazz met them? The police had questioned everyone but come up with nothing. She had not pressed on with the matter. Was she really surprised? Many times she had picked him up from strange houses. People he had just made friends with that evening. She calls the real estate woman and tells her that her plane is late. She is stuck in Dallas and will not be able to see her until the morrow.

From the Quai St. Pierre, she can see the château set upon the hillside. The iron key, which she keeps fingering, weighs heavily in her skirt pocket. She can sleep there tonight if she wishes. The servants have been notified. The cook can be called at a moment's notice.

She cannot bring herself to sleep in Chazz's château. The last time she was there was her birthday two years ago. They had fought. Something trivial that had escalated into her running to the airport. She felt she couldn't breathe. Always their fights were so dramatic. Everything the end of the world.

It takes her ten minutes to get to the main street and book a room at the Hilton. She is trembling by the time she lies down to rest. In the morning she will gather her strength to visit the house, first thing. She skips dinner and falls into a deep sleep. She dreams again of the night he called. The phone is ringing, it is the first of his two phone calls, and the house is thick with fog. She doesn't want to pick it up if it is his second and final call. But she doesn't want to miss it if it is the first. Life hinges in between the calls. No matter, she tells herself as she tosses in bed, for she cannot find the phone.

Morning breaks through the sliver of the black-out curtains. Again she postpones her visit to the château, glancing briefly in its direction but averting her inner gaze. With a staidness she did not know she possessed, she overshoots her thoughts, skipping over the château to Les Muscadins, the *ristorante* overlooking the Bay of Cannes where they celebrated her birthday. It had been July then. There was laughter, she remembers. The earth strewn with fallen purple lilacs. The quaint stone inn covered in climbing magenta bougainvillea, the blue folding chairs on the terrace where they dined.

She boards the train, avoiding his picture at the station. Skirting the area where he fell. She pretends it is a different station and not the one where her husband met death.

Aix is as she remembers. All stone and shade of trees. Down to the left, she knew a family that once lived in the large three-story ochre-colored house. Had known them intimately, in fact. She stops to gaze at the house. As a child, Claudette would stop her playing and reach for a brown woven basket as Madame Barr roped down a handwritten list on vanilla-scented stationery from the first balcony: *Two cloves of garlic. Green peppercorns. Three potatoes.* With an extra two francs for Claudette and Laurent. In the kitchen of that house, Madame Barr became like a second mother, since Claudette's came alive only to the tipping of a bottle of *vin*. Otherwise her *maman* slept like a vampire, craving and rising only for blood-red wine.

In Madame Barr's kitchen, she learned a guarded family recipe, how to boil peaches and watch as they glowed like orange orbs, and then she and Laurent would undress the fruit, the skins slipping off like silk, to prepare the preserves.

Then, as a grown girl, she and Laurent studied in the kitchen near the snacks. Many evenings she spent on the black wrought-iron terrace. She wonders if the Barr family still lives there and what became of Laurent after she gave him back her engagement ring. It seems like a lifetime ago. Before her chest was this heavy and her head splitting in such a way. She turns from the memory and strolls straight down the main thoroughfare of shops on Mirabeau. It is Saturday and the market is laid out in the middle of the crowded street.

In Aix she can breathe. No one is staring at her. People are too busy buying heads of garlic placed without fanfare on a folding table. Just the garlic, heads piled one on top of another in a white-and-purple mound, without a tablecloth. An elderly gentleman sits beside the table in a lavender dress shirt rolled up to his elbows, wearing a beret and counting out the change to customers. Women haggle over prices and stuff fruits into woven baskets, composing their faces to haggle again a few rows down.

A new beauty salon, Caritas Paris Institut Coiffure, has opened on the right. Pale green boxes in white trim stacked neatly in front of the window. *Would you like to go in?* she can almost hear Chazz leaning over to whisper in her ear. He was attentive that way. He delighted in things that interested her. She turns away from the salon. This season women are wearing triangular sequined sashes knotted to ride low on their waists in taupe, black, white. They wear them over jeans, peasant skirts, and dresses. "You should get one, Dettie," Chazz would have said.

Across the way are the cafés, La Belle Epoque, arched trees, Pizza Capri with its orange awning, the stone floors dappled with shade and sunlight. A waiter at the Café de Paris takes a cigarette break and stares at one of the large stone fountains in the center, where an Irish wolfhound has decided to jump in to take a bath. People point and laugh at the large goateed dog as they stroll. A purple banner advertises the *Galerie d'Art at 2600 Cours Mirabeau. "Les Amis des Arts. Bédarrides Exposition du 5ième Juillet au 1er Août 2002."*

People carry plastic bags from the market with a green clover logo and a red ladybug with the caption *Scènes de la Vie*. Koala Voyages. Le Grand Hôtel. The *librairie* above the hamburger café. The wail of a distant siren. All this food and she feels nothing.

The people are still laughing at the bathing dog. He is now drinking the water as he bathes. Their laughter hurts her head and her eyes are sensitive from the sunlight. She heads east, off Rue d'Italie and toward the quiet street and tiny intimate plaza of the Musée Granet. A small black poodle, skinny as a cat, runs desperately through the crowd, searching for its owner. It darts left and right and Claudette shades her eyes to see if it will be reunited.

She turns off one of the narrow side streets and continues on until she faces the church next to the Musée Granet. The tall houses leading up to the church are muted tones of apricot, beige, rose. A row of parked cars line one side of the street. She has forgotten how small the cars, how tiny the streets. She will go to see Cézanne's paintings at the museum. Visit the other room of stone artifacts, sarcophagus lids. The door to the museum says that the Cézanne section is closed for renovation. The urge to grab one of the handles and shake and kick until they let her in is overwhelming.

She can feel the church, to her left in the small courtyard, watching her. Its beautiful presence pressing in on her. *Won't you come in?* it asks. *All this way just for this tiny museum? Is that what you told yourself?*

She takes a deep breath and faces the St. Jean de Malte church where she and Chazz were married. The twelfth-century architecture is beautiful in the daylight. Its simple cross atop a triangular point. The thin turret. The matching circular windows, the smaller one up top and then the larger one above the red wooden double doors. The images rush her at once. Her simple wedding gown, taupe-colored, with one delicate detail of mauve and lavender rosebuds at the center of her sleeveless bodice. A bouquet of dusk-colored roses. Her father had walked her down the aisle with tears in his eyes.

He was still alive then. Her father, Michel Dumont. He had raised her single-handedly. Her mother, sure to be found nursing a bottle at all hours, was present without being present. An empty beautiful bottle of a woman. Sober for Claudette's wedding day because her father had willed it. But the strain was showing, her mother wearing a brittle smile. Such a happy and sad time. Her father so sad she was leaving for America. So angry that she had turned down the opportunity to teach at the Lycée Français. "Why must you give up your dream for his?" he had asked. "First this dream. What next?"

She had been angry then, too. She had wagged a finger at her father while clutching her train in the other arm. "You favor Laurent over him. Simply because Laurent is French. You wish I had chosen Laurent. But I haven't." Her father! Whom she adored. Had she really wagged her finger under his nose? She saw his shoulders fall then. The realization in his eyes that he would need to relinquish his throne to Chazz.

"No, *chérie.* You misunderstand. I only wish for the two of you to start out equal. Why must you give up your dreams? Which one shall you give up next, and after that? Why is there a need for you to sacrifice? If he loves you there must be some compromise."

"But whatever I planned to do here, I can do in America, Papa. That is the compromise."

How flushed her face had been. How disbelieving that her father would choose that day to ask such a question. And how right he had been, looking back. What had she done but give up her dreams one by one as Chazz's illness took over? And now, the church seemed to ask, *Was it worth it? Your sacrifice? What if you had stayed the course? What if you had married Laurent instead, with his mother, who loved you?* Only now did she allow these questions to wash over her.

For two years her marriage had been easy, full of smiles and evening walks. Then little by little Chazz had started to crumble before her. Little incidents that she at first did not understand. The first was the party at the house of her new friend Virginia. "Why must we leave so early, Chazz?"

"I have a headache, darling."

"I can get some pills. There is a *pharmacie* around the corner."

"No." His voice was sharp. Then more gently: "I can't move. You don't know how it feels. Everyone laughing and asking questions. And inside I just want to die."

She hadn't understood then. He hadn't told her yet. That was the first betrayal. That is what caused the first tear. Then the bigger one at his best friend's wedding. Chazz was the best man, and he had to leave before his speech.

"You cannot be *sérieux*? How can you be so selfish?" she asked, following after him as he stormed out.

"What do you know?" he shouted. And the guests looked their way in the parking lot. She was mortified, but still she followed after him.

Later, after he had coaxed her into forgiving him, he told her: "My compass is broken."

"What?"

"I have a problem. Something wrong with my thinking. I get confused."

"Tell me," she said, taking his hand. Was that it? Only a problem? That was the cause of the terrifying pressure building in her chest? The unnameable fear caught in her heart banging the walls to get out? Just a "problem"? She could manage a problem. Hadn't she cared for her mother? She even said so to him. "A problem? Then we shall fix it." But the incredulous look in his eyes had sunk her stomach for good. "What, Chazz?"

The saddest one had been at a big Christmas party for his father's company, held at Boulevard Restaurant, with its delicious tiled floors and cavelike interior. Chazz had been sleeping well. He was no longer afraid to go to the market. Such a relief after months of terror, where simply purchasing socks became such an effort for him. So humiliating for a man who loved to purchase clothes. But somehow it lifted. Perhaps it had worked, her insistence that he not lie in bed all day. That he get up. *Get up and do one thing. Go to the market. Buy something.* Whatever it was, the therapy or the shelves of medication, seemed to be working.

In a matter of days it was as if he had been returned to her. They got dressed; there was a big Christmas tree and red wine. He squeezed her hand throughout the evening, and Claudette was certain his anxiety had left them. They had conquered it together.

But then at the dinner table, Chazz's speech became stilted, halting, and then very confused, as if he were speaking to them from underwater and the messages were getting to them in delayed time. He hadn't understood a question an associate's wife had asked: "Where are you planning on staying in France?"

Silence. A muted smile on Chazz's lips. The whole table waiting. How charming he looked in his tuxedo. There was chuckling. A joke said lightly. Perhaps he had had too much to drink already? How Chazz liked to think a question over. But Claudette saw, her wine glass frozen at her lips. She saw his hands were shaking in his lap. She was so confused. Should she answer for him? And then what seemed like five minutes later, after they had awkwardly moved on to another topic, Chazz said, "We have a home in Cannes." And everyone had looked quickly from one to another.

And then the horrible "Where in Cannes?"

Claudette had wanted to die. Not from embarrassment but from her need to help him. Ten minutes elapsed; the conversation moved on, but stiff, very awkward now. And finally the manager of their northern region, whom Chazz worked with intimately, asked, "Are you all right, Chazz?"

And he answered, "That's a very good question." He stood abruptly, the wine and Champagne glasses overflowing and clinking as he banged into the table like a blind man without his stick and walked off without asking to be excused. Claudette followed after him, wanting to rock him in her arms. She caught up to him in front of the gift table, next to a giant ficus with tiny Christmas lights woven into its branches. She led him away gently to the curb, to wait for their silver Mercedes. She remembered rubbing his back with the palm of her hand as they waited for the valet. Chazz's face had broken out into a thick sweat. "I just want to go home."

She took him to the doctor instead. He had a seizure in the car. She screamed and honked the horn and drove on the sidewalk. At the hospital they were told that the various medications he was taking for his depression and his mania had conflicted with one another.

"Nothing that can't be fixed," the doctor said. "A simple change in the combination of pills. A lighter dosage of one, heavier on the other." Claudette remembers how nonchalant the doctor had sounded. As if he were simply fine-tuning the knobs on a stereo, and the static between stations so unbearably loud it had brought them to their knees that day was just routine, searching for the next clear station. As if the episode had not chipped a large piece of Chazz's dignity away and left a gaping, irrevocable wound. As if the doctor were the one experiencing these inexplicable outbursts with her and the incidents rolled off both their shoulders like rain on a slicker. "No damage," the doctor said.

He seemed to know intimately this demon Claudette could not see, was helpless to fight. If her father had seen Chazz that way perhaps he would have understood how Claudette had delayed and delayed the offers of a teaching position, first in Aix and then later in California. But Chazz was so careful not to let the episodes show. She understood his need to hold them close to himself, to keep the episodes from eroding what little confidence he had left. He trusted only Claudette with them.

They were both gone now. The two men who had defined her. Were they in the same place?

Aix was as she remembered it. Beautiful Aix, but that was a lifetime ago. Another lifetime, when the future had stretched out full of endless paths and opportunities. Before the darkness had settled to envelop and choke them like untamed ivy.

Claudette Dumont, daughter of a fisherman. As a girl accompanying her father to the markets to sell his catch, she had known these stone streets, these scrub oaks and plane trees as if she owned them. She knew all the storekeepers, the priests, the museum and gallery attendants. "Dettie, time to go," her father would call up to a tree, and with a shaking of leaves Claudette would shimmy down the tree like a monkey.

Well, will you come in? the church asked. Inside was coolness and shade and memories. "No, some other time perhaps." She backed away from her memory of herself in the wedding gown, from the sound of her delicate heels tapping on the stone streets with one arm laced in Chazz's and the other holding her train. From the memory of sipping chilled peach Champagne afterward in her *grand-mère*'s tiny cottage, which had fit a reception of twenty sweetly. Grand-mère had made a special white princess cake filled with strawberries and marzipan topping. No bride and groom on top, just beaded white frosting. *No time for this.* She needed to check on the mansion in Cannes. She was to meet potential buyers this evening.

"Claudette?" For a moment she feels as if the church has spoken aloud.

A hand at her elbow. She turns to face a tall, slender man in tan corduroy pants and a blue polo shirt. He is wearing designer sunglasses. Calvin Klein, she thinks. "Claudette?" he says again. There is a smile in his voice. Dark brown hair.

The eyes come into focus, the dimples. She places her fingers reflexively to his cheek. "Laurent?" She steps back. "Laurent!" She throws her arms around him as if he is a piece of wood from a sinking ship.

"Claudette," he laughs and embraces her. He tries to untangle her arms, but she is afraid to look at him. Afraid he will see her eyes. He lets her stay for a moment. He knows her well. "I read in the newspaper," Laurent says, bringing a gentle hand to the back of her hair like one would with a child. "It is true then? It was your Chazz?"

"*Oui,*" she says into his shirt collar.

"I am sorry. It was in the papers. I could not remember his last name. And I have never met him personally. But the first name stuck. And again, I was certain because they mentioned his father. The American millionaire."

He bows his head, putting her at arm's length but still holding on to her elbows. "I have just come from Maman." He gestures down the street, toward his old house. "I stepped out to buy tea at her request."

"Yes? She still lives there?" Claudette asks. "I wondered."

"*Oui,*" he says, suddenly quiet.

She is struck with the memory of their last talk. It had ended bitterly five years ago. She had placed the ring on the dining room table of that house, and in an uncharacteristic fit of anger he had taken the ring and flung it across the room. "You're marrying him for the money. You would never have looked at another. We've known each other since we were children."

She had let him rage. She had been seven years old when they first met. Twenty-three when she last laid eyes on him. "I was going to visit the museum," Claudette says.

"Do you have time? Have you had lunch yet?" he asks.

Lunch? Of course, it was noontime. The thought of lunch repulses her, but she says, "I could have a glass of water."

"Come then, around the corner. A new restaurant. Can you stay awhile?"

"Yes." She allows him to lead her, and she marvels at how different he looks. "Have you grown, Laurent?"

"Yes. Strange, isn't it? Two more inches! I suppose I am a late bloomer."

She smiles. How easy it is to place her hand in his arm and be led away from her memories.

The waitress seats them at a window table. She grabs his hand without thinking. "A ring! You are happy?"

He avoids her eyes. "Yes. You would like her, I think. Maman, on the other hand . . ." He lets his hand drop. "She was partial to you."

He stares at her then. Claudette blushes. In his look there is no wife standing between them. He gazes at her as if five years have not passed. Finally he notices her look of concern. "Forgive me. I have often wondered how you are. How you look now. And here you are. It is as if I have willed you here."

She reddens even more.

"Your work, Laurent. You are a big engineer now, yes?" she teases.

"I am happy." He gazes at her entire face. "With that I am truly happy." He nods. "And you? Your students. What age do you teach now?" He smiles.

A pained expression flits across her brow. "I—I never used my studies. I have not taught yet. But I've been meaning to. There was just no need, you see."

His face cannot deny the shock. "But, Dettie. That was your dream." It takes a moment for him to compose himself.

"Yes. But I had other dreams as well."

At this his lips twist in a wry smile. "Ah yes. To be a millionaire's wife. How silly of me."

"Laurent?" she asks, her voice wavering. It feels as if he has stabbed her in the chest.

His face is instantly sorry. "Claudette," he says, taking her hand in his, "forgive me." He is quiet for a long moment. "I suppose the bitterness still lingers, though you wish it gone." He sighs and looks up at the trees. His glasses reflect the sky. "That was bad of me."

"It is all right. I understand."

"Do you?" His eyes are sad. "But what am I thinking? Would you like to visit my mother? I stepped out for her errand and I saw you. I have completely forgotten. She would like to see you, you know. Have you eaten at all today?"

"Yes. Yes. No." She smiles as he pays the bill, when what she really wanted to say to all his questions was no.

From Laurent's house she calls the real estate agent. "Madame Guerlain, I am so sorry. Again the flight will be delayed. Thank you. Tomorrow morning? *Oui*. There are many takers? And how many viewings have you had? Eight days. *Oui*. *Non*, I do not doubt that it will sell immediately. *Oui*. So good of you, Madame Guerlain. *Merci*."

"Oh my, look who is here," Madame Barr exclaims as she walks across the hall. She takes Claudette's face in her cold hands and kisses each cheek. She seems tinier than Claudette remembers. Her shoulders so narrow now. Her blond hair, her only beauty, lacks its former luster. She is still wearing her *chai,* the necklace that she treasures so much. She wraps her arms around Claudette.

Claudette feels such a relief of belonging. The house is the same. Large and cavernous. This would have been her mother-in-law if she had married Laurent. Not the one in America who barely embraced her at the news of Chazz's death.

"But let me look at you. So thin you are."

"It is so good to see you, Madame Barr," Claudette says.

"Laurent! Why do you not feed your cousin? Josianne, your mother will be angry if you do not eat more."

Claudette's mouth parts open, and she has to consciously force it closed.

"Maman, this is not Josianne. This is Claudette. You remember. She was like a second child to you. We were engaged once."

"What? Of course I remember. How can I forget my cousin's child?"

Laurent sighs. "No, Maman. Claudette. Monsieur Dumont's daughter, the fisherman. Do you remember our neighbor? His daughter."

"Ah." Madame Barr blushes. "Of course." Her eyes are lucid. "Forgive me. Claudette Dumont, Claudette. The two of you were engaged once." She repeats Laurent's words, so that Claudette is still unsure if she remembers her until she says, "I sent all those invitations. All those invitations." She clucks her tongue and shakes her head. "This brain. This memory of mind. It grows so feeble. Forgive me, Dettie."

"No, Madame Barr, forgive me. To drop in on you like this. Without calling first." Her words are firm, but Claudette feels nervous inside. As if she has just taken aspirin on an empty stomach.

"What are you saying, child? You are welcome here always. Laurent. She is hungry! Where are your manners?"

He laughingly shrugs. "I just found her. I brought her home to feed."

"Oh no. I could not eat. I'm not hungry," Claudette says.

"Please. Please, you two catch up. I will show Serena to her room and then I shall join you."

"Serena?" Claudette asks after his mother leaves the room.

"My wife. She has severe migraines from time to time."

"Oh. I intrude. Laurent. Why did you not say?" Claudette stands in horror.

"No. Claudette. Sit. Please. I told her I had bumped into an old friend. She sends you her apologies, but sometimes these headaches. They are debilitating. They cause her to lose her sight at times. They can be very severe." He begs her to stay with his eyes.

"Lose her sight?"

"Temporarily. Very blurry." He gestures into the air.

Claudette stares at him. She knows this. The irritation at the illness. The exhaustion he tries to hide that seeps out anyway. The constant caring for someone that consumes you whole. Consumed the both of you so that there was no longer a you or a he but an illness.

"I'm sorry, Laurent," she says.

He puts his hands into his pockets. "Do you remember that room?" He nods down the hall.

"Yes," she giggles. "That time you tried to show off and your foot went through the table? Your *maman* was so mad. Her favorite table."

"Ah, but I am her only son. That room belongs to a family now. That and the adjoining one. Maman rents it out. She gets lonely from time to time."

Claudette nods. She can still see the laughing long-haired girl she was then. Twirling away from Laurent's antics. Twirling away from standing still. She had not known then that she was dancing away from herself, from her independence.

268 / Tess Uriza Holthe

"I'm sorry, I should have warned you. Maman's memory has gotten worse. Most of the time she is clearheaded. But certain things. Certain things confuse her. She had her necklace stolen the other week. It started the confusion. I had an identical one made. Though if you look closely, the garnet is different."

"Yes, I understand. She loved that necklace." Claudette nods. "Somehow it triggered the confusion."

"Yes—'triggered'—that is the word the doctor used. And the necklace was her aunt's. So." Laurent pressed his lips together in a helpless smile.

Claudette smiles sadly out the window. She knows that word, *triggered*. How often Chazz's own doctor used it to describe his episodes. Did Claudette know what "triggered" it? Had he done something to "trigger" it himself? On and on.

"What will you do now?" Laurent asks, standing so close behind her, his chest to her back without touching. So easy for her to lean into him. When she turns to look over her shoulder he is there gazing down at her. She knows in that instant he will always be there. That he would kiss her if she let him. And she realizes that she wants to be kissed. Not because she harbors any feelings for Laurent, but because she misses Chazz so badly. Misses being held. Misses being cared for. Being the center of someone's world.

"I should go," she tells him.

"But you only just arrived." He is desperately trying to think of some reason. She can see his mind working.

She lifts a hand to his brow and brushes away his hair. She loves him for making her feel at home. For giving her his unspoken support. For these memories of herself he allowed her to touch, if only for a moment.

"Claudette," he says, "Maman will want to talk to you. She was there, you know. When your husband was hit by the car. She did not know at the time who he was. It was only later in the papers when we talked."

Claudette feels her heart stop. Had the whole world witnessed him die but her?

"Will you not wish to speak to her?"

"He was already dead?" she asks.

"Yes."

"Then there is nothing more she can tell me. It will only bring me pain."

"Let me drive you home."

"No, Laurent. It was a blessing to see you again. It was meant to be. For fortitude, I suppose. I have to visit Chazz's château in the morning. I am to sell it, you see. But I must do this alone. No more pushing back the inevitable."

The château is heartbreakingly beautiful in the soft twilight. Mauve and rose light upon the clay-colored exterior and black wrought-iron railing. A fanlight over the doorway. If there ever was a house to fall in love in. Blue cornflowers and red poppies rustling in the warm breeze. Cypress and plane trees leaning in to shade the house. Ivy climbing alongside magenta bougainvillea. Two small red birds flutter and hop on the faded red-tiled roof, craning necks down, small jerks of their head as they listen to her fumble for the copper skeleton key, her hand shaking.

She imagined cobwebs, dark corridors, a giant urn in the center of the large dining table. A Gothic feel, when the house has never been so. The house is just as they left it. Big windows filtering in the light upon the stone floors. The thick walls cooling the interior. The scent of fresh-cut cedar, wood smoke from the chimney ingrained in the walls.

Their beautiful oil paintings, purchased together during bundled winter months in New York, San Francisco. David Hockney's lighthouse, Claude Lazar with his incredible lighting that darkened with the night, Anne Bachelier's magical children. Hanging over the length of the sofa is the Modigliani oil on canvas of Chazz's grandparents. Dignified, seated on a sofa. Claudette's body reacts with familiarity. She knows this house. This portrait. The elongated figures, in ripe green, red, indigo blue. The artist has painted the grandmother with copper-red hair, though she was a blonde. It intrigued her, Chazz said, to see herself through the eyes of an artist. Modigliani had a fondness for redheads.

The shutters are thrown open. The house smells fresh. Even when Chazz is gone, his households work like clockwork. Someone has taken the initiative to phone and ready the house for her.

A note on the hallway table where she places her keys. Her heart jumps. A mean unconscious joke from the caretaker. Chazz used to leave her such notes when he had woken early to go to the beach. *At the beach. Come join me.*

The note read:

Madame, the address for the Monsieur is listed below, along with the hours. I have filled the refrigerator and cupboards for your convenience. The cook's phone number. The real estate lady, Madame Guerlain, asked that you phone her tomorrow at nine—Antoinette.

The address for the Monsieur. Claudette brings her fingers to her lips. Such a civilized way to say your husband's ashes can be picked up at this address at these hours. Right before the message about the refrigerator. She walks through the first floor with a steely resolve. The bedroom window, when she opens it, still has the sound of the sea. The closet still holds their evening clothes side by side. A slinky silver dress. A burgundy ball gown. Her strappy heels. His tuxedo and, beneath, a pair of black Armanis creased where the instep of his foot bent. Ready to be worn for a night of dancing. She takes a deep breath and opens more windows to let the fresh air in.

She goes to the living room to turn on the stereo, intending the radio; instead, Chazz's CD of Ella Fitzgerald and Louis Armstrong plays "Tenderly." The trumpet starts and the piano, and Claudette's knees buckle beneath her, bending slowly until her fingertips touch the floor and she sits that way.

He always played this one. *The evening breeze caressed the trees. Tenderly. . . . I can't forget how two hearts met. . . . Tenderly.*

She feels suddenly tired, as if hit by the flu. She has a vague feeling of crawling toward the cushions; next, she is lying on her back on the cobalt-blue sofa, eyes closed, one arm thrown over her head. Is she crying? She isn't sure. Her stomach is racked with the motion of sobs. She can hear herself breathing brokenly. Her mind winds round in circles . . . *I am to blame. I am to blame.*

So selfish. She, who had the luxury to pull away from him when he needed her most. Was it so bad that you had to leave him? Think of how hard it was for Chazz, who couldn't leave. Who couldn't step out of his illness as if it were a pair of trousers. So good he had been to her when she'd asked for the time away.

"Of course, sweetheart." He had kissed her forehead. "I'll be fine. It's a lot. I know. It's a lot. I'll call you tonight to make sure you're all right. Don't cry, Dettie." Always so good to her.

Does it feel so necessary now to have asked for that—what did you call it? "Breathing space." What had she said to him again? "To remember who I am in all of this." How silly, how frivolous to ask for such a separation in light of all that has happened. Listen to yourself. "In light of all." Where had she picked up that phrase? Recently, at the reading of his will, at his doctor's?

A better wife would have stayed beside him through the worst of his crisis. A good wife would have held his hand when he was so racked with paranoia that he couldn't get up to bathe himself. A decent woman would not have sat day in and day out, resenting him for the life she had thrown away. Ignoring the changed husband in front of her and waiting, eyes shaded, looking to some far-off horizon for the old Chazz to return to her. A good wife would not have wondered what it would be like to be teaching instead of coaxing him to take his pills. A loving wife would not have said those words: *"Chazz, it's too much. I need some sunlight. I miss your company."* What she meant was I miss having a normal life. I miss having a husband. I miss having nothing more to worry about each evening than what it is we are going to eat.

And he hadn't known. The night he called her from Milano Central when he was supposed to meet her that day to discuss the possibility of a divorce. He was running from her verdict. He hadn't given her a chance to say how she had spent the day buying new sheets that he would like. He would never know that she had cut her hair even shorter and bought a dress to welcome him home. Had filled the kitchen with things he loved. How she wanted to tell him that it was a stupid idea and to come back home. A new start. They would face it together. He had died thinking she had left him.

She needed to get up. *Get up.* She rolls to her side and pushes her hands down on the sofa to rise. Her left hand slips in between the sofa and touches paper. She remains very still and pulls the folded paper out slowly. A note dated two years ago. The last time they were here together. The paper is soft and wrinkled. Chazz's writing. Her throat tightens. Someone is playing a horrible joke on her.

Dear Dettie,   *July 1, 2000*
   Same story. The last few days have been such a reprieve. Everything all sunshine and laughter. But I feel the anxiety of it creeping in. The way it does when the days are good. The

anxiety that it will return soon. So even when it is good I can only enjoy the days for so long. Because I know it will return. I am anxious that I will soon be anxious! And so I go in circles. And soon I am not talking. I hate this disease. I hate it. Why me and not that asshole who cut us off this morning? So I take it out on you. I'm curt when a moment ago I was hugging you. Quiet when an hour ago I couldn't stop teasing you. It must drive you insane. And yet you stay. You are not to blame. Never think that. When I am clearheaded, I realize how hard it must be for you. And yet you stay. Thank you.

—Chazz

She remembers now. The last time under this roof they had had an argument. She was touchy. The newness of their marriage was wearing off and he was beginning to let his real self show, his impatience to get away from the crowds. His refusal to visit her father. "You go, darling. I'm feeling a little worn."

Or perhaps the extreme joy he had been riding was starting to spiral downward. That was the pattern of his disease. The illness was unique to each person. But she had had enough. Like a spoiled, petulant child she had stormed off in a taxi to the airport. Not intending to leave him, not intending anything but to show him how upset she was, how it was her turn to be paid attention to, cared for, and armed with the supreme knowledge that she would see him back home and they would resume their normal life.

Their normal life. It was never again normal. Never again. So this note. It was so like Chazz to sort out his feelings on paper and hope for the best from her. Hope that she would return and read it and they could continue as always. A walk on the beach. Not a visit to her father. A concession of her anger. But she had never returned. She had gone straight home. And after a day he had followed her, as always.

She picks up the phone and dials Madame Guerlain. *"Madame? Oui,* I am finally home. I arrived just an hour ago. Forgive me. I have had a change of heart. I cannot sell our house. There really is no need to. *Merci.* Yes, thank you for being so understanding."

In the morning she will pick up Chazz's ashes. She will open the urn and place it by the window. She will let him fill the sea air outside so that he will be around her, yet always free. Finally free. She falls asleep listening to "April in Paris." And she dreams the same dream she has every night for the last week, since his death. It is the afternoon they are supposed to meet. The first of his last two phone calls.

She picks up the phone smiling. She can barely contain her excitement. He doesn't see the white candles she has bought, the largest of which she is staring at as they speak.

"Dettie?" he says.

"Yes," she answers, arranging the bouquet of roses. She knows as she speaks to him she will not be able to wait for him to arrive. She must tell him over the phone.

"You sound happy," he says, the concern in his voice turned to amusement. "Are we still meeting this evening? Do you want more time?"

In her dream she does not wait as she did that day but tells him immediately. "No more time. I cannot stand the time away from you. It was a mistake. I bought candles, and dinner is waiting to be cooked. I even bought a new dress." She laughs. "I cut my hair even shorter!"

A pause and then a deep breath. There is a definite smile in his voice now. "Can I bring anything?"

"Just come home, Chazz. I miss you."

about the author

tess uriza holthe is the author of *When the Elephants Dance*. She was born in San Francisco, California, and has a bachelor's degree in accounting from Golden Gate University. She lives in northern California with her husband, Jason.